ISBN: 978-0-6151-5903-4

Foreword

I started writing this novel in November 2005, during Nanowrimo, the National Novel Writing Month. Back in 2001, my first crime novel was published in Denmark, and I wanted to have a go at writing a novel in English. I finished the first draft during that long month and spent most of the next year revising and editing. The result is what you see here.

Frank Cash is designed to be an open-ended character, possibly someone I could use again in a later novel. In fact, durung Nanowrimo 2006, I did start a sequel to 'Ghost Whispers', but the main storyline didn't hold up. Several sub-plots did, however, so just know that there is a lot more to Cash and his team, than this novel covers.

If you want to know more about my writing or would like to leave comments about this particular novel, feel free to contact me. You can find my current contact information on my website, rasmusrasmussen.com.

This edition of 'Ghost Whispers' is the final draft version. This means that though some very intelligent people have read it and given me pointers, an actual editor has not been involved in the process. Any mistakes left in these pages are mine and I apologize for them in advance. That said, I hope you will enjoy this story.

GHOST WHISPERS

by Rasmus Rasmussen

Chapter one

PRISTINA, NOVEMBER 2000 – Branko looks down at his hands, wondering if he is strong enough. Stretched out, his fingers could be mistaken for a pianist's, were it not for the scars. When he makes a fist, it looks like a well used mallot, big and rough, like the rest of him. Still, he has his doubts. It will take more than physical strength to take on the responsibility, that lies before him. He had hoped for a quiet life, eventually, with the end of the war. He had hoped to retire from the life of a soldier, to help his father run the coffeeshop in Pristina. Now those hopes are gone, along with his family and the coffeeshop, lost in NATO's bombings of his hometown. And it is no longer safe to be Serbian in the city of Pristina.

Though the city has its hidden gems and beautiful details, a large part is made up of concrete apartmentblocks and older brick townhouses, Pristina is like a grey, old lady who wears her fine and intricately detailed jewelry hidden amongst old and dirty rags, full of holes and patches. She is a woman of many faces, all of them have their own sad story to tell and all of them have scars. Bombs and bullets do not discriminate between old and new, delicate and practical.

The task in front of him now, seems straightforward and though there will certainly be obstacles along the way, he knows it is what he must do. It has taken him many prayers, to get the courage built up. To believe that he would actually be able to restore the family honor. As Branko looks at his hardened hands, he sees the blood that is already on them, and it is not from the men he has killed, but from her. It is his own blood that he sees. It feels like the whole war has been for this very purpose, to harden him for this task. To track down and bring to justice the man who took the life of Jovana, his little sister. The one to whom all his letters had been addressed. The one he should have been there to protect.

Jovana's bright green eyes were as mild as the morning dew on the farmer's field and truly mirrored how she was. Whenever she played the piano, everyone else would just listen and watch, as her long, slender fingers seemed to take on a life of their own. They were the same long fingers, her brother had. She wanted to be an astronomer, she said. Maybe even an astronaut. She could have been anything, she wanted, Branko was saying to himself.

His hands are making fists so tight, as he thinks about her, he feels his nails bite into the flesh of his palms and it makes him clench even harder.

If she had died like the rest of his family, in the bombings a year earlier, it would not have been so hard to take perhaps. But it was a far more gruesome death, that had taken her, before the bombs had started falling. It was a death no one should have to suffer. One that Branko could not learn to live with. One that had to be avenged.

He had never actualy seen her body himself. Not with his own eyes at least. Jovana had been killed and laid to rest almost six years ago in 1994. Branko had not known about it until he came back to the city, trying to find out what had happened to his family after the uprising, the fighting and the air strikes. But he did not blame his father for not telling him. It was not right to blame the dead. Had it not been for a helpful policeman, he may never had known of Jovana's fate. The police had recorded the crime, written a report and taken some pictures. But that had been the end of their investigation. Though the war did not rage in the city of Pristina at that time, it was still a time of unrest, and the overworked police force quickly dropped the case. Yet, in a way

Branko was lucky. Had it happened a few years later, there would not even have been an investigation at all.

The pictures were in his suitcase now, along with the report that proved nothing. There were no obvious clues to find in them, nothing except the brutality of what had happened. And the insanity. Branko knew that something like this could only be the work of someone. who had seen the horrors he himself had seen. Done the things he had done. But someone who unlike him, had taken pleasure in doing them. Someone evil and twisted enough to rape and murder for their own sick entertainment. One of the foreigners, he thinks. It had to be one of them.

There were four photographs in the A4 envelope inside his suitcase. Three of them showed her from various angles, as they had found her, her face partially covered by what looked like a pillowcase or a sheet. Two holes had been cut away, like a child's ghost costume, revealing those once mild eyes. Even in the pictures, the horror in them was present, as they stared lifelessly into nothingness. Her legs were spread and tied to the bedposts and the bruises inside the thighs spoke of the abuse, she had endured before dying. Her arms had been placed across her chest, her hands crossing over her heart. The police had said that the bruises on the wrists indicated, that the killer had handcuffed her and probably taken the cuffs off and placed her hands like this, after she had died.

In the last picture, the ghost mask had been removed and her face was fully visible. Branko had to force himself to look at this image, but he did it, so he would not forget. Jovana's mouth was open and her tongue hung half-way out. There were more bruises on her neck and the side of her face. The harsh light from the camera's flash washed out the already pale skin and made her light brown hair seem darker. He saw the flakes of dried out tears on her unbruised cheek. She had not had fast or painless death. She had been raped, beaten and finally strangled.

The weight of the moneybelt is heavy around Branko's waist. He has enough American dollars to pay for information and maybe even buy an old car and some travelling papers. In the long run, he knows, he will have to get more money, but he has decided to worry about that, when he has to. First, he must concentrate on finding someone who knows about the foreign mercenaries and their movements, or more preciely, who and when any of the companies were in Pristina. Someone who can help him pick up the scent of his sister's killer.

He starts frequenting the backrooms of seedy bars, gambling dens and whorehouses. Getting anyone to talk is expensive these days, because nobody trusts anybody and everyone could use the cash. The city is running on survivalist instinct these days. Everyone has lost relatives, loved ones or friends, and while there are enough that are willing to help, no favors come free.

After a couple of weeks and couple of thousand dollars, Branko finally hears about a man, who may be able to help. They call him The German and rumor has it that he can get you anything for a price. Weapons, passports, information. The German is both well-connected and filthy rich, and to be both of those things as well as alive in a city where lives run this cheap, can only mean that he is tied to some kind of organisation. This is the kind of man, who might know about the comings and goings of foreign mercenaries, or known someone who does.

The meeting is set up in an Italian restaurant and the first thing Branko notices, is that The German is a short man, almost dwarflike in stature, with short legs and arms but broad shoulders and an almost square head, on which a dark purple baret rests. His skin is very pale and his eyes are sparkling green. His handshake feels like his hand is made of pure steel.

There are no other people at the table, which helps to create a friendly atmosphoere, but Branko knows that it is just a front, and that somewhere very close by is a man with a gun probably already pointed at him, ready to pull the trigger on The German's command. Espressos are served in silence, as Branko takes a seat, and the waiter moves away immediately, without asking if there is anything else, they would like. The conversation is short. The German asks what it is Branko wishes to know, though he has certainly already been briefed by the man who referred him, Branko explains his situation and the little man nods and listens. He seems genuinely interested in hearing about Branko's sister and agrees that finding the man who did it, will not be an easy task. And he is certain, that he will be able to help for the right price.

Through The German, Branko is referred to another man, who turns out to be simply a henchman for someone else. He talks to drug dealers and a man who offers Branko young boys and girls, and Branko has to listen to him brag about the children he traffics, because one wrong step and the chain of referrals is broken for good. And every link in the chain costs him more money than the previous. It is a slow and painful process, during which Branko prays hard every day for the Lord to be his guide. After months of delays and going from contact to contact, he is finally referred to a retired, Russian officer, who is supposed to know everything there is to know about the mercenaries and their ways.

Chapter two

SEATTLE, NOVEMBER 2005 – Even before he was conscious, he knew that the phone was ringing. It was on his nightstand, next to his clock radio, which was supposed to wake him up at seven, but like so many times before, the clock was going to miss out on that today. On the fourth ring, Frank had rolled over had picked the reciever off its cradle. It took him another few seconds to find his ear.

"Are you alright?" said a voice on the other end.

"What is it, Laura?"

"I had a dream just now," she said. Frank sighed heavily into the mouthpiece, not caring whether or not she heard him. "I dreamt you got shot, Frank."

"Hold on, let me check," he answered and paused for just a second before continuing. "Nope, I'm fine. No one broke in and shot me in my sleep, sis."

"Don't talk like that," his sister replied. "I was just worried is all."

"And I love you for it," he said and meant every word. She was his only family after all, and even if she had become a bit mothering since that day in 1999, when he had taken a bullet, he still loved her. "I'm sorry," he said.

They said their goodbyes, which were awkward and seemed even more so, because it had been so long. A year almost, last christmas, had it really been that long? Frank's heart was beating too hard in his chest. The clock read five thirty, but he knew there would be no more sleep. It was going to be one of those days.

The meeting was finally over and Frank rubbed his temples slowly, trying to rub the headache away. But it was not that kind of headache. He finally got up with the others and shuffled out of the briefing room. No one was bantering or exchanging stories. They were all busy digesting the news. The three teams of six men that was the homicide division were to be re-organized, as lieutenant Redding had called it. What it really meant was, that they were going to get cut. That the manpower of the SPD Homicide Division was going to be halved.

During the briefing, they had been presented with all sorts of explanations, from dropping crime rates to the large number of retiring detectives over the past three years, which had left a shortage of qualified personel in other departments. It was a half truth at best. Everyone knew they had let cops retire, without bringing in new detectives to replace them, so in the end they could justify their so-called rotations, which were in fact just budget cuts, and Frank was sure his friends and colleagues were thinking the same thing he was: that homicide had been a victim of its own success. They were solving too many murders, which by the bureaucrats had been interpreted as a green light to transfer resources to other departments with lower successrates. It was all about statistics to the them, because statistics were great to quote in politics. They would see how much they could cut away while moving cops around, hoping to balance the statistics and keep the overall percentage of solved crimes at what they had referred to as "tolerable levels". The fact that homicide had one of the best rates in the department, meant they they could afford to lose a little, to boost the less successful divisions.

Frank was one of the lucky ones who got to stay in homicide, and had he not, he would have fought for it. There was no doubt, that if he was ever taken off homicide, now that he had finally made it there, he would hand in his resignation. Of course, as head of his team chances were slim of anything like that happening, unless he personally fucked up in such a way, that the department would have to let him go to cover the ass of someone more important than himself. Another reason to hate politics, he thought to himself.

Homicide was where he had always wanted to be, ever since a bleak afternoon many years ago, when he had discovered what loss meant. He had been nothing but a boy, when his father had been murdered. That was when he had decided to make finding murderers his trade, and though these memories were now buried way in back in the archives of Frank's mind and only rarely popped up, they had been very clear always present over the last couple of weeks. Ever since lieutenant Redding had given him the heads up, on what was about to happen to the department. Redding had called him and the other team leaders in for a need-to-know-only meeting, where he had asked them to pick which detectives they wanted to keep with them and which ones would be transferred elsewhere. Of course it was only a matter of minutes after that meeting had ended, before everyone knew, or at least had a pretty good idea, about what was about to happen. The decision had meant many nights without any sleep, which was probably why he was so tired now and certainly one of the reasons his head was pounding. Over the past four years, his six-man team had worked together as one unit, with everyone knowing their place, their own and each other's strengths and weaknesses. They had a perfect record for the past eighteen months, solving twelve homicides within Seattle and helping to solve three others. Sending off half of his friends to do jobs in other departments just to satisfy some stat-junkie in administration, made him feel like the biggest asshole on the planet, even if none of his now to be former team-members had even hinted at blaming him for this.

Joel Burns had been an obvious choice. He would spend endless hours pounding on doors, day or night and never complaining about it. In the past Frank had asked him to chase down even the tiniest leads, and he had disappeared for a few hours and come back with everything there was to know. No one ever asked Joel how he did it. Three years of undercover work for Vice, helping to blow a major drugring in the early nineties, had given him respect amongst his peers as well as a network of informants and contacts in the underworld. Right now, Joel was sitting in his beat up chair, that he had brought in to the office himself, staring out the window. His feet were up on his desk, as they often were, showing a pair of well worn, brown, Italian leather shoes that had a replaced heel on both feet and almost no sole left in the center. He was chewing slowly on a ball-point pen, not much thinner than his fingers, his bony jaw seemingly working hard at crushing it.

Frank's second choice had been much harder. No one wanted a transfer, and Frank could easily find a use for every single person. But in the end he had chosen Elouise Jackson. She was insurance and a good balance for Joel. She too was sitting at her desk, which seemed too small for her, even though everything was neatly organized on it. Frank watched her, as she scanned her desk from left to right, correcting the piles of paper, the phone and the computer keyboard. Her face was tight mask that made her look, at if she might explode if someone poked her hard enough. Frank knew what the expression meant, and that there was nothing he could say to change it.

Next to each other, Joel and Elouise were like night and day. If she was night, she was a dark and dangerous one. She never talked about it much, but Frank knew she had been an MP during the first war in Iraq. As a black woman that could not have been easy, but her large, muscular frame would have helped. She always had perfect creases in all of her clothes and never wore short sleeves. Frank expected the two detectives to bump heads more often now than in the past, since they would all be forced to work closer together. He was already planning on talking to them about this, as soon as the initial shock from the *re-organizing* had settled. The truth was that they were perfect together, not in spite of their differences, but because of them. Joel was sometimes a little too quick to speak and certainly had a temper, but he kept all that at bay somehow, when they were in the field. Frank had never seen Elouise lose her temper, but he had a feeling, he would not want to be around when it happened. Once he had seen her beat two men singlehandedly, to get them to give up a third guy. She could play the bad cop to perfection, and shake it off just as easily. The truth was, that Frank never knew what she was really thinking. But she got things done, and like himself, she liked being systematic about it.

His colleagues were starting to leavie the office, as he sat there, going over these things in his mind. When it came to handling internal disagreements on the team, that always brought on the headache. His strength was in the work itself, not the administration surrounding it. He wondered whether there would be more headaches now, that his team had to do double work.

The room would be much too big for the homicide division. It was a fairly large room with clusters of desks, one for each team, seperated by filing cabinets holding the paperwork of years of old cases, some of them still open. Everyone had done their part to cover their grey, metal surfaces. Some had hung drawings by their kids, reminding them that there was a life outside work. Others had hung printouts of jokes, photographs and newspaper clippings. The people who were now being transferred would be missed, not only in person, but physically in the room, when they took all these things with them.

Frank's own desk was not much to look at, he thought. There were no photographs or children's drawings, no photocopied Calvin and Hobbes strips or anything like that. There were stacks of file folders and forms, a couple of them looking like they might fall at any time, spilling all over the floor. His eyes lingered on them for a while, but he made no effort to straighten them out. He had a pack of Oreos and a small tower of Starbucks paper cups. He thought about throwing them in his otherwise empty wastebasket, but did not do it.

Driving across the bridge toward his home in West Seattle, Frank felt his throat tighten and a burning behind his eyes, as he tightened his grip on the wheel of his dark red Mustang. He felt tired, suddenly, fast approaching his 37th birthday, still unmarried with no kids and living in a rented apartment. It was the stereotypical life of a homicide detective, but the truth was, that Frank was the only one who actually lived up to the stereotype. He kept telling himself, that he could never ask any woman to be a cop's wife, and he had seen too much evil in the world to ever want to put children into it. As he drove the Mustang through the pouring autumn rain, he was wondering if he had given too much to the job. It wasn't the first time, he had had these thoughts, but the answer was always the same. This was what he was good at, what he had been meant to do. He had known this ever since that night, when he was a just a boy. He still remembered the look on the face of the cop, who had come to the door. He had been an older guy, probably around fifty, with a bright white mustache and eyes as blue as the ocean, surrounded by the fine lines of a man, who smiles a lot. But he did not smile that day, and his voice was so soft, as he spoke to Frank's mother. He smelled like sweet pipe tobacco. Frank remembered his mother crying a lot. It took several days if not weeks, before he had understood, that his father was never coming home.

Frank had always been ambitious, knowing exactly where he wanted to be. Friends had made jokes about him becoming the next chief, but he was never going to go that way. Homicide was what he wanted to do, and he was doing it. And with that in mind, the question of whether he was giving too much to the job, seemed less important.

It was almost 8pm when he pulled into the designated parking spot. He cut the engine and sat there for a while, listening to the sound of the rain hitting the roof of his car. He grabbed the sixpack he'd picked up on the way and opened up a bottle. The rain and the beer made all thoughts of department politics and early retirement fade away. He was tired and hungry and his mind started drifting towards ordering delivery, hoping that he'd stay awake until it arrived. He stayed in the car until the first beer was gone, put the bottles back in the bag and went inside.

The apartment was dark, stuffy and smelled like dirty laundry. He put a load on in the washer and turned on the television as he took out a second beer. The local news channel was on, but Frank wasn't really paying attention to what the newscaster was saying. He just let the images float by, sipping his beer without a thought in his mind. The beer dulled the headache and the world grew hazy around him.

Suddenly Frank was thrown back to reality by the sound of his doorbell. For a second, he thought it was the pizza, but then he realized, he'd never gotten around to ordering one.

Chapter three

Rosa Perez looked up at Frank with her familiar, wide smile that held teeth that seemed much too big and bright, for such a small woman. She held out an orange, plastic plate that looked like, it had come from one of those picnic sets, they sell at the supermarket every summer. On it was a couple of sweet smelling tortillas, covered with a thin layer of sauce and surrounded by salad. Frank often wondered, how Rosa had attained her plump figure, with the kind of food she prepared and all the hard work she did. They had been living next door to each other for three years, and though neither had ever set foot in each other's apartment, Frank felt that he knew mrs. Perez very well. All the fights he had overheard before her husband finally took off. Once, he almost burst in there, when he thought the guy was slapping her around, but then the oldest son came home and things settled down. On happier days, he would hear her sing through the walls. Though he did not understand the lyrics, he always thought there was a very genuine sadness behind the words.

Mrs. Perez had four kids, two of them living at home with her, the other two dropping by all the time, it seemed. When Frank thought about the size of his own two bedroom apartment, he tried to imagine all those people sharing a similar one.

"I thought, you might be hungry, mr. Cash."

"Thank you, Rosa," Frank replied, as he took the plate. "You are too kind."

"Mr. Cash," she said and smiled. "You work hard for all of us. Just leave the plate in front of my door, when you're done."

"Thank you. Good night, Rosa."

He took the meal inside and opened another beer to go along with it. Ever since he had told her what he did for a living, she had started bringing him food from time to time. Frank had wondered about the connection between the two, but had never found any obvious explanation. Perhaps it was simply a sign of appreciation, he thought, or maybe one of her friends or family members had been murdered long ago, and this was her way of staying in touch with that. Or maybe she was hoping Frank would protect her, if her husband ever came back. On a couple of occasions, he had tried to return the favor, by bringing her a bottle of wine, but somehow that always felt awkward, so the last time he did it, he had simply left it outside her door with a card on it.

The food always made little beads of sweat form on Frank's brow, as he scarfed it down, which for some reason, he always did with her food. Some day he would find a good way to repay her for her kindness, he thought as he emptied his bottle.

The flat, plastic sound of his cellphone playing the theme from Hill Street Blues, tore him out of sleep. Frank was still on the couch, the only light in the room coming from the flickering images of the muted tv. His clothes felt sticky.

"Hello?" He said.

"Hey, Fax," said Burns's voice on the other end. "We've got a call."

"Where?"

"Downtown studio apartment. Vic is a single, white female. You'd better get here quick. This looks like a big one."

"How so?" Frank replied, now completely awake.

"Just get here, Frank. You'll see."

Frank got the directions and hung up. His back was aching from the awkward position he had been sleeping in. The green numbers on his VCR showed it was two in the morning. He had been out for about four hours. Before leaving, he allowed himself a few minutes to change his shirt and freshen up, brushing his teeth to get rid of any left-over beer breath.

On the way out, he grabbed the neighbor's plastic plate, which still had a few leftovers on it. He normally washed off the plate before returning it, but this time, he settled for scraping the leftovers into the garbage disposal.

"I'm sorry, Rosa," he said, as he put the plate down in front of her door.

Fifteen minutes later, Frank met Joel in front of an older apartment building on the corner of Boren Avenue and Seneca, just outside the Downtown core, a couple of blocks from Seattle's convention center. Compared to the glass and steel towers of Downtown, this building was decorated with classic terra cotta designs and like many other buildings like this in Seattle, the higher you got, the more intricate the and detailed were the patterns and gargoyles. The yellow streetlights and the blinking red from the cruiser parked out front made the patterns and carvings look deeper and sinister. Besides the patrol car, Frank spotted Joel's car and a white forensics van.

"I see our friends from the media haven't arrived yet," Frank said to Joel and the uniformed officer, standing outside the lobby entrance. "Get those lights shut off," he pointed towards the cruiser. "No need to attract them faster than necessary."

"It's a weeknight," Joel said, while the other cop cut the lights, "they're not out in as big numbers. But they'll be here shortly."

"Tell me about the scene," Frank said, as he started walking inside without waiting for Joel to follow. "What are we looking at here?"

"We're looking at a twisted one. I'd say someone who's done it before. Maybe even a serial."

"That bad, huh?"

Joel did not reply, but he did not have to.

The lobby was spacious and decorated like Frank imagined a fancy Parisian hotel would be. Red and white striped couches were carefully placed on each side of the room, along paneled walls and under crystal chandeliers. There were matching carpets with a tiled passageway in the middle, leading up to the elevators.

As soon as Frank entered the apartment itself, he could smell it. His throat tightened and he felt the Mexican dinner try to work its way back up to his throat. He was not sure, if it was the sweet, familiar thickness of stench or the knowledge that he was breathing in particles of a rotting corpse, that always made his gag-reflex set in. Years of practice had taught him to hide and fight it, but he had never gotten used to it.

"Neighbor called it in." Joel said.

"No kidding?"

The two walked slowly through the apartment towards the bedroom. A couple of technicians were standing by, waiting for the detectives to finish.

"Where's Elouise?" Frank asked.

"I couldn't reach her on her cell."

"Did you try?"

"A little."

Frank turned towards Joel, who immediately held up his hands.

"I called her twice, okay?"

"Keep calling."

As impressive and countrystyle posh as the lobby had been, the apartment looked and felt like any other apartment. The walls were painted white, the floors were carpeted, there was no fancy paneling or decoration, apart from what the tenant had put in. Which in this case was very little. The short hallway featured a large, wallmounted mirror with a simple black frame, under which was a shelf. On it was what looked like unopened mail. On their way to the bedroom, from where the stench was coming, the passed through the living room, which in one end was dominated by a black leather couch, designed to look as square and uncomfortable as possible. It was facing a flat, wallmounted plasma television. A glance at the coffee table in between, revealed only what you expect ot find there; a remote control, a cordless phone, an empty glass, a couple of magazines and more mail. At the other end of the room, near the kitchen, was a simple, dark wood dining table, which looked like something out of a medieval castle with a thick top and legs that appereared to be attached with large, black iron nails. On it was a silver candleholder with a half-burned candle in it and a grey vase with a handful of long dead daisies in it. Were it not for a large, abstract painting with a red and orange pattern, the flowers would have been the only color to be seen anywhere.

The only other piece of furniture was a shelving unit with a few books, cds and and a stereo on it. Both the shelves and the stereo were black.

Frank and Joel arrived in the bedroom. The bed was a queensize, covered with a once white sheet, under which the form of a human body could be seen. The white linen had since been stained by the fluids released from the body. Frank noted a darker, brown stain between the legs.

As Frank came closer, he saw that two holes had been cut in the sheet. One over each eye of the victim, each about two inches in diameter. A pair of lifeless, almost completely grey eyes were staring out from underneath the ghost costume.

Turning his attention away from the dead woman, Frank looked up and saw two windows, both of them closed and filtering sunlight straight onto the bed, no doubt helping the decomposition along in the process. He felt his insides turn again and swallowed a mouthful of saliva. Trying to focus, he finally looked over at Joel, who was still trying to reach Elouise. Joel hung up and sighed, shaking his head. Frank wondered if he was shaking it just to say, that she still was not answering, or if there was more.

"Anyone pull the sheet down yet?"

"I took a quick peek, while I was waiting for you."

"And?"

"Looks like strangulation."

Frank put on his gloves and slowly peeled the ghostlike mask from the face.

The woman must have been around his own age. A good looking mid-thirties woman straight out of "Sex and the City" with long, deep brown hair, a fit figure and healthy skin. Except this one had been dead for a while, and now her skin was yellowish white and her shape bloated. There were dark bruises on her neck and throat indicating strangulation, just as Joel had said. Her blodshot eyes supported the theory, still Frank knew, that only an autopsy could give a certain cause of death. For all he knew, she could have been held down by her throat but killed some other way. Joel finally got through to Elouise and used it as an excuse to leave the scene. As if the dead woman was making too much noise.

With help form the forensic technicians, Frank gently removed and bagged the stained sheet, exposing the woman's naked body fully in the process. As they did it, the sweet smell of rotting flesh got so intense, Frank's eyes were watering, and it took a minute, before he could see again. She appeared to have been posed on the bed, laying completely straight, her arms folded across her chest. If there had been a fight, the killer had removed all signs of it. Were it not for the bruises on her wrists, ankles and throat, she looked like she might have died a peaceful death in her sleep.

"This guy has definitely killed before," Frank said without taking his eyes off the body. Around him the techs had started their evidence collecting, taking pictures and preparing to take the dead woman to the morgue.

"I got through to Elouise and described the scene to her. She's at the office working on cross reference right now," Joel said as he came back into the bedroom.

"Good. You get a statement from the neighbor yet?"

"Not yet, just the 9-1-1 call, but we've got a guy waiting with him."

"ID on the vic?"

"I think it's the lady who lives here. Caroline Saunders, psychiatrist."

"A shrink, huh?"

"I always knew that was a dangerous line of work," Joel said.

"Maybe this is the work of a disgruntled client, then."

The two men looked at each other, then went off in different directions, not having to talk about what needed to be done. Joel would go knock on the neighbor's door, while Frank would continue working the crime scene.

On the floor next to the couch in the livingroom, he found a brown designer handbag with a matching wallet inside. In it, he found a driver's license. The picture showed a brunette with a wide smile and bright eyes, who even in the flat light and washed out colors of the driver's license picture, had an aura of confidence about her. He recognized the face, in spite of the bloating and discoloration of the body in the next room. Their victim was indeed Caroline Saunders.

There were also a few of Caroline's businessbards in the wallet. Frank put one of them in his pocket and bagged the wallet and handbag for fingerprint processing.

Nothing seemed out of the ordinary in the apartment. There were no signs of struggle, no indication that she had had a visitor or that anyone had broken in. In fact, he thought, the clutter on the coffee table suggested, she was not expecting company at all. He found the base for the chordless phone in the kitchen and noticed a blinking icon in the display, indicating voicemail messages. Carefully, he lifted the phone up with his gloved finger, carefully pressed the voicemail button and held it close enough to his ear to hear, without touching the phone directly.

The phone contained eight messages. Five of them were from what sounded like a young man, asking where she were and when she was going to show up. On the third message, he said that he had started telling the clients, that she was sick and begun rescheduleing their appointments. On the fitfh message, he said that he was closing the practice and leaving a notice on the door and answering machine, saying they would be open again tomorrow. All five messages were from Monday.

The three other messages were from a person calling herself Anna. The first two had been left on Saturday, a little more than a week ago. Anna appeared to be heading up to the touristy town Leavenworth, a couple of hours north of Seattle, and from the sound of the messages, it appeared that Caroline had been supposed to join her there. Anna was calling to confirm on the first two messages. The third message was left on Wednesday. Anna said that they were having fun in Leavenworth, but that they missed Caroline's company, and would she please call back.

Given that it was now early Tuesday morning, the phone messages gave Frank some idea of the time elapsed, since anyone had last seen Caroline Saunders alive.

Frank got out his notebook and started writing all this down. He would need to find the young man, who sounded like he might be an assistant of Caroline's, and he would need to locate this Anna and find out who *they* were. For all he knew, either caller could be the killer trying to establish an alibi.

Having found nothing else in the apartment, the rest would be up to the forensics people. They'd go over the place with a fine tooth comb, looking for anything the human eye wouldn't catch. Frank had great respect for their work, even if some of the younger ones seemed a little full of themselves, after the "CSI" shows had become such a success on television. Frank's strategy was to treat them as part of his own homicide team while on the scene, and then just stay out of their way and wait to hear their findings. Other detectives put pressure on the lab, trying to get their evidence processed faster. Frank suspected that this kind of pressure only led to sloppy work and fewer result. So, instead he did his best to compliment their efforts and save the phonecalls for when he really needed them. So far that had never led to anything but perfect cooperation and respect for his authority on the scene.

"Do you want to go down to the office and kick it off right now?" Asked Joel, tucking away his notepad and looking at his watch.

"You said Elouise was down there already?"

"Yeah, I talked to her again though. Says she hasn't found anything. Might need something more to go on, she says."

"You got the testimony and the info on the neighbor?"

"Uh-huh."

Frank looked at his watch. It was a little over four in the morning.

"Let's get some sleep," he finally said. "We'll meet at the office at nine thirty."

"Will you let Elouise know?"

"Sure, Joel."

Without another word, Joel swung around and left the apartment. Frank waited a little. They were loading the body into a bag and onto a stretcher and the lab people were finishing up as well. He looked at the bed, wondering what had happened to the psychiatrist. He got out her businesscard and his cellphone and dialed the number printed on the card.

Chapter four

BULGARIA, FEBRUARY 2001 – It's cold in the backroom of the Russian restaurant. From the pale winter light coming through the cracked window, Branko watches the steam of his breath, as it twirls slowly in the air. His fingers are numb and he doesn't feel the other man's hand, as he grips it for a handshake. Oleg is Russian and former KGB, if the rumors are true. Supposedly retired, but according to the information Branko has bought, Oleg is currently involved with a group of Russian 'entrepeneurs', who occasionally need him to procure what he has heard them refer to as strongly motivated personel for what they calll pro-active security detail. In other words, the Russian is renting out soldiers to whoever has the money to pay for them. Branko is not sure, how much of his information is correct, but he has high hopes nonetheless. It's been more than a year, since he set out to find Jovana's killer, and so far, he has gotten nowhere. Branko has already decided what to do, if the Russian can not help him.

Not a word is exchanged between the two men, as Branko hands over the envelope containing the police pictures and report. Oleg pours them both a shot of vodka, and like the old traditions dictate, he raises his glass to their health, before pulling out the contents of the file. Branko leans back and feels the back of the rickety chair give under his weight. He watches a fly, slowly crawling across the table, no doubt dying in the cold, as he waits for the Russian to speak.

If the crime scene photos have any effect on the old man, he does not show it. Slowly, he goes through them one by one, pausing to look closely at each one, before putting it at the back of the pile. He does so at least twice without offering any expression or sound. The room is quiet except for the shuffling of the pictures, the occasional buzz from the dying fly and the muffled sounds from the kitchen behind them. Oleg carefully slides the photographs back into the envelope, before lifting his head. His steel-blue eyes pierce Branko, as he hands it back.

"This was your sister?"

"Yes, sir."

"And this happened in '94? In Pristina?"

"Yes."

Oleg pours another shot for the both of them and dedicates it to Jovana's honor. The old man grows quiet for a while after that, sitting completely still as he looks out the window. In the dark room, the single shaft of white light hits his face and reminds Branko of the face of someone who has already died of old age, his hollow cheeks and sunken in eyes, framed by the deep wrinkles and scars. Only his grey eyes are clear and full of life. Another shot of vodka is poured before he speaks again.

"I do not know this man," he says, pointing at the envelope. "But I know who knows."

"Will he help me?" Branko asks, knowing all too well, that the circles in which mercenaries travel are hard to penetrate. Most of those he has spoken to so far, have not been willing to help. Some because they are afraid to incriminate themselves, some because they fear what will happen, if the information is ever traced back to them.

Finding Oleg was not easy or cheap. Had it not been for the Lord's help, Branko is sure, he would not have gotten this far.

"He will," the old man says, as he gets out a brand new cellphone and dials a number. "I paged him. He will call back soon."

The old man speaks Russian on the phone. He talks in short bursts and seems to listen a lot. His eyes never shifting from Branko's, his face never giving anything away.

"I am told, the man you are looking for was recruited by a Dane. This Dane was known to my contact, but even he did not personally know the man you are looking for. We believe he might have been a one-timer."

From his own experience with the PMC's in the war, Branko knows about the one-timers. Men with something to prove to either themselves or someone haunting their minds, who thought themselves tough, but who soon discovered that the reality of war was far from the Hollywood-reality from the movies they had seen. Those men never went back out, either because they had been broken by what they had seen and done, or because they were dead. No man could walk into war and come out without wounds one way or the other, and those who came unprepared or for the wrong reasons often left with the deepest ones. Branko thought about the things he, himself had done. Things he never thought, he was even capable of.

Another vodka is poured and though Branko is starting to feel the effect of the previous ones, warming his body and casting a slight haze over this thoughts, he picks up the glass. It would be an insult not to. As they drink, he shuts his eyes, hoping that the Russian will give him more information and less vodka in the minutes to come.

"Go to Denmark," Oleg finally says. "Find the recruiter. His name is Jacob Hansen. A fairly common name, unfortunately, but that is all I can give you."

With that, Oleg gets up and leaves the same way he came in. In spite of the vodka, the cold is already creeping back into Branko's bones, as his mind races, trying to process this new information. He has another name to go on, but no way of knowing if that person is still in Denmark. Or even alive.

But there is hope and faith.

He has to go to Denmark, which means going into the European Union. That will not be easy. He will need new papers, a car to replace his worn out Jeep and more money. He has only a couple of hundred dollars left now. Not enough at all. Once again, he must arm himself with patience and do things, he does not like doing. There will be plenty of opportunities to earn some cash along the way. Small banks, gas stations, supermarkets. All of them good targets.

Only the small places will do, where security is not too tight. And he must spread it out, over time and geographically to keep it from becoming too dangerous. If possible, it would be best to avoid having a price on his head. He must have patience and courage, if he is to survive.

"For Jovana," he says to himself, lifting his still half-full glass toward the winter landscape outside. "I will do anything for you." As he puts his glass down again, he notices that the fly is no longer moving.

Chapter five

Three hours of sleep was not enough. Great amounts of coffee would not do anything but upset his stomach. Not even a cold shower brought Frank back to reality. As he got ready to go, he let the news roll in the background. The murder was mentioned, but no critical details had apparently leaked to the press yet. Instead, they used the killing to segment into a story about the recent restructure of the division. He knew, they would have to hold a press conference sooner or later, before the vultures started digging too deep, or at least issue an official statement. He would have to talk to the lieutenant about that.

The office was completely empty, when he walked in, carrying his box of doughnuts and the triple-shot latte from the Starbucks across the street. On his desk was the first report from Elouise on top of the one he had written himself, straight after leaving the crimescene earlier this morning. Joel's summary of the interview with the neighbor, and the first respond report was still to be written. As he placed the reports into a fresh binder, his cellphone chirped. The number seemed familiar, but he could not quite place it.

"Homicide, detective Cash."

"Eh ... hi. It's Darryl from the clinic."

"Caroline's assistant," Frank said, suddenly remembering the number being the same one he had dialed last night.

"You asked me to call you?"

"That's right, Darryl. I'd like to talk to you, but not over the phone."

"What's this about?" The voice sounded nervous now, like people often did, when he talked to them.

"It's about Caroline Saunders."

"Is she alright?" The sound of Darryl's voice told Frank, he had not watched the morning news on tv. Or he pretended not to.

"Why don't you come in, Darryl, and we can talk about it?"

Frank gave Darryl the directions and hung up. In the meantime, Joel had arrived and started writing his report. It was a quarter to ten and Elouise still had not arrived, but before he could finish the thought, his cell rang again. It was her. She told him, she'd been on the phone with Caroline's parents, who were coming in to formally identify the body. She would meet them at the morgue, talk to them, and come up when they were done. Frank hoped, Elouise had gotten a hold of them before they had had a chance to hear the news elsewhere

Already, Frank was starting to see how difficult it was going to be, to work with a three man team. He was used to holding these meetings every morning and evening, and often one or two detectives would not be there, because the case would not necessarily be waiting for a meeting to be over. Before, that was not a problem, as the detective could read up on the case on the summary written at the end of each meeting. But with only three people on the team, everyone would have to be there. Now, Elouise was at the morgue and he was expecting Darryl to show up at any time.

"How long will it take you to write that?" he said, nodding at Joel's computer.

"About an hour," Joel said without looking up from the monitor. His skin looked grey in the light from the monitor on his desk. It made the dark rings under Joel's eyes stand out and reminded Frank of cheap zombie movies.

"Elouise is at the morgue with the parents. If she shows up while I'm gone, send her down to me. I'll be talking to Caroline's secretary."

"Will do."

While he was waiting for Darryl to show, Frank called the lab to get an update. They had a preliminary report, which was mostly a list of the evidence collected on the scene, and some pictures ready. The autopsy was still pending, which was the best answer he could get. The report and pictures would be arriving by messenger shortly.

Darryl wore a dark blue polo shirt with a lighter blue stripe across the chest, khaki pants and big, square glasses. His two front teeth stood out, as if they were trying to escape from his mouth, made worse by his almost non-existant chin. He did not appear like someone who would be a threat to anyone, but Frank knew better than to judge by looks alone. He had seen scrawny guys perform feats requiring great strength, just like he had met shy, quiet men, who turned out to be sadistic, cold-blooded killers. Darryl did not have a record, but that was no guaranteee either. Frank hoped that this interview might give him an idea which kind of man Darryl was.

"Could I have a glass of water?" Darryl asked, before sitting down.

"Of course," Frank replied. "Just wait here."

When he returned with the drink, he put it down and waited for him to take a sip, before sitting down across from him. Darryl's hand was shaking.

"Shall we get started?"

"You said this was about Caroline?"

"Yes. But before we get to that, I'd like to ask you a few questions?"

"Sure," Darryl fidgetted in his chair. "What about?"

"When was the last time, you saw Caroline?"

"Last Friday."

"Not this Friday, but the one before?"

"Yeah. The clinic was closed last week."

"Why is that?"

"Vacation, I guess," Darryl shrugged slightly, but at the same time, he was gripping his glass so tight, Frank wondered if it might break.

"You don't know?"

"It's Carol's clinic, she can shut it down for a week if she wants to, can't she?"

Frank nodded and looked straight at the young man in front of him. It got so quiet, he heard the seconds tick by from the watch on Darryl's wrist.

"She didn't tell you, why she closed it down?" he finally asked.

"She was going up north. Leavenworth, I think."

"What if there's an emergency with one of her patients?"

"She has clients, not patients," Darryl explained. He had stopped moving around in his chair, Frank noticed, and he was no longer clinging to his glass of water. "They are mostly people who suffer from midlife crisis, mild depressions and every day stress. No real loonies."

"Alright," Frank said, deciding to change the pace a little. "So, the 'clinic' was supposed to re-open on yesterday. When it didn't you called her, and when she didn't answer, you simply closed up shop?"

"That's right."

"It didn't occur to you, that something might be going on?"

"I don't know," Darryl said, suddenly seeming uncertain again. "What's this about? Why are you asking all these questions?"

"Caroline was found murdered last night, Darryl."

"Murdered?"

"Yes. That's why you're talking to me. I'm a homicide detective, remember?"

Darryl didn't answer. His eyes and mouth were wide open, like he was too shocked to speak. There was a knock on the door, and Elouise popped her head inside.

"Fax, I need you outside for a sec."

In the hallway, Elouise told him that the parents had identified the body as Caroline Saunders, and she gave him a fast rundown of the package from forensics, which contained no surprise clues.

"She was raped prior to being strangulated. They found residue from a lubricated condom as well as bruising. No seamon or hair. No sign of a break in, and the fingerprints they pulled have not been processed yet."

"In other words, nothing at all."

"Pretty much... We can hope for a surprise to turn up during the autopsy, but I wouldn't count on it."

Elouise held out an envelope containing the images from the crime scene, but Frank waved her off.

"I don't want Darryl to see those. I don't want him to know exactly what happened to her."

"Think he did it?"

"No," Frank replied. "But if he did, he'll know what she looked like. And if he didn't, I don't want him accidentally letting any details slip to the press later."

When Frank came back into the interrogation room, he had already decided to go easy on Darryl. He was pretty sure, the assistant was not the vicious killer, responsible for Caroline's death, but just to be sure, he did not want to spook him more than necessary. Short of a confession, they didn't have anything to hold him on anyway.

"I'm sorry you had to hear about it like this," Frank said. "Would you like some more water?"

"No thanks ... Is she really dead?"

"I'm afraid so, Darryl. Now, is there anything you can tell me, that might help us find out who did this?"

"I don't know. I don't think so."

"Did you know of any jealous boyfriends? Any pissed off patients? Anyone who might have it in for her?"

"No, no one. But I didn't really know her that well. I've only worked for her a couple of months."

"Do you know, who had your job before you?"

"No, but I'm sure there must be some records at the clinic." Darryl's voice trailed off and his face became vacant. "I can't believe she's dead."

At this point Frank decided to let the guy go. It seemed obvious that he knew very little, and he certainly did not look like a suspect. Just to make sure, he would have Joel dig around and see what would come up on both the current and the previous clerk. He thanked Darryl for coming in and sent him home.

Joel had his feet up and was munching on a doughnut, and Elouise was flicking through the case file, when Frank joined them in the office. The nonchalant attitude of Joel's bothered Frank more than it should, and he felt his jaw tighten. Lack of sleep, he told himself, was wearing his patience down.

"Let's get lunch," he said. "Bring the file."

Instead of going to some diner, the trio got a bagful of sandwiches from Subway and drove down to the water. It had been Elouise's idea, and Frank had liked the idea of being able to talk freely, without people eavesdropping from the tables next to them.

"So, tell me about the neighbor," said Frank, as he bit into his BLT sandwich.

"Seems straight forward," Joel replied, his mouth full of food. "He noticed a smell and called us."

"Nothing else? Didn't hear anything?"

"Nope. He said ms. Saunders – he called her that – was a good neighbor. Never any noise, never any parties, apart from the occasional coming home late."

"Boyfriends?"

"According to the neighbor, she was single. If she ever brought a man home, he never noticed it."

"Seems a bit odd," said Frank.

"Maybe not," Elouise interrupted. She had barely touched her sandwich. "She might be the type to go home with someone, but never take a guy to her place. A lot of women do that. You'd both know that, if you'd go out more."

"Hey, I'm married," protested Joel.

"Yeah. Proves there's someone out there for everyone, don't it?" Elouise replied.

"You think he could have done it?" Frank broke in.

"Nah. Not the type at all," Joel replied.

Had it been any other detective, Frank would not have been satisfied with that answer, but that was why he'd picked Joel to be on his team. He had a gift for reading people, like no one Frank had ever seen. Often, Joel would be able to call a suspect's guilt or innocense in a matter of minutes. Elouise knew this too, and like Frank, she did not question Joel's conclusion.

Eating their subs side by side on the pier, looking out over Puget Sound, Frank started to think, that perhaps this new three man team was not as horrible, as he had feared. Stopping himself from becoming too sentimental about it, he started recapping the interview with Darryl, ending with the conclusion that he too, should be written off as a suspect. That left them with the clerk at the clinic, Darryl had replaced, and the mystery girlfriend, Anna. Joel pointed out, that it was very unlikely that Anna had raped her friend, to which the two others had to agree.

"I'd still like a word with her," Frank said.

"I bet we can find her number on Carol's cellphone," Joel suggested.

The phone, along with various other personal accessories, had been handed over to the crime lab for processing. According to the report from them, they had already taken the fingerprint samples they needed from this, and it was ready to be released. Frank thought about this for a second and decided to cut his lunch short. He excused himself and left the others by the pier, turning his red Mustang straight towards the lab.

It was nearing two in the afternoon and the autumn clouds had given way to the afternoon sun, which was beating hard through the windows at the office, creating an almost sedating, stuffy heat in the room. Both Elouise and Joel looked just as tired as Frank felt. None of them spoke and the only sound was the soft humming from the computers and the almost inaudible clicks, every time Frank pressed a button on Caroline's cellphone.

Frank noted Anna's number on a legal pad and tossed the phone over to Joel.

"I want you to call all the other numbers in there, and find out what their connection was to Caroline," Frank said before turning to Elouise. "And I want you to get us into Caroline's office. If there's anythng in there, I don't want it gathering dust."

"Got it," Elouise said and got up. She towered over both Frank and Joel. "I'll call you, when we're ready."

"And what are you going to do?" Asked Joel.

"I'm going to put together a summary for the big bossman," Frank said, trying to look like he'd gladly swap tasks with Joel. "I'm sure he's anxious to put out an official statement to our friends in the media."

"I bet."

"And when I'm done, we'll hopefully have access to the office. After that, I'm heading down to the lab again. You're welcome to join me, if you'd like."

"Gee, thanks, Fax."

Fax had been Frank's nickname for years. Whenever he was asked about it, he thought about making up some fantastic story about heroics or savvy policework. Or even something funny involving a fax machine. That was was most people thought it came from, but the truth was far simpler and infinitely more boring. They called him Fax as a contraction of his first and middle name: Frank Alexander. Frank had never liked it, mostly because he too was reminded of fax machines, an invention he considered pure evil. Complaining about the nickname would not change anything though. It was just one of those things that stuck.

Flicking through the pages of the reports so far, he hoped something would leap out at him. It happened sometimes, which was why he never minded the paperwork as much as most cops. At least in that respect, he did not live up to the stereotype. Paperwork tied everything together and ensured nothing was missed in the confusion. Most often, when something did turn up in the paperwork, it was much further into the investigation or on cases where the amount of information was staggering. Neither was the case here, and the fact that they had so little to go on, became clearer every time, he re-read the contents of the folder. .

Writing the summary report, he felt a knot forming in his guts. He wondered if there was anything they could have done differently. If the team had had six members like it used to, they could have been done with the numbers in her cellphone and the processing of the clinic by now, possibly finding a lead through there. As he saw it, those two were the best hopes so far, along with the autopsy or some other forensic surprise, and though he knew that either of these might prove to provide them with the lead they needed, writing the summary of what they had so far, still made the entire investigation feel half-assed. But it was not, he reminded himself. His two investigators were working it as good, as they could, with all the thoroughness and diligence a murder case required. The lack of speed was a direct result of the lack of manpower.

Lieutenant Redding, or Big Red as they called him behind his back, was usually pretty good at listening to his detectives. This time, however, Frank was not expecting too much understanding. Redding was not used to recieving such thin summaries. The time since the cutbacks had been hard on everyone in the office, and Big Red was no exception. Everyone had known some sort of cut had been coming, and the lieutenant had probably known the details ahead of the rest. Frank had no doubt, that Redding had done his best to fight the cuts, but he would have been going up against both the chief and the mayor's office at the same time.

Big Red got his name from his size. He was a huge man, once one of the best homicide detectives to ever work the department. Seven years earlier, he had been shot in the line of duty, and though he survived the incident, he was left with a permanent limp and a deskjob. Since then he had gained at least a hundred pounds, and people who didn't know better, often assumed that he walked with a cane to support his massive weight. Frank was happy, that he answered to a man, who knew what the game was about. He never interfered with how investigations were run or the internal workings of a team, but cared only about getting the guy and securing the evidence. Frank was not sure, how Big Red would see their lack of leads or progress after the first 24 hours.

He had just put the summary report on the lieutenant's desk, when Elouise called to say, that she was waiting for them in her car outside Caroline's clinic.

Chapter six

SERBIA, MAY 2001 – The gun is cold and smells like burnt oil. The smell is overpowering and hangs in the car like a thick, invisible fog. Everything else is hot, the sun is beating hard through the windshield of the car. Even in the shade it is almost intolerable. His head feels heavy and from the heat and the fumes, and if he closed his eyes for more than a few seconds, Branko fears he would fall asleep. For three days, he has been parked across the street from the bank, getting out every hour to walk around the streets in the neighborhood and get familiar with it. He has been in every little shop in the area at least a handful of times. The town is a small one, basically just a crossroads where to main roads cross. At the intersection, where he is sitting there is a post office, a general store, a bakery and the bank. He knows the layout of the bank very well. As you come in, you enter a plain, small white painted room, where two tellers at seated at worn wooden desks behind an old, scratched up counter. To the left of them is a small office with glass windows and no door, where the manager is. The walls inside the bank were once white, but are now yellowish grey, covered by years of filth and nicotine. There are two cameras inside, but Branko is not worried about those. He is not even convinced they are working. Still, after three day, he has not been able to pull it off. Weighing the pistol in his hands, he prays to the Lord for guidance.

The cash ran out almost a week ago, now there is just enough left for food and gas. He did not think, it would be so hard to do a simple bankrobbery. Preparing for it was easier. He has switched the plates on his car, stealing a set at a rest area across the border. Even if they are reported stolen, it will take longer for the local police here to find out. It is not much, but anything to throw them off will be a help. He is not planning to stick around, anyway.

Perhaps it would be easier, he thinks to himself, if he had actually gotten any closer to finding Jovana's killer, or The Ghost, as he had started calling him lately. He talks to him sometimes, at night, before he goes to sleep. Usually, he asks The Ghost why. Whenever he answers, Branko realizes that he does not really want to know, and he has to shut him up. The Ghost is a faceless man to him, but he is not without expression. Branko sees his smile, as he talks about how he raped Jovana, whispering softly into her ear, as she struggled with the handcuffs. He sees those black eyes come to life, as The Ghost describes her last twitches, before death finally came to set her free. And he screams, hoping to drown it all out, but somehow the words are always come through in a hoarse whisper.

"You will never succeed," he says to his own reflection in the rear view mirror, "in turning me into another one of your ghosts."

The last few months were spent searching in vain. Branko could not afford the false EU passport, which would allow him to travel unhindered within the European Union, so he went back to Kosovo, looking everywhere he could think of for more information, hoping to find out more about the Dane, Jacob Hansen. But no one knew him or could give him anything to go on. He had gotten in touch with The German again, who seemed like he might be able to help, but the more questions Branko had asked, the more distant the little man had become, until he had finally asked Branko to leave and come back, when he was ready to pay for the passport.

Ten thousand American dollars is what he needs, and robbing banks is how he plans to get it. He can only hope that The German is still around, and that the price is still the same, when he finally has the money. It is not the type of merchandise that goes on sale. As he stares at the door to the bank, he wonders if The German knows anything about the Dane.

The church belltower plays a short melody that sounds sad in Branko's ears, followed by twelve strokes, indicating that it is noon. With a light sigh, he puts his left hand on the car door while clutching the gun in the right, and is halfway out of the car, before he realizes his mistake. He puts the gun in his pants instead, pulling the T-shirt out over the handle. It is not very well concealed, but it will have to do. From the backseat, he grabs a cotton sack, the kind made for laundry. That is as much of a giveaway as the gun, so he crumples it up in his hand. Finally, he pulls his American baseball cap down low and takes the sunglasses from the dashboard. It's now or never, he thinks. For Jovana.

As he opens the door, Branko does not hear anything but his own pulse and a sharp ringing. His feet feel lighter than normal and everything seems to move in slow motion. He knows this feeling well from his time in the Yugoslavian People's Army. There are two women and one man inside. The blond behind the counter stares straight at him with a helpful smile on her face. Maybe she recognizes him, from when he was scoping out the place, exchanging a few dollars as a cover. At one of the desks further back in the room, an older woman is typing something on a computer. At first she does not even notice his entrance, but when the blonde sees the gun, she stiffens and lets out a small sound, that causes the older woman to turn around.

From his own office, a short and barrelshaped man sees Branko before any of the others, maybe even before he enters the bank itself. In his right hand, the fat man is holding a sandwich of some kind, which he is pointing at Branko like a gun, as he storms out of the office, yelling something Branko does not hear.

The gun is already in Branko's hand and no longer feels heavy, but like an extension of his arm. He does not have to stop to aim, and the one shot he fires hits exactly in the middle of the manager's forehead. In a red mist, the back of his head explodes, and he stiffens for a second before tumbling backwards still holding the sandwich. The two women do not move a muscle.

"Fill it! Dollars and Euros only. Everything you've got!" Branko yells, as he tosses the sack to the blonde. She works fast without looking at him.

The older woman looks white like a sheet. She turns to look at the dead man, and she begins to shake. A scream is slowly forming in her throat and appears to be struggling to come out of her mouth. Without getting up, she leans across her desk, reaching towards the body.

"Not a word," Branko says, shifting his gun to the older woman. "or you will be next. I would prefer not to shoot a woman."

He heas the Ghost whisper to him. "Do it."

But the woman does not seem to hear him. She is getting up slowly, her arm still stretched towards the lifeless figure on the floor. Branko feels his finger tighten on the trigger, as she edges around the table. He pans with her, until his line of fire is broken by the blonde, holding out the bag, still not looking at him. He grabs it and runs.

It feels like there is a block of ice in his stomach, heavy and with a pain so cold he almost cannot breathe. As he steps on the gas and speeds out of town, he is barely able to focus on the road in front of him. There is no one chasing him yet, but he knows it won't be long.

Killing had not been part of the plan. Branko had hoped, he would not have to take another life, until he took the Ghost's, but war had taught him to take life as a defense, and he did not even realize what he was doing, until the explosion from the chamber of his gun mixed with the ringing that was already in his ears. In that instant, all he wanted was to drop the gun and get out of there, but the soldier in him took over and finished the job. Just like before.

He knows, he must be more careful now. He had comitted a murder and a violent robbery, and the story would be spreading to other towns in the area. People would be on the lookout for a car matching Branko's, for a man with his build and clothes.

There is nothing else to do for him, than to keep going. He plans on getting to one of the deserted farms, somehow get a new car and burn this one. There are plenty of suitables hidingplaces in these parts, but hiding is not what he needs to do. He decides to keep going at least a couple of hundred kilometers east, then switch cars and drive south and west towards Kosovo.

As he is thinking through his next moves, he feels his grip tighten on the wheel. The first blinking lights appear in the mirror. He suddenly sees Jovana in the backseat. Her eyes are teary and she sounds like she is about to cry, as she says: That man did not have to die. He had a family too. Who are you to say, that my life was worth his?

Chapter seven

Caroline Saunders' clinic had no fancy sign or logo out front. It simply had her name and the word 'therapist' in friendly, gold letters on the window. You could not see in from the street, because the lower half was covered by a plain, black curtain. If you wanted to look inside, you would have to step all the way up to the glass and stand you your toes. Inside, the half-covered windows had a nice effect too, giving the reception area an openness from the light coming in, but also a enough privacy, for the any waiting clients to remain comfortable. The floors were dark hardwood, the furniture looked like it was designed by some Scandinavian with a name Frank would never be able to pronounce, the center piece being an almost cubistic black, leather sofa with a matching low table. On it were neat stacks of magazines bearing names such as GQ, Empire and Vogue. The walls had abstract paintings decorating them, similar to the one on the wall in Caroline's apartment. Frank wondered if they were from the same artist, and whether or not that would be a clue, were it the case. In the back of the room was a tall black counter with a black leather-bound ledger and a slim cordless phone on it, another painting on the wall behind it and a barstool. This, Frank guessed, would have been Darryl's corner.

"Was she a shrink or a fashion guru?" Joel asked.

"Looks like she was targeting a very specific set of clients," Frank added. "Where did you get the key?"

"From her mother," Elouise explained. "She had it with her own house keys at the morgue. She's also the cleaninglady."

"How sweet."

"Where do we begin?" Joel was asking and putting on his latex gloves at the same time.

"You can take the lobby," Frank said. "I'll take the office. What else is there?"

"There's a small kitchen in the back, a bathroom and what looks like it might be a storage," Elouise explained.

"Good," Frank said, looking at her. "You get those."

The inner office, where the actual therapy took place, was decorated with more simple, clean furniture. A set of comfortable looking chairs in the same series as the sofa in the lobby, a small, low glass table with a handful of rounded rocks about the size of a a small egg, a black teapot and exactly two little cups on it. At the far end of the office was a rather large desk with lots of sharp corners and very little clutter on it. A Dell desktop computer with a flat screen monitor, a coffee mug, which to Frank indicated that the teapot was more for show than for actual use, and a leatherbound notepad.

In contrast to all the square black furniture, were the off-white walls and a large tapestry, which in soft pink and light blue colors depicted a giant orchid on a rocky background. Very zen, Frank thought.

There was a distinct lack of paper in the office. No books, no diplomas, no photographs and just a small, discreet cabinet partially hidden by the desk. A quick glance at the contents, revealed mostly financial records and a lot of space. Frank turned his attention to the computer, turning it on with a latexgloved fingertip without touching anything else. Slowly, the computer started up until it stopped at a login screen, prompting him for a username and a password. He sighed and turned it off again.

Instead he opened the notebook, but found only the blank pages of a yellow legal pad. There were a couple of drawers in the desk, containing standard office supplies, a small box of artificial sweeteners and a shrink's first-aid kit; a healthy supply of Kleenex. Frank bagged the sweeteners for analysis at the lab, knowing that they would probably turn out to be exactly what they claimed to be. In the bottom drawer, he found what appeared to be a small make-up kit, complete with hairbrush and an expensive looking glass bottle of perfume. He bagged it all.

After a good half hour, he was done looking through Caroline's office, but he had not found a single thing that looked, smelled or felt like any kind of smoking gun. He met up with the others back in the front room. Neither of them had found anything either. Joel had even taken a walk around the block and had time to small talk with the forensic technicians, who had arrived in the meantime. None of them spoke, while the techs started doing their bit. They all stood in the middle of the room, looking around as if something hidden might magically reveal itself.

"You'd think," Joel began, "that a shrink would have clients, that'd qualify as suspects, wouldn't you?"

"Yeah," Frank answered. "I'm still trying to figure out who her clients were."

"From the looks of it," Elouise said, "I'd say most were thirtysomething, well-off types. Men, judging from the magazines there. Some might be a little older, dealing with mid-life crisis issues." She smiled at the two men in front of her.

"Impressive," Joel said. "Can you tell if any of them's the killer too?"

"Just thinking out loud, Joel."

"Wow," Joel said, turning towards Frank. "She thinks."

"Hey," Frank cut him off. "We're all frustrated, but let's stay focused, okay? Besides, Elouise is right. The only problem is, that this narrows it down to those, who'd be most likely to kill someone like that anyway. White males between thirty and fifty. And let's not forget Darryl's predecessor, whom you'll be tracking down, Joel."

The two techs were done collecting prints, tagging and loading the bagged and boxed items into the van, and Frank used that as an excuse to unload the paperwork on Elouise and Joel, and leave the clinic behind, following the forensics van away from the office. But he did not go to the crime lab. Instead, he turned east towards the Harborview Medical Center, home of the King County medical examiner.

On the drive there, Frank's thoughts were circling around the case and the very few clues they had so far. He knew, that the more time that went by, the less chance they'd have to ever catch the guy. As he was repeating this to himself, for the thousandth time in his career, the images of Caroline Saunders flashed before him. She'd been tied up, raped and stranguled. No signs of break-in or struggle. Everything pointing towards someone she knew or at least trusted enough to let into her home voluntarily. If experience had taught him anything, it was that in cases like this, the fastest way to the killer would be through the victim. They needed to understand who Caroline had been, but so far Frank had not found anything, that really painted a picture in his mind. It was as if she in life had been a kind of ghost, like the one she had been dressed up as in death. Maybe the neighbor was worth a second visit after all. Or Darryl the clerk. Neither of the two were good suspects in Frank's mind. The killer had been careful to leave no clues behind and, more disturbingly, he had known exactly what he wanted and how to go about it. He had done it before. So, on one hand this looked like a crime of passion, committed by someone at least fairly close to the victim. On the other hand, it looked like the work of a cold blooded serial killer. Instead of looking at Darryl and the neighbor, Frank was starting to hope that the girlfriend Anna or the former assistant, would be able to provide a few of the missing pieces of the puzzle.

The Harborview Medical Center loomed like a fortress in the afternoon light. All it needed were a few gargoyles and a couple of towers, and it would become the perfect home for the spirits that no doubt already haunted its halls. Like all major hospitals, it was a place where people were born and healed. Just like it was a place where people withered and died. Frank had been there once as a patient, on his last day as a patrol officer. The day he had taken a bullet to his face. Whenever he as much as drove by, the scar on his cheek would start to itch and burn, the way it had done when it was still a fresh and healing wound. He parked the car and sat there for a while, eyes closed and taking deep breaths. It always took him a few minutes to get past that feeling of having been so close to dying right here, in this hospital.

Walking through the pale lit halls on his way to the morgue, the smell of industrial disinfectants mixed with decaying human flesh grew stronger and stronger, the closer he got. Frank swallowed hard.

The autopsy of Caroline Saunders was being performed as he arrived, which was exactly what he had been hoping for. These procedures, gruesome as they were, often ended up providing investigators with crucial leads, and even the slightest thing could mean a world of difference in cases like this one, where there was little else to go on. Frank crossed his fingers and whispered "Please,

please, please," as he entered the room, where the autopsy was being performed.

Frank had attended plenty of autopsies before. An opened up body on a metal slab did not scare him or make him sick, the same way it did for some detectives, like Joel Burns. The sound of the saw cutting through bone and flesh, the slithering of insides being pushed around or removed alltogether, and the medical examiner's monotone and clinical listing of facts and findings, was all too much to handle for a lot of people, but Frank had gotten used to all of it but the smell. He was hit by the same nausea, he had felt in Caroline's apartment, the contents of his stomach flip-flopping around, wanting to spill out. The cool temperature inside helped a little, but he could not help thinking, that he was in fact breathing microscoping particles of a decomposing corpse, and it was this thought that got him time after time.

Caroline Saunders was far from one of the worst bodies Frank had seen or smelled. It was nowhere near as bad as some of the floaters, after a few days in the waters of the Seattle harbor. As in any port cirty the occasional floater was unaviodable, though most often they turned out to be drunken accidents. Those were the worst.

Dr. London was a methodical lady who took her job very seriously. She never small-talked during the work, talking only to the microphone hanging from the ceiling, listing her observations as she saw them. Frank had asked her questions once, only to be told to stand back and shut up, until she was done. If she found anything, she would inform him afterwards. Since then, whenever he had been present at one of her autopsies, he had kept his distance, offering only a cordial nod as he entered the room.

Frank liked watching Dr. London. He wondered how old she was. He had never seen her in civilian clothes, and the shapeless, white plastic aprons she wore while working obscured most of her features. Judging from her face, he would place her anywhere between thirtyfive and fortyfive. Maybe she looked a little older, because she had no make-up on, and because of the circumstances under which he always met her. Was he weird for checking her out, while she was cutting up a dead person? Part of him said yes, that it was a little on the gross side. Another part of him, however, said that he was a man and she was a woman, and checking her out was the most natural thing in the world. He wondered wether she had ever secretly checked him out too and what she would look like with a tan, a little mascara and lipstick, maybe wearing an evening dress.

As she finished up, he finally approached her.

"So, what's the verdict?" He said.

"She's dead," Dr. London replied, looking straight into Frank's eyes. Hers were pale and blue, as if all those dead eyes she'd seen, had sucked a little life out of hers as well.

"Well, thank you, doc," Frank replied. "I had perhaps hoped, you could be a little more specific than that."

"It's pretty much what it looks like," she said. "She was tied up, raped while struggling and finally strangled to death. You'll find the details in my report."

"If you could tell me now, it might be a big help."

She looked at him again, like no one had ever been so bold as to suggest something so outragous before, and he felt like a schoolboy about to be told off by his teacher.

"My guess is," she finally said, "that the killer also had some kind of noose around her neck as he raped her, tightening slowly, as he went about his business."

"So, he was killing her at the same time he was raping her?"

"That's what it looks like to me. She would have been on her knees, and he would have pulled on the rope. Bruises on her throat point in that direction."

"Who would do such a thing?"

"That's your job, detective Cash."

"Call me Frank," he said, hoping she would offer her first name back to him. When she did not, he went on. "Any traces of drugs or alcohol?"

"No, but I did find this." Suddenly she smiled at him. It was a wide smile showing a set of porcelain white teeth. She was pointing to the back of her neck, turning Caroline's head a little to let Frank get a better look. "I found it just before you got here, but I think it may answer your question."

On the back of the neck were two small marks, looking almost like a snakebite. The edges were dark and slightly bruised.

"Tazer?" He said.

"Yes. She was probably pacified with it. The effect would last long enough for someone to bind her."

"What about undressing her?"

"She wouldn't be out of it long enough for that."

"So, she was either naked when she got stunned, or undressed after being untied. Perhaps even post mortem?"

"I see why they made you a detective."

"Thank you very much, doc."

Dr. London nodded to him, covered up the body and took off her latex gloves. When Frank did not leave, she turned around again.

"Anything else, Frank?"

"Yeah," he said. "I was wondering if you'd go out for a cup of coffee some time?"

"I don't drink coffee," she said.

"Oh." Frank suddenly felt incredibly awkward.

"But I wouldn't say no to a glass of wine and a good steak," she said, suddenly smiling again. Frank stood frozen as she brushed past him, grabbed her purse and dug out a small card. "Call me. But never before noon. I work nights."

He did not even look at the card until he was safely back in his car. His eyes searched for her name on it and found: Dr. M. London. An initial was all he got. This would be the first time, he had a date with a woman, whose name he did not even know. The mere fact that he had asked her out, had surprised him. Perhaps, he thought, he had been more surprised than she, and maybe that was part of the attraction.

Chapter eight

PRISTINA, MARCH 2002 – The rain never seems to end in the city and the concrete apartment blocks seem greyer than ever. Still, everyone but Branko seem engulfed in conversations of hope and renewal. He passes a couple of old men on a streetcorner, and overhears them talk about the rebuilding of the city. It could be the next Berlin, one of them says. On cold stone steps, a young couple is sitting, holding each other, laughing and kissing. Branko can not remember the last time, he has seen so many smiling people, but he does not feel welcome among them. There was a time when the Serbs ruled this city, but those days are long gone, and Branko's people are now almost completely gone. Only a couple of thousand Serbs are left in a city of half a million people. Branko tries to stay in the shadows, going out mainly after dark, if at all. There is peace in Kosovo, but it is a fragile one that may still shatter.

The window does not open in the room, he has rented, and the air inside smells like stale sweat and molding leftovers. He has a lot of money now, stashed away, and soon he will have the passport and hopefully enough new information to continue his quest. He does not sleep much anymore. Most nights he will doze off briefly and suddenly find himself in a car that does not run. The police are closing in. The dead bank manager sits in the passenger seat, leaning over towards him, so the gaping hole into the back of his head is visible. There are little bits of skull and brain tissue in his hair. Branko hears the ghost laugh at him, as the blinking lights of the policecars surround him. Then he wakes up, and only a couple of minutes have passed.

At first he would pray a lot, hoping the Lord would take away the evil dreams. Eventually, he felt that every patrol car slowed down, while passing him, and he started crossing the street rather than walk past any bank. His prayers were not being answered, and he was hearing a rumor, that there was a price on his head. Anyone having any information on the bankrobber who killed a manager, loving husband and father of three would be rewarded five thousand dollars. The Lord had done this, he says to himself, as a test. He has to get through this on his own.

But the bank manager still haunts him in his dreams. None of the others, the ones he killed in the war, have ever haunted him like this. This one is different. His only prayers now, are the He may protect and bless the family of the man, he has murdered. After he hit the other banks, it suddenly became news. Brank read about his own crimes without any interest in anything but the people. After that first robbery, he had taken great care not to shoot again. According to the newspaper, the bank manager's widow had been the older lady in the bank. The one he had almost shot too. In his prayers, he also thanks the blonde girl, who stepped into the line of fire, saving the other woman. And making sure the children did not become orphans.

Sometimes the pain is so hard to bear, that he questions whether he should go on. He knows, Jovana's killer might never be found, but he also has no choice. He hears the Ghost laugh, whenever the doubts appear. He mocks him, whispering in a hoarse, almost inaudible voice, that he should give up and give the Ghost his final vicotry. He stares out windows that have never been washed, except by the rain, at the dimly lit streets below. But he doesn't really see anything.

Earlier his meeting with The German was confirmed. Getting the false papers will not be a problem. Supposedly a passport that was stolen from some tourist and then altered. He feels a knot in his stomach and his hands are shaking at the thought of the meeting. It is strange that he should be this nervous, but he can not shake the feeling, that somehow The German is tied into Jovana by more than a simple passport.

Maybe it will be a new beginning, he says to himself. As soon as he gets his new identity, he will be able to enter the European Union and go north to Denmark, where hopefully, this Jacob Hansen will be able to help him.

Branko finally takes his eyes of the wet windows to get out his notebook and look through the pages again. Slightly torn in places and covered in the grime that has settled on the pages after all this time, these pieces of paper contain everything he has found, since he started looking for Jovana's killer. Right now, he is looking through his own scribbled notes on Jacob Hansen. For the fourth time today.

Hansen was a mercenary involved in the conflict against the muslims in the north. From what Branko has learned, he at one time headed a small batallion of men by the name The Spectres. In Branko's mind, this could not be a coincidence. The Ghost would have to have been one of the Spectre soldiers under Hansen's command. If that is true, Branko already knows what kind of man he is looking for.

The Spectres were rumored to be ruthless killers, not caring who or why they killed as long as they got paid for it. Children and women were no different than trained soldiers to them. They were at war with the muslims because the opposing side paid better, and for a while, the only good muslim was a dead one. While he had been driving around the countryside, looking for banks to rob, he had met Ahmad, a young man with dull grey eyes and a stare that would never fully return from whatever horizon it was on. He had survived an attack on his village by The Spectres, and he had told his story to Branko without looking him in the eye even once. If he had, he might have seen the Serb looking back at him, and decided to keep his mouth shut.

Ahmad started by saying that he was ashamed, for he had run for his life without trying to save his family, and for that, he feared that Allah would send him to Hell. Branko listened without interrupting, as he tried to remember the faces of all the young men just like the one in front of him, who had not been smart enough to run, when Branko had aimed his assault rifle at them.

Ahmad had seen the trucks come in and had been hiding in a shed. At first, he had thought of his uncle's rifle, and whether or not he could sneak in and get it. The first truck unloaded about a dozen men in plain view of the young man, and as if to get everyone's attention, one of the soldiers pulled a pistol from his belt and shot an old lady in the head right there in the street. It was then, he said, he saw the whole village freeze, everyone looking at the bloodpool forming on the ground and for a second, it seemed that there was no sound in the world at all. The silence hung heavy in the air, as the whole village held its breath, trying to understand what they all knew would be coming next. That was when Ahmad made a quick decision and ran for the woods.

Three days after the attack, he returned to the village. Half the houses had burned to the ground, some still smoldering softly in the already hot sun. Every remaining surface seemed to be riddled with bullet holes. At first he could not find anyone, but as he got closer towards the center of the village, the wind changed and brought a sweet smell with it that made his blood curlde and his stomach churn. Ahmad followed it to the marketplace, and there they all were; men, women and children piled on top of each other, most of them killed by a single shot, just like the old woman, others nearly torn in half by bullets. Those were the ones who had tried to run like him, he thought, or perhaps the men in the trucks had gotten tired of shooting them one at a time, and had decided to take them out in groups. And at the top of this pile of death, was planted a white flag with two holes cut in it, like the eyes of a ghost. The flag of The Spectres.

Branko stayed in that area for almost a month, looking for others who knew anything about the Spectre group and its commander, but everywhere he went, he was told to let the past be the past, and that was when he was lucky. Most of the time, no one wanted to speak to him at all.

The next time, Branko hears about Jacob Hansen, is when he talks to The German. Before any business is done, there is the obligatory small talk. He asks about the passport, and what Branko intends to do with it, and once again he tells the story of his sister and the hunt for her killer, ending with his plans to go to Denmark. The German listens and nods a lot, and when Branko is done, says he remembers the last time Branko told him that story. Back then he was not sure what to think, he says, but now he understands Branko's dedication and sees that he is telling the truth. A rare thing, these days, he adds, looking away as if getting lost in his own thoughts. For a couple of mminutes, he does not say anything else, but leans back in his chair, sipping his espresso and smiles like a buddha in a purple baret. It makes Branko want to grab the little man by the throat and shake him until he reveals, what it is he so obviously knows, but he rethinks it and realizes that it might just be a test. Tomorrow, he says to himself, when he goes back to pick up the new passport, will he make the German tell him all he knows.

To complete the deal, the two men meet up in the Split Bean Café. The place used to be Branko's family's worst competition, located only a block from where his father's coffeeshop had been. But theirs had been lost in the Nato bombings, and the Split Bean had been spared. It still feels like betrayal, as Branko steps inside.

Nothing has changed since before the war. The same dusty armchairs, the same tables that are all different and the same candleholders lighting up the place. The brown walls are covered with nicotine stained paintings of streetlife, as it used to look in Pristina a hundred years ago. The owner is Albanian and during the conflict, that would have been another reason for them to hate each other, but times are at least a little different now and he nods at Branko, as he enters the café. They might have been competitors and even enemies once, but in a sense, they had also been colleagues. He knows it could just as well had been the Split Bean that got hit. Stray bombs do not care if your Serb or Albanian, muslim or christian.

The German is in the back, close to the fireplace and easily recognizable by his purple baret, and though the room is cold from the bad weather outside, no one else is sitting close to the fire. They obviously know him here, and people know to give him his space.

When Branko sees him, he is once again surprised by the man's short stature, but it only makes him act even more humble. He would not want to upset The German. At least not yet.

"Good to see you again, Branko."

The owner comes over and serves him a cup of pitch black coffee.

"Coffee is on the house for you," he says to Branko.

As the man leaves, the German takes out an envelope from his coat pocket and puts it flat down on the table between the two.

"This is the new you," he says, almost whispering now. "You name will remain the same, but you are now a German citizen."

"Will that work?" Branko blurts out, forgetting for just a second that the man across from him is a gangster whose business, he is now questioning. There is a pause and he sees the little German's wide mouth split open in a smile that is too wide for his face.

"Of course it will. There are lots of Yugoslavs in Germany."

Branko knows that he calls him a Yugoslav on purpose. Most would find it offensive these days. There are now many groups and regions in what was once known as Yugoslavia and much of the war was about the independence and seperation of each of these. But Branko lets it slide without comment, focusing on the envelope instead.

"Do you have something for me as well?"

"I do," he says, putting a small plastic bag on the table. Inside it is a roll of American dollars. Five thousand of them in hundred dollar bills. The German hungrily grabs it and looks inside.

"Looks good," he says. "I trust it is all there?"

"Five thousand, as we agreed."

"Good. We are done then," he says and pushes the envelope with the new identity papers towards Branko. But Branko lets it stay there and drinks from his coffee, instead of getting up.

"Not quite," he says. "I want to talk to you about something else."

"The Spectre merc, yes?"

"Jacob Hansen."

"There's not much to say. And why would I tell you anyway?"

"Because I need to know."

"I would imagine that such information would be worth quite a bit to you, yes?"

Branko speaks slowly, as he leans forward just enough to tap the German on the knee with the barrel of his gun. "Consider it included in the price of the passport."

Branko knows he is playing with fire, but he does not care. For a long time, he has been ready to die, and if he never finds Jovana's killer, death is still the best alternative he has been able to think of.

"You've got some balls, I'll give you that," the German says, not moving an inch but his voice sounding like his mouth is suddenly dry. "I respect that." Branko leans back, knowing that the German will talk now.

"I know that mr. Hansen was a veteran merc, but not affiliated with any particular PMC. He was too much of a loose cannon for that," the German says, looking at Branko with eyes that shows no emotion. Branko knows that that by PMC, the German is talking about 'private military companies', small armies of professional soldiers for hire by anyone willing to pay. The German continues. "He was rumored to be a real sick fuck. Liked his job a little too much, if you know what I mean. But he never lost control, because he was good. His men, however, were nothing but a band of bandits. Rejects from other companies, criminals and murderers, wannabes and perverts. One can only guess how Hansens kept them in control. They fought as The Spectres in the north, but they have had other names in other wars."

"What happened to him?"

"He was wounded in combat. Not sure how exactly, but as far as I know, he left the country and went back to Denmark."

"And? Did you help him back to Denmark?"

"He couldn't travel on the papers he had on him, so the Spectres came to me. I did for him, what I did for you. Except I never actually met mr. Hansen."

"How do I get in contact with him or one of his men?"

"I don't know where he is now, but I know who he went to first."

Branko is back in his room. The rain is still pounding on the windows, as if it is trying to brake them. His most promising lead is a new name and a new address. This time in Amsterdam, Holland. Maybe he should be afraid, he thinks. Maybe the German is sending him there and straight into an ambush. But he does not believe that to be the case. The German is a businessman after all, and one who has undoubtedly experienced more dangerous situations than being threatened in a coffeeshop. Branko feels certain, the German will let this one slide.

The open suitcase on the bed holds everything Branko is bringing. Two pairs of pants, a handful of T-shirts, one shirt, one tie and some socks and underwear. Along with the sweater and coat he is wearing, that will have to do. Together, all of this takes up about half the suitcase. The other half is full of money. Five, ten, twenty and hundred dollar bills. Hopefully, he will only need to hide this, as he crosses into the EU. Once inside, he can pass from one country to the other without even stopping.

As he puts the suitcase in the trunk of his car, he makes another decision. Driving across the river, he makes a stop on the bridge, gets out and tosses his gun over the side. He watches it hit the water and stays for a few more seconds, as if there is a chance the thing will float back up to the surface. Finally, drawn out of his trancelike state by the cold rain making him shiver, he gets back into the car and starts heading for the border.

Chapter nine

Back from his visit at the medical examiner, Frank found a couple of messages for him on his desk. It was hardly as a surprise, that Big Red wanted to have a meeting with the team first thing in the morning. Before any such meeting, he would want to update the file. The second message was from Joel, saying simply that he had tracked down a woman, who had worked as the clerk at Caroline Saunder's clinic before Darryl. The message ended with three words: Not suspect material. Besides himself, Elouise was the only one working at the office, which indicated that the other teams were busy with cases of their own.

The paperwork did not take long, because there was very little new to add. There was still the chance that the lab would find something in Caroline's office, or from the samples taken at the autopsy, but he was not counting on it. Whoever killed Caroline Saunders was careful enough not to leave anything for the cops to find. And unless the killer had made a mistake somewhere, Frank knew they would get nothing from the lab.

"What are you working on?" He asked Elouise.

"I made som calls to some of the other people in the phonebook, trying to identify them all and maybe find a jealous ex or something."

"And?"

"ID is going fine, but when it comes to the case, there's nothing so far. I'll keep at it though," she said, pointing to a thermos and a cup full of still steaming coffee. "Got a message for you."

"What's that?"

"Big Red is bringing in an advisor tomorrow."

"The feds?"

"A profiler, I think. There's nothing here for the feds, Frank."

"They still might be able to help," he answered. "Why didn't I think of this sooner?"

Frank finished off the workday by faxing over a copy of the summary report to Jeffrey Bernstein, a very capable researcher from the FBI, Frank had worked with before. If something like this had happened elsewhere, perhaps Jeff would be able to dig up some information on that. If someone at the bureau knew anything, even sneaking suspicions from older cases, that would not show up in any database searches, Bernstein would be able to find it. For good measure, Frank spent another hour searching the various databases himself, but as he had expected, there was nothing there for him to find.

Driving home, he looked out at the rain falling on the West Seattle Bridge. It was no wonder, so many people were suffering from depression in this city, where rain seemed to be the most common weatherforecast eight months of the year, and this year, he thought, it seemed worse than usual. But the rain never made Frank depressed. It felt like a cleansing process, he thought, washing away the stench of urine and garbage from the narrow alleys downtown and calming everyone down. Fewer people got killed in the rain than on hot, sunny days. He looked at the reflections on the road in front of him from the taillights of the other cars gliding across the tall bridge and he thought of M. London, medical examiner.

Eric was letting himself out, as Frank was walking up to the front door. Eric was mrs. Perez oldest son, a slender and almost sculpturelike cut man, pretty enough to be a model, and always impeccably dressed. Tonight, he was wearing a navy blue suit and a fresh shave.

"How're you doin' mister Cash?" he said, as he held the door open.

"Pretty good, Eric. How about yourself?"

"Not bad. On my way out on a date, man."

"What does your mom think about that?"

A big grin spread acress Eric's face. "She thinks I am going over to Roger's."

"Dressed like that?" Frank said and they both laughed. "Don't worry, Eric. Your secret is safe with me."

"Thanks, man."

Frank turned to let the door fall shut behind him, but just before it closed completely, Eric reached back and opened it back up.

"By the way, mr. Cash ..."

"Yes?"

"Some guy came by here today, looking for you."

"Really? What guy was that?"

"No one I'd seen before. Looked like a bill collector or something. Dressed in a cheap suit, you know?" If anyone wold know a cheap suit when he saw one, it was probably Eric, Frank thought, suddenly feeling very selfconscious.

"Probably a colleague from the sound of it," Frank said. In all his years on the force, no one had ever paid him a surprise visit at home, and fellow cops would probably not do it without checking the office first. But he did not say that out loud. "Thanks for letting me know, Eric."

Chapter ten

AMSTERDAM, APRIL 2002 – Everything is so expensive in the EU, Branko wonders how anyone can afford to eat, and the food he has been getting has been so greasy and salty, he wonders how they survive. It is no wonder so many of them are overweight. He feels like he has entered into another world, a world of self-centeredness, greed and stress. And he has only just arrived. Getting into the EU was easier than he had expected. He did not feel nervous at all, when they checked his passport at the border. Nothing to declare. No one even bothered to check his suitcase. He could have kept the gun.

He has driven for two days straight, stopping only to rest a little here and there, eat at roadside fast-food restaurants and to put gas on the car. His skin is sticky from the many hours behind the wheel and no showering. A little cold water, splashed in the face, combined with cheap deodorant is all he has been able to do, to refresh himself.

The hotel he checks into in Amsterdam is small and cozy. At the cashier they ask for ID, when he wants to pay cash for the room. Branko finds this oddly amusing. If you pay with a plastic card, no one asks any questions, but for some reason real money is a cause for suspicion. This part of Europe is more different than he thought it would be. Everyone looks tired and depressed, when they have no reason to be. These peope have not seen war, hunger or real poverty in two generations, yet they seem almost less happy than the people who have experienced all those things.

The room is stuffy but clean. He opens the window before jumping in the shower. He stands there for a long time, feeling the hot water peel the layers of dried sweat and dust off his skin. His eyes are closed the whole time, as he tries to shut out the feeling of being alone in a strange new land, where everyone speaks in tongues and the only familiar voice is that of a ghost, whispering over and over: "I already own your sister's soul and soon yours will follow."

A couple of hours later, Branko is walking through the streets if Amsterdam. It is pretty city, with small canals and quaint, old houses along their sides. Even though it is a weeknight and late, young people seem to be partying everywhere. Two staggering teenage girls, lost in a world of giggles, makes Branko think of lost sheep heading toward the forest where the wolf waits. One of them is singing the words from some pop-song, the other looks like she is just trying not to fall. The ghost whispers about them in Branko's ear, so fresh and innocent.

Suddenly, Branko finds himself in Amsterdam's famous red light district. Beautiful, half-naked girls stand behind tall glass windows, beckoning passers by to come inside. In some of the little booths, a curtain has been drawn, indicating that there is a customer with the girl. A plump, black girl with enormous breasts passes him on the street and slaps Branko gently on the ass.

"I've been looking for a man like you," she says in English.

"No thanks," he says. His cheeks feel a little warm, which surprises him as he tries to hide it.

"Don't be shy, big man. I bet you've got a big, fat cock under there," she continues, rubbing herself against him.

"I said, no thanks." He starts walking.

"Fuck you, asshole!" She yells after him, as he hurries down the street. A couple of other guys point and laugh, immediately heading over towards the black girl, who, as soon as she sees the two men, seems to forget everything about Branko. There is another voice laughing with them, inside Branko's head.

Before he goes to bed that night, he folds his hands and mutters a prayer to God. He prays for the black girl and all the other whores in the red light district. He prays for the two teenage girls out so late at night. They were so vulnerable, he thinks, like Jovana was before she was killed. And he prays for his own soul. When the black hooker touched him, he felt the echo of something he has not experienced in a long time, and he finds himself praying for more of that too.

Praying has helped him a lot lately. Every night, he has prayed to God for guidance, and the more he prays, the more it feels like God wants him to find Jovana's killer. He hopes that he will have patience to kill the man slowly. To make him suffer as much, as he made Jovana suffer. And he knows that this is God's will, because the only time the Ghost does not dare to speak, is whenever Branko is praying.

SEPTEMBER 2002 – Nothing is going as planned. The man Branko is supposed to meet in Amsterdam has disappeared without a trace. He called from the hotel and left a message at "The Split Bean", trying to get in touch with the German again, but never got a call back. There is a woman living at the address Branko was given, who first refuses to talk to him at all. Finally, after he offers her a hundred euros, she tells him, that the man he is looking for was in some kind of trouble and has left the country several months ago. She does not know where he is or how to reach him. That is all he gets out of her, and keeping the house under surveillance over the next two months has gotten him nowhere. Branko is stuck in Amsterdam for the time being. All he can do is wait and hope his money does not run out.

Chapter eleven

The woman sitting next to lieutenant Redding was almost bigger than him, together the took up an entire side of the table in the crammed meetingroom. She was dressed in a white shirt that had little red flowers printed on it. It was thin enough to hint at the pink bra under it and stretched across her breasts and shoulders. She had big, green eyes behind black-framed glasses and a narrow, but full-lipped mouth, painted thick with a glossy, dark red lipstick. It made her look almost girlish in spite of her size. Elouise sat on across from Big Red, looking manlier than both of them, wearing an expression like the coffee had kept her up all night and now, she was at the point where even the caffeine had stopped working. Joel sat at the opposite end, his elbows resting on the table and his head in his hands. Joel's hair looked greasy and he had bags under his eyes. Frank looked from one to the other, as he sat himself between his two detectives, imagining that he did not look much better than any of them.

"This is Christina Quick," Redding began. "She's a profiler on loan to us. She's been going over the reports from you guys and forensics, and hopefully tell us a little bit about what we're looking for."

There was a pause, as if everyone expected everyone else to say something.

"Okay?" Frank finally said and decided to direct his inquisitive look at the fat lady.

"As you have probably guessed," Quick began, "we are looking at someone who has done this before. Also, we are most likely looking for a white male between thirty and forty years of age, who lives alone, have sexuality issues and all that usual stuff. So, now that we've gotten the basics out of the way, let's dig a little deeper."

"Please do," Joel said, stretching before pouring himself a cup of coffee from the thermos on the table. Frank wondered whether the coffee inside was from today or left over from the last time someone had used this room. He did not see any steam rising from Joel's cup, but if the coffee was bad, Joel never showed it.

"The rape is significant," she said. "For most serial killers, the killing itself is what gets them off. I'm guessing the rape is a form of foreplay for this guy. From the forensics report, I could see that though the bruises indicated rape, there were no traces of seamon. I'm guessing he is unable to come from the rape alone, and that he probably finished himself off after," she paused and looked at her notes, "Caroline Saunders was dead."

"And good morning to you too," Joel said.

"Shut up, Joel," Redding and Frank said in unison.

"Jeez, you two become more alike every day."

"Go on," Frank said, nodding to ms. Quick.

"Right. He might still have used a condom, just to be sure. And he might have even saved finishing for later"

"For all we know, he might go home and hump the wife," Joel said.

"Isn't that a nice thought," Frank added.

"Another theory," Elouise said, "could be that he didn't rape her at all. At least not using his penis. There were no pubic hairs, other than the victim's own, found at the scene."

"That is a possibility," Quick said. "And that would still fit with him finishing off elsewhere. He might have raped her with an object, though I don't think so. Given this guys attention to detail, I'd say he checked for pubic hairs afterwards. He might even have gotten an extra kick out of that."

"But how does this bring us closer to having a suspect?" Big Red asked, looking very uncomfortable with all these details being discussed in front of him. Everyone in the department knew of Redding's weak stomache. Some even said that was the main reason, he had pursued a desk job career, rather than remaining in the field.

"I would start looking at previously convicted sex offenders whose MO, and especially the attention to detail, matches what we have here. Ones who might have been recently released from prison," Quick answered. "Obviously, I am not able to provide you with a complete bckground, based on this little information, but I am willing to bet, that this guy started with rape and went on to kill people later. I'm guessing that is why rape is still part of the ritual for him. I am also guessing that he is anal retentive about a lot of other things in life."

"Ms. Quick will continue to work on this as the case progresses," Redding went on. "She is on loan to us part time, but this case has first priority, so don't hesitate to make use of her expertise."

"Honestly," Joel said. "I don't see a lot more information showing up at this point. We're pretty much stuck."

"Listen," the lieutenant said, leaning forward and pointing a short, stubby finger at Joel. "I know the work is harder, now there's only three of you, but I will not accept giving up on a case like this one, just because we haven't found a smoking gun within the first 24 hours. Is that clear?"

Silence. Everyone looking from Big Red, whose face was quickly taking on the color of his nickname, to Joel.

"That's clear, sir," Joel finally said.

"Good. I'm not expecting miracles here. I'm facing the press in a few minutes. I'll keep them off your backs, as long as I can, but you can't give up in the meantime, dammit. Keep the ball rolling."

There was a gloomy atmosphere in the office after the meeting was over. The three detectives seemed to be lost in their own thoughts. There were still leads, but they were growing thinner for every hour, it seemed. Caroline's friend Anna was on her way downtown, but if she could not provide some new information, things were looking bleak. Frank's thoughts drifted to what the profiler had just told them. She was undoubtedly good at her job, but still the information she had given them was pretty general. Joel broke the silence after a while.

"How can someone so gigantic be named Quick?"

Frank felt a smile form on his mouth and he immediately looked over at Elouise, only to see that she was doing the same. A second later, they were all laughing.

"Elouise," Frank said when the laughter had died down. "Run that check on the known offenders. And Joel, I want you with me, when I interview Anna."

Both the others nodded.

"I take it," Frank said to Elouise, "that you had no luck with the phone numbers last night?"

"Too early to tell," she said. "I've got a date with a couple of guys later tonight. Both are coming in voluntarily."

"Who'd have thunk," Joel said, "what kind of services did you have to offer?"

"Shut your hole, Joel," she retorted.

"Hey, that rhymes," Frank said. "Come on, Hole. Let's cozy up the interview room for our friend Anna."

Joel shot him a dirty look, but Frank pretended not to notice. Joel had started the wisecracking, and he should be able to take it as good as he could give it, Frank thought. Taking Elouise's side was his way of telling him so.

As soon as Anna walked into the room, Frank shot a glance at Joel, just to make sure he was not about to do something stupid. She was tall and most of her seemed to be legs and breasts. If she was not already working as a catalogue model, she certainly could, Frank thought. Her hair had been dyed bright red, which Frank guessed was just an enhancement of her natural color, judging from her pale, milky skin. The green eyes were almond shaped and seemed naturally watery and perfectly balanced against a set of very kissable lips.

"Ehm ... hi," Joel said, wiping of his palm on his pantleg before sticking it out for a shake. Anna shook it without smiling or saying anything.

Frank settled for nodding, as he held the door into the interview room. Someone had been using it straight up til a few minutes prior, and the place was still heavy with the smell of nervous sweat and attitudes being thrown around. Funny how you could sense things that had happened in a room, Frank thought, even after they had happened. Anna either did not notice or did not care. She sat down, crossed her legs and folded her hands in front of her.

"Thank you for coming. As you know," Frank started, "we found Caroline dead a couple of days ago. I am sorry for your loss. We understand that you were close friends?"

"That's right," she said. Her voice sounded dry, as if she had been screaming a lot. "What happened to her?"

"We were sort of hoping, you could help us figure that out," Frank said.

"I mean, how did she die?"

"She was strangled," Frank said. "Again, I am sorry."

"I don't know of anyone, who would do such a thing to her."

"Did she have any jealous exes? Any patients who might have known where she lived?"

"I don't think so," Anna started. "Carol didn't have any ex boyfriends. Or any boyfriends, for that matter. She had lovers."

"How do you mean?" Joel was talking now.

"She was not interested in settling down with one guy. She liked the single life."

"Did she ever mention anyone in particular?" Frank said.

"She usually told me about her conquests. But if you mean anyone who broke her heart, the answer is no. I'm sure if you asked them, they'd say she was the heartbreaker."

"Why is that?"

"The truth is that she was a strong woman. Very independant. And she preyed on weak men in her job and in her bed." Anna paused and got out a pack of cigarettes. Thinking that the smoke might actually take away some of the stench in the tiny room, Frank conveniently forgot to remind her of the no smoking. "I want you guys to find whoever did this," she continued, her voice sounding thick through the smoke, "but I just don't have any idea who might've done it. Like I said, she only let weak men into her life."

"Where did she meet these men?"

"Bars, clubs, wherever. Carol got around."

"How about at her clinic?"

"No. She was very strict about that."

"How do you know?"

"She did it once," Anna said, "and it got very ugly."

"Do you know that person's name?"

"No, but even if I did, it wouldn't matter. The poor guy jumped out of a 12th story window four months after she'd dumped him."

There was a pause while Frank processed this information. Anna stared out into nothing and her watery eyes looked like they might overflow at any time. Joel got up and offered to get coffee. Everyone wanted some. Neither Frank nor Anna said anything, while he was gone.

Over the next two hours, the two cops asked Anna about her and Caroline's relationship, trying to get as much information on Caroline's life as they could.

The two had first met in junior high. Caroline had moved to Seattle with her parents from a small town in Ohio. Their family had felt compelled to move, after a disagreement with an uncle on the mother's side. The uncle had been none other than the local sheriff, so rather than cause a stir, they decided to move away. Anna described the Saunders family as good people, describing the parents as church going Christians but without being ignorant bible-bangers. When asked, Anna said that Caroline had grown out of Christianity by her senior year in high-school.

In those early and mid-teen years, Caroline had gone from being the quiet girl to being a man eater by her first year in college. It was as if she had an unsatiable hunger for boys, yet she somehow avoided the slut label and remained popular with the other girls.

Only after she got deeper into her studies to become a psychiatrist, did she seem to calm down. It was then, that she had finally told Anna her dark secret. There was a pause, and both Frank and Joel put on their most expressionless faces. The air was thick with cigerette smoke and suspense. So far Frank had kept himself busy with questions as Joel was taking notes, but the further into the interview they had gone, the less he had had to ask. Both cops knew that this was the moment, Anna had been warming herself up to. Whatever important thing she had to tell them, was just about to come out. Frank did not look at his partner, but he knew that he would be sitting at the edge of his chair.

Anna looked Frank straight in the eye, as she continued. Caroline's sheriff-uncle, she said, had been visiting the young girl in her bedroom on several occasions. Over the course of two years, he had regularly molested her, and he most likely would have continued to do so, had her father not walked in on him one day.

She had finally told Anna the story, because her psychology studies had opened her eyes to the traumatic experiences of her past. She knew, she had issues with dominant and powerful men, and even joked in private, with the fact that she was getting her revenge by breaking the hearts of as many men, as she could.

From this point on, it was as if Anna was talking to herself. Frank and Joel kept quiet mostly, taking notes along the way and asking only a couple of follow up questions here and there. Anne described as many of the men in Caroline's life, as she could remember hearing about. She went back about a year and the list was staggering, and consisting mostly of one night stands. Anna also told them about, how Caroline was seeking therapy for her own problems, while still treating mostly men at her clinic. Near the end of her life, she was dating fewer men and spending more time, trying to understand herself. She cried a lot, Anna said, wiping away her own tears, as she spoke. As friends, Caroline had used Anna as a shoulder to cry on, someone to brag to and bounce thoughts and feeling off on, and Anna did the same. Their friendship had evolved over the last couple of years, she said, to the point where Caroline had been more of a sister than a friend.

"Do you know who her therapist was?"

"No," she said. "I never asked and she never told me." Anna stared at the wall for moment. "There might not have been one."

"You mentioned that she had started therapy."

"I thought she was seeing someone," she replied, still looking at the wall. "But now I'm starting to think it was always just me and her and that our talks were some kind of self-therapy."

To Frank, Anna painted a picture of a deeply troubled girl, alone with an almost unbearable pain from her past. From what Anna had said, she had not kept many friends other than her. Not even her family was close to her any more. Since realizing her own problems, she had started blaming her parents for taking the easy way out in running away from the abusive uncle. Mostly, the blame had been directed at the mother, whose brother had been the man responsible for ruining her life. She had told Anna, that she could not look into her mother's eyes, without seeing the uncle there.

While Joel walked Anna to her car, Frank went to the bathroom to freshen up. The stuffy room and the story Anna had told, had all but worn him out, and even the cold water did not seem to have the desired effect. The smell of cigarette smoke hung heavy on his suit and in his hair. What he really needed was a shower or a drink, he thought, but either one would have to wait.

Joel was already back in the office when Frank returned, the two started comparing notes, starting by eliminating Anna as a suspect. The new information made it likely, in spite of Anna's opinion, that the killer was to be found among one of the men, Caroline had seduced. There were a few names, that they started by writing down and handing to Elouise, for her to use as yet another parameter in her search through the list of recently released sex offenders.

Still, Frank found it hard to combine the two different profiles; the weak, easily broken men that Caroline favored, and the serial rapist turned killer portrayed by ms. Quick. Perhaps the profiler would be able to come up with something new based on their interview with Anna, he thought, getting to work on the summary right away.

An hour into the paperwork, Elouise came over to his desk, dragging her feet and looking like her eyeballs were about to fall out of their sockets.

"I thought we had him," she said, as she collapsed in the nearest vacant chair.

"Who?"

"I checked the register for anyone who might be worth a second look, and found three guys, whose style matched what happened to ms. Saunders."

"But they didn't check out?"

"Nope," she said, checking Frank's cup for coffee she could steal but finding none. "One was already locked up, one is in the hospital from a car accident and one is out of town."

"How long?"

"What?"

"How long has he been out of town?"

"Forget it, Fax," she said. "The guy is a born again something or other. He lives with this sect in California. Hasn't left the temple in months."

"Hm."

"Exactly," she said. "I don't know about you guys, but I could use a drink."

"I know just the place," Joel said.

Frank sent the others off, wanting to finish the summary of the interview and add it to the file before doing anything else. He only hoped, the other detectives would be able to stand each other, until he were able to join them. Before leaving, he gave Redding a call.

"How did it go with the press?" he asked once the pleasantries were over with.

"As well as expected," the lieutenant aswered. "They were not happy with the standard were-working-on-several-leads song."

"Will there be trouble?"

"I don't think so," he said. "But there's a new crime-guy working at the Times. He might be out to prove himself. Worth watching out for."

"Alright," Frank said and continued by giving Redding a short recap of the meeting with Anna, before ending the call.

Chapter twelve

AMSTERDAM, JANUARY 2004 – Branko is drunk and staggers around like a blind man without his cane. The same thoughts go through his head night after night, about how God has forgotten him and his sister. Even the Ghost only comes around on rare occasions now. Tonight he stops at the dark canals to scream his lungs out, hoping that someone will hear. Anyone. But nobody pays any attention to the screaming man, and as he runs out of breath, the screaming is replaced by uncontrolled sobbing. He barely recognizes himself anymore, standing there in the cold January night, watching his own breath pour from his mouth in vapors of steam, tasting the salty tears that run into his open mouth. For a second, his misery is so complete, that he forgets why he is there, and he feels a little better. Then he remembers and the self-pity comes back. He knows that that is what it is, and he hates himself for it.

Branko visits the coffee shops almost every day, where there is a wide variety of hash to choose from. He has taken a special liking to som Moroccan stuff they call Amber Rose. Amber because of its yellowish color, and rose because it makes you feel like one. At least that's what they say. But for Branko it is all about not thinking, the hash is an excellent blanket to pull over one's mind. The heavy, white smoke clouds his thoughts and memories, as he smokes with a few of the locals, trying appear interested in them and their plans to change the world. But most of the time, all he really does is listen to the voices, like like a baby listening to the grown-ups, not understanding the words but taking comfort in the voices.

Dutch is a strange language, sounding like a mix of English, German and French. Branko finds that at least he can laugh at it, when he is stoned. Besides, his German and English skills are quite enough for him to get by here. Amsterdam is a mutli-ethnic cultural city, full of blacks, persians and whites, jews, christians and muslims all living side by side. And so many young people coming from all over Europe, to sample the temptations of the coffe shops.

Stopping on one of the many small bridges crossing the canals running through the city core, he catches a glimpse of Amsterdam's beauty. The dark water snakes its way, reflecting the golden orange lights streaming from streetlamps and apartments above. The streets are clean and full of small shops of every kind. At a glance, it looks so cozy and quaint, like something out of a fairy tale, but there is another side to Amsterdam as well, a raw and sinful side that will whisper false promises and pull those in who are weak enough to listen. The drugs. The whores. Both so readily available on every other streetcorner that they almost blend in with the boutiques, hiding in plain sight. Pulling and whispering.

A couple of months ago, Branko went back to the red light district. He searched for almost two hours, before he found the same black girl that had tried to get with him, the first time he had ventured in there. She did not remember him. He wonders if she will remember him now, though he doubts it. When you fuck a dozen men every day, how do you tell them apart.

She had led him to a narrow alley and down a couple of steps, and he had taken her right there. He remembers the thick stench of filthy, unwashed cunt that had hit him like a fist, as she had bent over to let him penetrate her, so powerful that it even overpowered the smell of piss in the alley, but he had taken her anyway, as hard and as fast as he could, holding the plump black girl's neck in an iron grip, as she whimpered in front of him. And the Ghost had been there the whole time, whispering in his ear: Kill her! Kill her! He starts to gag, thinking about it, before finally leaning out over the railing of the bridge, vomiting hard into the black water below.

As he spits the last of the döner kebab, he ate an hour ago into the water, he thinks of his sister. Perhaps for the first time all day. He will pray for her soul again tonight, he decides, if he does not pass out before that.

In the morning he seems to find a trace of who he once was. The face in the mirror screams at him, telling him to sober up, to move on with life and give up this pointless chase. It tells him to find a priest, so he can confess his sins. Especially the bank manager, who now seems to haunt Branko every night. And then, as he showers and shaves, and the hangover starts to lift a little, he catches a glimpse of courage. He reminds himself of why he is here, his purpose. His quest. Do not let her die without revenge, his mind says. His last clue led him here, to Holland, where there are no mountains and so much temptation. This is where he must stay, until God puts him back on track, or he perishes in a life of sin. It is a test of his willpower, he says to himself. God must have put him here for a reason. Only by being faithful, can he ever find out what that reason is.

So, he stays in Amsterdam. He still has money to spend, and he has found that he can make more by playing cards in a dive behind his hotel. In the army, they had played for cigarettes and vodka, as a way to pass time and shut out the horrors surrounding them every day. Today, he is not sure if he plays to forget or to remember. They always play for small change, but he makes enough to get high and drunk when he wants to and the occasional kebab when he gets hungry. The savings will pay for his room for at least another few months.

He sits on his bed, having just put his shoes on. Outside the sun is already preparing to set, casting an orange and pruple glow over the city. Branko's head still hurts from last nights drinking and his stomach wants food. He knows that a joint could take away the pain, or at least dampen it enough to make it tolerable. On the other hand, if he wants to go out drinking, he will need to make some money, and smoking will dull his ability to play his cards right. It is almost dark outside before the choice is made for him. There is a knock on the door.

"Mr. Petrovic?" the voice outside is calling. It is not the manager.

"What?" He says, as he opens the door.

The man outside is wearing a crumpled suit, like what you might expect a travelling salesman to wear. In his hand is a sturdylooking briefcase. He is a big man with deep lines in his face and a nose like a boxer's. The wrinkles around his big, blue eyes and flat, greying hair puts him in his forties, Branko is guessing.

"What do you want?"

"I have a message for you."

"Come in," Branko says, stepping aside. He shuts the door behind the man and sits back on his bed, gesturing towards the only chair in the room. "Have a seat."

" This won't take long," he answers, still standing. The suit puts his briefcase on the table, opens it and pulls out a large manilla envelope.

"A mutual friend is sad to hear, that you appear to be stranded in your efforts. He hopes that this might help."

Slowly, he hands over the envelope to Branko, who for a second has no idea what all this is about.

"Who is the mutual friend?" he finally asks, without having opened the envelope.

"I believe you call him German," the suit says.

"Why would he help me?" Branko asks, remembering how he had gotten the German to speak back in Pristina.

"Let us just say, that he stumbled onto this, and he knew it would have your interest."

Before Branko can say anything or get up, the man has left the room. Were it not for the envelope in his hands, he might have thought the suit's visit had been a dream. Branko pulls out a beer from his mini-fridge and moves to the chair, the sealed envelope placed on the table in front of him. His hands are shaking, as he downs the first can. Less so, as he empties the second. He puts the third and last beer in front of him, opens it and sets it aside.

"I might need it for after," he says to no one.

Branko's hands are trembling, as he tears open the top of the envelope. His palms are sweaty, and he stops to breathe before emptying the content out on the table. What he finds inside are a few sheets of paper, written in a language he does not understand and a single sheet written in German.

Petrovic,

It seems that we may be able to help each other. I have a feeling that the Dane has an interesting story to tell you. Call me.

He looks at the other papers again. They are printed forms with text that has been added by typewriter into the various fields. The words *politi* and *Danmark* are recognizable at the top of each page, and a few other words look familiar. He believes that he is looking at a Danish policereport. Wtihout being able to understand everything on the pages, Branko guesses that someone in the Danish police has been gathering intelligence on Jacob Hansen, the name which is repeated several times. The first page also has the word *adresse* which he immediately recognizes. The file contains Jacob Hansen's last known address, but the information has been obscured by a thick, black line covering the streetname. Suddenly he understands. This last piece of information will come at a price.

Branko tries to stand, but his knees refuse to hold him up and he collapses right back into his chair. He gulps down the already opened third beer, but does not try to stand up again. His mind and his heart are racing and he feels a cold sweat, he has not felt in a long time. It is the same feeling he used to have, before going into battle. Acutely heightened senses, adrenaline and fear mixed with a determination to harden up for inevitable. In his mind, he is already preparing himself for what is to come.

Chapter thirteen

Frank looked at his watch, deciding it was time to go home. It had been hours since he stopped counting the drinks and tomorrow was not a day off. Joel had already left, before Frank had made it down to the Shoeprint, which left just him and Elouise. She had had a shot of tequila waiting for him, even before he arrived.

The Shoeprint was located in a tiny little corner of downtown Seattle, and had specifically targeted Seattle's finest as its preferred patrons. The place looked like an Irish tavern, in good cop tradition, but the place served a lot more than Guiness and Bushmore Irish whiskey. After the first tequila shot with a beer on the side, he had moved on to gimlets.

Over the past three years, other people had started frequenting the bar, after it had appeared in an article in the Seattle Times. It had started with women, the kind who have a soft spot for men in uniform. And where women go, men follow. Now the bar was only frequented by a small group of cops. Most others had moved on to other places, where they could be among their own, and the Shoeprint had changed its image a little, adopting CSI inspired decoration, like police line tape and, of course, a number of plaster footprints. All of it mixed with the wood classic pub interior created a cheesy, half-assed image, which was what Frank liked about it. That and the women. More than once had he been picked up by women there, and he was not about to complain about that.

Drinking with a black amazon warrior of a woman kept any other women away this time, but he and Elouise had a good heart to heart which suited his mood a lot better than the small-talk and pick-up lines of bar conversations between strangers. It had been much too long, since the two of them had talked, he realized. Every time he had seen her in a casual situation like this, he had been surprised at how outgoing she could be, compared to how quiet and reserved she could be at the office. Tonight, after a few drinks, he had mustered up the courage to confront her with it, and she had told him, that she purposely stayed in the background, because she did not want any favors. When Frank had wondered what favors she would get for being more outspoken, she shrugged and said that it was probably a carry over from her time as in the military. She did not want anyone to think, that she was another minority, trying to make a career out of her sex and the color of her skin. Homicide was where she had always wanted to be, she said, which made Frank nod enthusiastically. He knew that this was her way of thanking him, for letting her stay on the team, but instead of making him happy, it made him think about the guys he had let go. How many of them had been in homicide, because that was their call? He felt his cheeks go hot with anger, when he thought about the pricks who messed with good people's lives just to make some statistics look good. And then left people like himself to make the hard decisions, like deciding who could stay and who would have to start over somewhere else.

The conversation had gone from there onto Joel, who seemed to act completely opposite of Elouise. At work, he was always the wisecracker and the loudmouth, but in social situations, he seemed to be a very private person. Frank could only remember seeing Joel's wife once at a fellow cop's funeral, but he had never spoken with her. They had worked together for a couple of years, but now Frank realized that he did not even know Joel's wife's name or anything about what their life together was like.

Frank wondered why Elouise wasn't married. When he asked her, she brushed him off and said, that that was the lamest proposal she had gotten all night. He knew that was a warning not to go there, and just laughed with her instead and offered a toast to the happy, single life.

It was nearly one in the morning, before he was home. He had stopped drinking an hour before having to drive, but his head still felt heavy and his body slow. He had some eighties song in his head, that had been running on the jukebox all night, and he still could not remember who had performed it. As he fumbled with his keys, he noticed a piece of paper taped to his door. He recognized the handwriting as belonging to Rosa.

He sat on the couch, still fully dressed and unfolded the note. The message said simply:

A man came asking for you. Did not give his name. Rosa.

And then he remembered that he had gotten the same message the night before. At the time, he had not given it any real attention, thinking that it had been Joel or someone from the department. But he had forgotten to ask and no messages had been left at the office or in his voicemail. Weighing the piece of paper in his hand, like it would somehow reveal the mystery man's identity, he thought about it and decided to keep his gun within reach, when he went to bed.

Frank woke to the sound of his cellphone ringing. He was still on the couch, still fully dressed and still holding the note. His head was pounding and he felt like, whatever he was carrying inside his stomach might decide to come out at any time. When he pushed the green button, his hand was shaking.

"Hello?"

"Where the hell are you, man?" Joel was whispering at the other end. "I've been covering for you, but we gotta talk."

"Why? What's up?"

"Red wants us to close the case today."

"Today?" Frank asked, for a second not even sure which day it was.

"Yeah," Joel said. "Says there's no progress and he either wants the case shut or put on the backburner. Says work is piling up."

"What?" He squinted and tried to think, but found himself failing miserably. "I'll be there in an hour."

It took a very hot shower, followed by a short, very cold one, a shot of superstrong coffee and a lightly toasted plain bagle with a thick layer of cream cheese to bring Frank back to reality. It had not even been a week, and he could not believe that the case was being put down. Especially right after the press had been informed. What about the bad publicity they were going to get, when the media heard, that they were giving up on finding the killer of a successful, white, well-educated woman? Something else had to be going on, and Frank would find out what. He would not let the death off Caroline Saunders turn into a cold case.

As he entered the office, he did not stop to greet his colleagues, but headed straight to Big Red's office. The big man's face was slightly pink even before Frank had begun.

"Yesterday you bring a profiler into the case and today you want to shut it down? What the hell is going on here?"

"Calm down, Cash. What are you talking about?"

"I just got a call that you're wanting us to drop the case."

"From who?"

"Joel," Frank said and was about to say something more, when he saw that the big man looked like he was either choking on something or holding back a chuckle. Big Red's eyes weren't on Frank, but looking at something through the still open door. Slowly, Frank turned around, and the entire office started laughing at him.

Then he remembered the tradition.

Whenever a lead detective did not show up for work on time, following a night of drinks with the fellow members of his team, tradition dictated that someone would play a joke on him the next morning. As he realized what had happened, his expression changed and Big Red gave in to his urge to laugh. Frank breathed hard a couple of times, trying to calm himself, before finally taking a bow to his colleagues, who were still laughing in the main office.

"Hard night, huh?" Redding said through his own laughter.

"We left at the same time," Elouise said to the lieutenant, "but didn't have a problem getting up this morning. And I'm a girl." She put her hand on her hip and shot it sideways, as she said the last sentence, making everyone laugh even harder.

"Alright, Elouise," Frank said, holding up his hands in surrender. "You take the lead on the next case."

About ten minutes later, the entire team was done pouring over the day's newspapers. The press had brought the story of the young, successful shrink, who had her own highclass clinic, but who had fallen prey to a burglary, that had gotten out of hand and turned into rape and eventually murder. Without outright saying it had been a burglary, that was how the lieutenant had formulated his statement. The articles contained no specifics about the condition of the body or any other details from the crime scene, all of which only made things easier for Frank and his team. The less the public knew at this point, the easier it would be to sort through the phonecalls that would be coming in. It was the double-edged sword of asking the public for help. Give away too little and the press would refuse to run with it, give them too much, and there would be too many bogus confessions and false accusations to sort through. Instead, the article went on to give some vague details about Caroline herself, but it was clear that the journalist had had very little to work with, relying heavily on the statement. Caroline Saunder's parents had been unavailable for comment.

Most of the articles, as well as local tv news stations, had used the same picture of Caroline, one taken when she was very much alive. In it, she was smiling brilliantly and with a distinct twinkle in her eyes, her long hair flowed freely down in soft curls, framing her face and long, pretty neck. She looked like perfectly innocent and like a girl with the world at her feet, Frank thought. Alive and loving every second of it. He wondered now, how much of that had been a lie. None of the papers had printed the story about her sexlife and the many men in it. Neither had they uncovered the story about the abusive uncle. He could only imagine the kind of picture they would be painting, if they had known the full story. When he thought about it, Frank was not even sure he had the full story. It seemed that, for every truth he uncovered about her, a new set of secrets appeared. He could only wonder what would be next.

A couple of the more detailed articles mentioned Frank and his team by name and made comments about the recent cut in homicide manpower. Everyone on the team could see the potential advantage of getting that in there. Best case scenario being, that the cuts in manpower and the murder of a pretty, successful woman, in her own home no less, would cause an outcry in the public, which would cause the powers that be to panic and in the end might lead to a budget increase. Probably at the cost of some other department's budget, but such was the game of politics. They could only hope.

Frank was just finishing the article this morning's Seattle Times, when a light on his desk phone lit up, informing him that he had a call. None of his colleagues used this line, and he suspected it would be the first of the tips being called in.

"Homicide," he said, as he picked up his phone.

"Adam Langley, Seattle Times," said the voice at the other end.

"Adam, old buddy," Frank said, though he had never spoken to this man before. "How are you?"

Adam Langley had only been writing crime stories for the Times for a short while, and though he probably had some contacts on the force, Frank had never dealt with him before. Rumor had it, that he had been an up and coming reporter on the east coast, but that he somehow got involved in a scandal that forced him to move away. Frank wondered what that scandal might have been.

"Is this a bad time?" said the journalist.

"No-no," Frank said, trying to sound fatherly. He always got suspicious, when reporters were polite. "We're never too busy for the Times."

"Is this detective Frank Cash?" Adam said, suddenly sounding a little unsure.

"It is."

"I was wondering if I could somehow set up a meeting with you as soon as possible."

"A meeting? Like an interview?"

"Not exactly. I was thinking we'd be able to help each other out?"

"Really? How so?"

"I'd like to discuss it face to face," Adam said. "I might have some information for you."

Frank knew better than to fish for information from a journalist. That was their specialty, so he agreed to meet up with Adam over lunch, which was coming up soon anyway. He made it short notice and picked the place on purpose, to show the reporter who was in charge, even if he did get hes "meeting". After he had hung up, he passed the information on to his team members, and for a few minutes they sat around speculating about what mr. Langley might or might not know. Talking about it was pointless, of course, but it beat having to face the fact that nothing they had uncovered so far, had brought them any closer to finding a real suspect.

Frank met Adam at The Hurricane, a divey 24-hour diner where the customers ranged from old, dusty beatniks to young goths and everything in between. Frank liked to go there every now and then, mainly because he enjoyed the diversity and the fact that no other cops were among the regulars, and that, combined with the fact that they served alcohol, meant that he could have a drink after lunch, without risking that any of his colleagues saw it and felt it necessary to make a fuss about it.

Even though Frank had never seen Adam before, he recognized the tall guy, as soon as he entered. The way he was scouting across the landscape of booths gave him away, and Frank stuck up he hand and waved him over. He was in his early thirties. His face was smooth and shaved to a shine, though from the looks of it, Frank guessed that facial hair had never been a problem for this guy. His trench coat looked like it had just left the dry cleaner, and that he only wore it, because someone had told him that that was what real reporters had on. At the end of perfectly pressed pants, dark brown leather shoes shone, as if he had just bought them minutes ago. Frank thought, he looked more like a lawyer than a journalist.

"Mr. Cash," the young reporter said, holding out his hand. Frank shook it and gestured for Adam to sit across from him.

"You must be Langley," he said.

"Call me Adam," he said and fidgetted his way into the red vinyl seat. "I'd like to say right away, that this is an off the record meeting. At least unless we agree otherwise."

"That's good with me," Frank said. "But you were the one with the information."

Adam smiled almost apoligetically while Frank's blue cheese burger arrived along with a pint of Pyramid Hefeweizen. The waitress was a bored looking twentysomething with dyed black hair, pale white skin, piercings in her lower lip and left eyebrow and a shuffling walk. If she thought the two men were out of place, she did not show it. Instead, she turned to Adam, who ordered coffee only.

"So," Frank said as the waitress left. "What've you got."

"If I tell you," Adam said, "will you agree to let me get an exlcusive when the case breaks?"

"First of all," Frank said with his mouth full, "I don't know which case you are talking about. And second, I'm not promising you anything, until I know it's worth it."

"Fair enough," the journalist replied and fidgetted some more, eyeing the burger as if he had not eaten in weeks. Coffee arrived and was being poured, when he finally took his eyes off the food and started talking. "A while ago, I was contacted by a man, wanting to know if any women had been killed in the Seattle area."

"Wow," Frank said. "I immediately see the connection."

"Hold on," Adam said. "this guy was very specific. He said that he wanted to know about women who had been raped, and left with a white sheet over the body. More specifically, a sheet where holes had been cut for the eyes."

The little hairs at the back of Frank's neck suddenly stood up and he nearly dropped the much coveted burger. This information had not been released to the public. If someone had told Adam Langley about it, it meant there was a leak. Or that he had been at the murder scene before the body had been removed.

"Tell me more," Frank said.

"There's not much to tell. I was new here at the time, so I researched it in the Time's archives but found nothing. I passed it on to the guy, he thanked me and I never saw him again."

"Who was he? How did he look?"

"Foreigner. He spoke with a heavy accent. Could have been German or something. Fairly big guy, dark hair, bad complexion. Around my age."

"Did he say why he was interested?"

"Said he was writing a book," Adam said, looking calmer now that he obviously had Frank interested. "Said he wanted to make sure, he didn't write about something that had actually happened."

"And when was this?"

"About three months ago."

"This is very interesting, mr. Langley," Frank said, picking up his burger again. "And I will grant you your exclusive on one condition."

"What is that?"

"You tell me who your source was."

"I can't do that," the reporter said, holding his hands out flat, as if to show Frank he had nothing more to give. "Without protecting my-"

"Forget it," Frank cut him off. "I've heard this song before, and it's lost its charm. I'm going to find out anyway, so you're not really protecting anyone here." He finished the burger and was drying off his mouth with the napkin as he spoke. "And I hope, I don't see any of what you've told me in the paper."

"I can't-"

"Yes, you can," Frank said, as softly as possible. The effect seemed to be exactly the one he was going for. Adam started fidgetting again. "You're still new in town, mr. Langley. You need good contacts and a good reputation. If you print any of this, I'll see to it, that no cop in Seattle will ever share anything with you again."

Neither man said anything, as the waitress came back to re-fill the coffee and take Frank's plate away. He ordered another beer, being extra nice and smiling in the process, to show the reporter, just how calm and collected he was.

"Alright," Adam finally said. "I never planned on printing any of this anyway. I'm a good guy, detective Cash. On your side. And I'm sorry if we've gotten off on the wrong foot here."

"Not at all," Frank said. "I'm just telling it like it is. You've got information on the case that was not meant to be publically known. I'm trying to protect that information, just like you are trying to protect your source."

"Fuck it," Adam finally said. "I got it from my girlfriend, okay?"

"Your girlfriend?"

"Yeah. She works down at the crimelab. We were talking about the murder in casual conversation, and she said it spooked her, when she heard about the ghost costume. Naturally, I asked. When I put it together with that guy, who had contacted me, I tried seeing you. I've been trying to reach you for days, man. Even before a statement came out."

"Why didn't you just leave a message?"

"I left one with your neighbor last night."

"You came to my home?" Frank asked, remembering the mystery man, who had been to his apartment two days in a row.

"I live a block away. I used my girlfriend to get your address."

"Okay fine," Frank said. "I don't appreciate you coming by my home, Langley. I don't know you and I don't really take well to unannounced visitors."

He dug out a card from his wallet and slid it across the table. "Next time just call me on my cellphone."

"So, are we cool?"

"You'll get your exclusive, if that's what you're worried about. But tell me, what's your girlfriends name?"

"Why?" Adam asked, his eyes widening.

"I have to check that she really exists," Frank lied.

The reporter looked at Frank for a long time before answering, probably knowing that no matter what he answered, he would be in trouble one way of the other. Sighing, he finally said: "Jennifer Richford."

"Now, get the hell out of here and let me enjoy the rest of my beer."

Adam Langley nodded, fidgetted his way back out of his seat and left the diner, his head hung low. A few minutes later, Frank left the Hurricane behind as well, heading straight to Harbor View Medical Center. There was no reason to wait, when he might as well have a word with ms. Richford right away.

Once he got there, she was easy enough to find. Flashing his badge and asking for her at the desk, was all he had to do. They paged her and left him to wait. The scar on his cheek started itching again, like it always did, when he was there. Memories flashed back into his mind, little pieces of that day playing themselves out like a movie.

It was one of those blistering hot days, July 13th 1999, where the air was still as a corpse and everyone seemed to be on the brink of overheating. Frank responded to a domestic disturbance in West Seattle, not far from his own apartment. A neighbor had reported screaming and noise from what was either shattering furniture or someone getting their head kicked in. They had not been sure. Someone was overheating.

The house was a small and partially hidden behind a hedge, someone had allowed to grow out of control. It occurred to him, that he must have passed the place a hundred times, yet he had never noticed it before. He heard the screaming before he had even left his car and quickly radioed for back-up, before stepping out to take a peak at the house. If he stood on his toes, he could look over the hedge, but there was nothing but a shaggy, yellow lawn and the house itself. It was impossible to see anything through the filthy windows, but now that he was that much closer, he was able to hear everything that was going on.

The male did most of the screaming, and all of what he said were profanities and curses. It was unclear what he was upset about, but whatever it was, he obviously felt that the female was to blame. Her presence was limited to a low sobbing, bare audible through the flimsy walls, under the man's screaming. At first Frank heard nothing to indicate, that this was more than a simple argument, even if it was a loud one, but all that changed in an instant, when the sound of a gun being fired, suddenly tore through the heavy summer air. The woman let out a yelp and the screendoor flew open. Frank only had a moment to react and instinctively, he reached for his own firearm, crouching down slightly behind the hedge. He saw the gate fly open a yard away from where he was standing, and a woman flew past him into the street.

She was dressed in nothing but a tattered, faded bathrobe, her hair disheveled and her face puffy from crying, but she did not appear to have been shot. Frank's eyes met her for a second, and she seemed to look right through him. Her face was a hard with deep lines and sunken cheeks drawn up in a mask of fear. With a sudden jerk, she looked back up past Frank and the gate she had come through, and when her eyes widened and another scream started forming on her lips, Frank knew that the guy with the gun was coming up the path and would be out in a second.

A block away, another cruiser came around the corner. Backup was coming.

Maybe it was the flashing lights of the second police car heading toward them, that made the woman realize what was happening, but she stopped screaming suddenly, and she turned back to look at Frank. He thought, he saw something resembling hope in her eyes then. The guy with the gun saw it too apperently, because when Frank turned around the corner, pistol first, pointing it up the path and yelling for the man to freeze, he had been ready for him. Frank remembered the flash from the muzzle and the look on the shooter's face. His eyes were wide and red, his nostrils flared like on a horse, and his mouth was moving so fast, that it seemed to spew out curses faster than the bullet, that was leaving the barrel, heading straight for Frank's face. For a split second, he actually thought, he might be able to dodge it.

When it hit, time sped up again. The sound came first. A sick cracking and popping sound, as bone inside Frank's jaw snapped an shattered. He didn't know exactly where it had entered, or if it had even gone out again. It fel like everything from his nose down had exploded in an inferno of fire. He heard screeching tires, shouting and more popping sounds from guns being fired, but saw none of it. Suddenly the world was slipping away too fast. Frank wanted to stay awake. He wanted to live.

The pain woke him up. He wanted to scream, but found that he had no control of the lower part of his face. He opened his eyes and realized that he was at the hospital, but his eyes could not seem to find their focus. He tried to listen, but hear nothing but a high-pitched tone ringing in his ears. For a while, he took comfort in the pain, because it seemed to be the only real indicator, that he was still alive. And then the world slowly faded away again.

The recovery took months. Frank had been lucky, they had told him, but with his jaw wired shut, reduced hearing and his entire face puffed up, it was hard to believe. Slowly, he began to realize that they were right. He wondered if he had been able to dodge the bullet anyway, at least partially, of if the shooter had just got unlucky. The bullet had entered through his cheek and shattered his jaw before continuing out just below the ear. He would be alright, eventually, and for his trouble, they made him a homicide detective.

Jennifer Richford was a short bone of a girl, on whom the nurse's uniform looked more like a white tent. She had a longish face with almond shaped, blue eyes, narrow lips and a nose that was too broad. Her skin was pale, like it is on people who work too much indoors and spend their time off collapsed on a couch somewhere. From her posture, with her arms on her hips and her head slightly tilted, it was clear she had no idea why Frank had asked to see her. So much the better, he thought. There had been a chance Adam Langley had phoned ahead to warn her.

"You the guy asking for me?"

Frank flashed his badge at her and nodded. "I wonder if I might have a word?"

"Well, I'm here, aren't I?" her back stiffened as if she was trying to look taller, and her mouth puckered, making smoker's lines appear all around her mouth.

"I understand you're seeing a man by the name of Adam Langley?"

"None of your business," she said.

"I'm afraid it is, miss Richford. Especially when you accidentally slip him information about an ongoing investigation. And even more so because of mr. Langley's occupation. Do you understand where I'm going with this?"

"I don't know what you're talking about," she said flatly.

Frank felt the anger building inside him and took a step towards the little nurse. She stepped backwards, but suddenly found herself up against the wall. They were standing in the corridor, right next to the information desk, but no one seemed to notice Frank standing a couple of inches away from Jennifer, pointing his finger at her face.

"Listen carefully," he hated this part of the job, but from time to time, it was necessary to do and say things, he would rather have avoided. "Your flapping mouth could easily have cost us this investigation, which I shouldn't have to remind you is a murder investigation. I don't like that and I don't like your snotty attitude about it either. If you like your job here, miss Richford, I suggest you start showing some respect."

The expression on the little woman's face changed slowly, as Frank stared into her eyes. He imagined that right then, she was wondering whether or not he really could get her fired, which he had no idea whether or not he could, but it had sounded like the best threat, when he said it.

"Do I make myself clear, miss Richford?"

Slowly, the nurse nodded and Frank stepped back and let her slip away from him and down the corridor. He did not watch her go, but started heading towards the exit, suddenly feeling short of breath. As he stepped outside, he found that his heart was pounding hard in his chest and his palms were sweaty. He did not like hospitals.

Getting into his car, he wondered if Adam Langley would be in trouble, the next time he saw his girlfriend. Part of him hoped so. Maybe that would teach him not to come around Frank's private residence in the future.

Chapter fourteen

HAMBURG, FEBRUARY 2004 – The German is already there, as Branko walks into the bar. He knows why he is there and what is expected of him, yet he still has a tight knot in his stomach. It is easy enough to spot the little man with the purple baret. The German smiles and nods, as their eyes meet across the room. It is too late now, there is no turning back. As if there ever was.

After the man in the suit had dropped off the file on Jacob Hansen, it had taken Branko two days to make the phonecall. During those two days, he had not gone out to the coffee shops or to the bars to drink. He had stayed in his room, praying to the Lord for guidance. And he had worked out. Push-ups and situps for hours on end, cleaning the poisons from his system, clearing his mind and find his purpose. The ghost had whispered in his ear, telling him to stay in Amsterdam and give up this silly quest for someone he would never find, but the more the ghost protested, the harder he worked out. He had scared it, he thought, finally shown the voice in his head, who was in control.

Branko knew that the German would ask him to kill Jacob Hansen. That was the only logical explanation to the sudden appearance of the file. Killing was a sin, and though Branko had already killed more than once, it had never been like this. In the army, he had been a soldier, killing for a cause. Even if what they did was sometimes less than human. The thoughts made images of ravaged women and executed children flicker in his memory. Still, that was war. War has no rules. And then there was the bank manager. An accident. But now he was going to commit a cold, planned murder. So he prayed for forgiveness, for what he was about to do.

The man who had answered Branko's call, gave instructions to meet the German in Hamburg, Germany. The time and place were already set. All he had to do was show up, and he had plenty of time to get there. He had spent a couple more days preparing himself before leaving Amsterdam behind. And as he left the city behind, he couldn't help laughing out loud. It was as if he had just woken up from a deep sleep, from which he had feared, he would never awake. Like he had been a prisoner there, held captive by broken dreams and a multitude of sins, and only now that he was leaving, did he truly see it for what it was. It was the laughter of a man, who thought his life had been over, but who suddenly discovered that it was in fact just about to begin.

"My client," the German says as Branko is sitting down across from him, "has a personal interest in this matter. And I know you are the perfect man for this job."

Both of them know what the job is. Spelling it out is unnecessary.

"It was lucky," the German continues, "that I still knew where to find you. I am sorry the contact I gave you down in Amsterdam did not work out. The guy was not very reliable, I'm afraid. Too nervous. Not like you, Branko. You are cold as ice."

"I just want to find the man who killed my sister," Branko says.

"I know, I know. And that is why both of us will win from this situation. I don't care what kind of information, you get out of mr. Hansen before finishing the business at hand, but I am sure he knows something that might help you."

"What do I do, when the job is done?"

"I will give you a number," the German said. "It will only recieve one call, so don't waste it. Call as soon as it is done. You will reviece instructions on where to go. There will be a small compensation waiting there."

"And then?"

"Then that's it. You will hopefully find your sister's killer and do whatever it is you need to do."

The two men sit in the low lit German beerhouse. Some jazz track is playing in the background and people around them seem to be enjoying themselves. It is almost exclusively middle aged men in the place, and from their conversations, it sounds like this place is where they all go after work to wind down, or perhaps to prepare themselves before facing their women at home.

"Don't be so gloomy, my friend," the German says. "At least you should be happy that you will never have to deal with me again."

Branko forces a smile.

"Look," the German says, leaning in over the table. "You're a driven man, and I respect that. You value your family, and I respect that too. What you did to me back in Pristina, I would have probably done too. I could have picked anyone else to do this job. But I picked you, Branko Petrovic. I want you to remember that."

The German gets up slowly, like an old man having difficulty walking. He stops and looks at Branko, and for a second, if seems like there is genuine sadness in his eyes. He pats Branko on his shoulder and leaves without saying another word.

Branko notices the plastic bag, the German has left on his seat. It is a half-empty bag from some supermarket. He does not look inside it. Instead he sits there, trying to make sense what the German just said, drinking his beer slowly. For the first time, he thinks of the German as another human being, with feelings of his own, dreams and hopes, and he wonders about the connection between them. But there are no answers, and finally, Branko drops the subject and begins to focus at the task at hand. Before going back to his motel, he picks up the bag and peeks inside. Inside there is a cigar box and an envelope. That is all he needs to see.

Chapter fifteen

Frank looked down at his cellphone and the number punched in on the display. All he had to do now was press the green button, but somehow that was a lot harder than it seemed. It was always like that, every time he met a woman who had something more, than the ones he would meet at the Shoeprint. That little button was all that stood between him and whatever the future held for him and this woman, There was more to it than that, of course. Nervousness and anticipation. What if they did not click at all outside the sterile environment of the morgue. Did it really matter? He finally closed his eyes and just pressed it, quickly lifting the phone up to his ear, at the same time, he put his car in gear and left the parking lot of Harbor View.

"Hello?" said the voice on the other end.

"Dr. M. London," Frank said. "How are you today?"

"Just got back from lunch and about to cut open a hit and run. How are you?"

"Good."

Awkward silences were part of the game, and this was one of them. He thought of her, in her lab coat, maybe standing in front of a slab. In his imagination, there was nothing resting on that cold, stainless steel surface. There was no need to ruin the moment.

"So," the pathologist said, "you decided to call?"

"Yeah, yeah, I did. I want to take you out for dinner."

"Really? Sounds nice."

Was there something in her voice? A smile perhaps.

"But first you've got to tell my your first name."

"No one calls me by my first name," she said. Frank thought her voice had a lot more melody to it, than he had ever noticed in the morgue. Maybe that was not so strange, when it came down to it. This was after all, the first conversation they had ever had, that did not somehow involve death.

"I'd like to," he said.

"It's Mary, alright?"

"Well, Mary, when are you free for dinner?"

"Tonight," she said. In the background, he could hear footsteps echoing in the long halls inside the medical examiner's building, heavy doors opening and closing. "Look, detective Cash, I've gotta go. But I am looking forward to seeing you."

"Likewise," Frank said, but she had already hung up by then.

There was a message for Frank, when he returned to the office, asking him to call Jeffrey Bernstein. His colleagues, however, were engaged in a conversation with Christina Quick, apparently trying to come up with something new, by discussing the old. This was not a sign of desperation, Frank knew. Quite often, details in a case that had previously been dismissed as unimportant, would be recognized as crucial when reviewed later. Going through the pile every now and then was part of the job. This was really where the great minds of the team members could come together and sometimes perform miracles.

"Anything new?" Joel asked as Frank sat down.

"Adam Langley," he started, "seems to have been contacted by someone who might have known about the killing. Only he was contacted a few months in advance."

"How so?"

Frank recapped the meeting he had just left, leaving out the part about Jennifer Richford. When he was done, there was a long silence, while the whole team digested the new information.

"It's strange," Christina said, "that the killer contacted the journalist like that."

"It's not unheard of. The Zodiac killer regularly wrote letters to the press," Joel answered.

"True," she continued, "but this is different. This guy checks in advance, as if he wants to make sure no one else has ever done anthing like what he is about to do."

"Either that," Elouise said, "or he already killed someone in the past, and he wants to see if anyone ever found the body."

"Why ask someone about that?" Frank asked. "Couldn't he just as well check newspaper archives himself and avoid the attention?"

"Maybe it wasn't the killer at all?" Christina suggested.

"Who else would have knowledge about the details of a murder that hasn't happened yet?" Frank asked.

The team sat around for a few minutes, no one saying anything, but trying to make this new piece of the puzzle fit into the bigger picture. Joel finally shrugged, got up and left the room.

Chapter sixteen

COPENHAGEN, FEBRUARY 2004 – The Danish capitol is freezing cold. Outside the people roll by on bicycles and in cars, running in what looks like small, black canals dug in the grey slush mix made out of roadsalt, exhaust fumes and halft-melted snow. Branko is staying in the Astoria hotel, right next to the central train station in the middle of the city, and from his room, he can look down on a broad and busy street, where cars, bikes and buses roll by in a never ending stream. Everything is grey in this country, where winter appears to have seeped into the buildings themselves, the asphalt and the neon lights. For a second, he is reminded of Pristina. It feels as if someone has taken an ice pick to his heart, as he thinks about the home he will never see again. His family. Jovana. Her name brings him back to the real world.

As focus returns, he watches a big, yellow bus pull into a bus stop and load a handful of people. All of them are dressed in heavy clothes and big boots. Even from this distance, Branko can see the frowns on their faces, and as the bus tries to leave the bus stop, the slippery road makes it slide right back to the curb. The bus lets out a loud sigh, as the driver tries again and finally pulls away.

"What a shithole," he says to himself and lights a cigarette.

Branko turns his attention back to the task at hand. He has Jacob Hansen's home address, an apartment complex in a part of the suburbs called Brøndby Strand, and now he is studying the maps of the area, noticing how all the blocks there have the exact same layout, as he to memorize all the names of the sidestreets. Without having ever set foot in Brøndby Strand, he expects it to be a sad place, juding only from the map in front of him. Tomorrow, he will go to see the area for himself, and see how close he can get to Hansen's apartment without appearing suspicious. After that, he is going to lay low for a few days, before returning to finish the job.

Getting into Denmark was just as easy as all the other European countries. His EU passport is like a golden ticket. Travelling through Germany, Belgium, Holland and now Denmark, he has not seen one single custom's officer. Had it not been for the signs by the side of the road, welcoming him to a new country, he might have completely overlooked crossing the borders. The fact, that he had been able to drive all the way was almost too perfect. Bringing a firearm aboard an airplane would have been a challenge, he did not need.

He smiles as he pulls the cigarbox out of the bag and opens it. Inside is a Walther PPK pistol. It is a fairly small firearm, easily concealed but still very effective. It had once been the favored gun of none other than James Bond. Branko takes the gun apart and puts it back together in seconds, getting a feel for the shape and weight of it. He would like to clean the gun, but he does not have the equipment for it. Instead, he inspects every single detail of the Walther. Looking through the barrel before clicking it into place, pulling the trigger a couple of times, putting a round in the chamber and taking it back out. His time in the Yugoslavian People's Army comes back to him in little flashes he would rather be without. The sound of screams, the smell of blood and gunfire. Finally, he puts the gun away and decides to try out the hotel bar.

The bartender is a little on the chubby side with a crew cut and a goofy look on his face. There are no other guests there, and the plump guy lights up, as Branko sits down at the bar.

"What would you like?" he asks.

"A beer. Whatever is on tap."

The bartender puts a pint glass under the Carlsberg tap and lets it run without looking. He could probably do this in his sleep, just like Branko can take apart and re-assemble a pistol.

"So, are you staying for business or pleasure?"

"Business. Pure business."

"What do you do?"

Branko gets his beer and looks at the tiny bubbles rising inside the glass for a long time before answering.

"Lifeinsurance."

"Sorry," the bartender says and laughs. "I already got one."

"Here's to life," Branko says, lifting his glass.

The freezing wind bites at his skin, as he walks through the streets of Copenhagen. The air is so moist, it feels like he is walking through ice. His feet carry him across town square, where an endless number of neon signs scream out at him. Among them, he spots a McDonald's and decides to get a bite to eat. Placing his order and getting his food seems to take forever. The food, once he gets it, has no taste. The seat is uncomfortable, as if it was designed to make people hurry up and move along. Why are these western Europeans always in such a hurry, he wonders.

A chill runs down Branko's spine, but it is not from the slightly stale-tasting cola he is drinking. This is a different kind of cold coming from within him. Sometimes he still wakes up in the middle of the night with images of torture and mutilation before his eyes. Pictures of friends with their limbs torn from their bodies by incoming grenades. Sounds of bullets rococheting around him. Those nights he can not go back to sleep for a cold coming from within himself, seeping out into the room. This is that same kind of coldness.

He sits by his small plastic table at McDonald's, looking out the window, wondering how his life would have looked, if Jovana had still be alive. Perhaps they would be rebuilding the coffee shop together. Maybe they would both be starting new families to replace the one they lost in the bombings. He decides, that if he ever has a daughter, he is going to name her Jovana. But he doubts, he will ever have children. Still, the thought of it is helping keep the anxiety at bay.

Maybe Jacob Hansen has children. How that will affect the job, he wonders. He sees himself poised above a dead man, as a little boy walks into the room and sees his father's lifeless form in a pool of blood. What will he do then?

He knows, he could never purposely kill a child. In his mind, he is playing out various scenarios. In one storyline, he takes the child with him and start a new life somewhere. The two of them live in a cabin in the mountains. They live off the land, working hard, and in the evenings, they play chess and laugh. In another story, he leaves the child alone for the Danish authorities to take care of. Surely they have homes for abandoned children in this country, but what kind of life would that be? He imagines a fragile boy becoming a young man, hardened by a brutal life among other rejects, and one day the young man learns of his father's fate and sets out to settle the score. His thoughts begin to drift. After all, he has killed children before. Children of the enemy that would some day become threats. But before he starts considering ways to silence a child, he does not even know if exists, he stops himself from thinking any more about it. Ultimately, it will all be in the hands of God when the time comes.

It has started to snow, as he leaves the fast food restaurant, and starts walking back towards the Astoria, he notices the small group of young men. They are hanging around a set of benches, as young men tend to do, until one of them points at Branko and nod to the others. Now they walk up to him, in the middle of town square.

The group catch up with him in the middle of the square, in the shadow of the castle-like city hall building with its spires and clock tower. Neonlights cast glows of many colors on the faces of the men in front of Branko, and apart from a few cars driving by near the edges of the square, there are no other people around. He recognizes them as muslims. Not that it matters. There are young punks in all ethnic groups, he thinks to himself, but if these boys only knew how many of their kind, he seen torn up by bullets, stabbed and gutted – and how many of them he himself has done these things to.

The group has almost surrounded him, when one of the young men says something in a language Branko can only assume is Danish.

"I'm sorry," he says. "I don't understand."

"Ah," the young man says and flashes a confident smile to his friends. "A tourist."

His friends smile back at him. Their clothes all look new and expensive and they are all wearing the same thick, black jackets. Brank feels like laughing at this pathetic gang of theirs, even as a couple of them pull out knives.

"Give us your money," the young man who appears to be their leader says.

"No."

The group moves in closer, an the air is thick with tension now. The smiles are all gone, and the young men shift their weight around, as if uncertain how to handle this. A single man refusing to comply. They must not be used to it. He knows this situation and what is to come, if he does not stop it. And he must, in spite of temptation of taking these punks off the street for good. Causing a situation here would jeopardize his mission. He looks the leader straight into the eyes.

"Do you want to die tonight?" The young man asks.

"If I do, it won't be by your hands."

"Tough guy, huh?"

The staring contest has begun. Branko does not blink and when he breathes, he does so without moving. Only the steam coming from his nostrils give away his exhales. The small stream pours steadily from him, unlike the man who's eyes he is staring into. His opponent is already breathing faster than he was a minute ago, and Branko knows that it is the adrenaline pumping through the young man's veins. As the seconds pass, the unrest within the rest of the group grows. One of them says something in Danish to their leader, but he does not answer. No one else says anything, and Branko knows they will not make a move until their leaders gives the sign. Branko starts to take his hands out of his coat pockets, as slowly as possible.

"That's right," another man in the group says, "take out your wallet."

Then Branko moves so fast, none of the others see it coming. He has pulled the Walther PPK out and taken two steps forward before any of them could even blink, now holding the muzzle about an inch from the leader's forehead. He is still looking into the young man's eyes, but his opponent is no longer looking at Branko. His eyes are crossed from looking at the muzzle and the excitement has left them for pure fear.

"Do *you* want to die tonight?" Branko asks, as he sees the faux courage fade from the group around him. He waits until the gang members have all taken a few steps back, before letting their young leader do the same.

Chapter seventeen

The final report on the fingerprints had come in with absolutely nothing to go on. Special agent Bernstein did not have good news for Frank either. No databases, investigators or archives had any unsolved cases matching Caroline's murder. Not even any solved ones where the killer was back out on the streets. If this guy was a serial killer, he must have recently changed his MO. Bernstein had not even been able to match this murder to any known serial rapist cases.

Frank got a list of murders and rapes that came close enough to be considered possible long shots, in case no other leads panned out, and he thanked Jeffrey for it. When their conversation was over, he sat down to read through the list. A total of seventeen murders and thirtyone rapes on the west coast involving binding and strangulating the victim, all done within the last three years, but none of them included any white sheets or other references to ghosts, halloween or even horror movies. Frank read through the list three times, hoping that something would pop out at him, but every time the cases on his list seemed to match Caroline's less than before.

"It doesn't make any sense," he said, as he got out of his chair, feeling frustrated and tired. It was becoming clear, that there would be no obvious suspect in this case, and what was worse, no obvious leads to follow either.

Frank put the list away and wished he was at home, watching a good movie to take his mind off things when he noticed a message blinking on his cellphone, indicating a voicemail waiting. It was from Mary London, who had called while he had been on the phone with Jeffrey. The message was short and to the point. She had taken the librty of reserving a table at The Buenos Aries Grill at eight thirty. Nothing else. This would be better than a movie, he thought to himself and smiled, as he closed his phone. But the smile disappeared just as fast as it had appeared, when his eyes returned to the desk and the work piling up in front of him. Joel and Elouise had both been following up on details, tracking down a couple of guys whose numbers had been stored in Caroline's cellphone and reinterveiwing Darryl the clerk, to check for possible jealousy motives. None of it had turned up any smoking guns.

This was homicide at its worst, Frank thought to himself. Not just a simple jealousy killing or gangs settling scores amongst themselves but a whodunnit case, with clues pointing either in all sorts of directions or nowhere at all. He had seen good men get too involved in too many cases like this, ending up breaking over a load of unsolved cases, or even worse, cases where they did have a suspect, but never got enough evidence to make the arrest. For a moment, Frank almost wished that were the case here, so that they at least would have had a suspect, but quickly dismissed the thought. As he did so, his thoughts wandered to those ended up so frustrated, that they grew too remote and detached from their job to remain focused, eventually getting sloppy and careless. In the relatively short time he had been in homicide, he had seen a few cases go to hell because of sloppy detective work, corrupting or even ignoring the evidence, and ultimately letting the killer go because of it. He had sworn not to end up in either category, though there were still days where a particular hard case would weigh heavy on his shoulders.

As he left the office, he put a cd in his car stereo and took the long way home, driving on some of the less busy streets, leaving downtown through 1st Avenue, heading home through first Pioneer Square, with all its old buildings and pick-up bars, coming into the more desolate areas passing the two stadiums side by side, almost empty parkinglots and apartment buildings that had not yet been turned into expensively renovated town homes. A few years ago, this had been a bad part of town, and though it was getting better as Seattle kept expanding and the value of real estate exploded, this was still a neighborhood on the border of the industrial area. The music blended with the flow of the traffic, and for a few minutes, he managed to block the case and all of the frustrations that came with it out of his mind. Music almost always did that for him, and especially whilst driving. Mary London was on his mind instead. He tried to imagine her in a different environment, such as a nice restaurant or a dimly lit bedroom. It was not until he pulled into his parking spot, that reality crept back into his thoughts.

As he tried getting ready for his date, the same things went through his head over and over, distracting him. The mysterious man who had been seeking information about the murder, even before it had happened kept popping up, while Frank was in the shower, while he was shaving and picking out clothes. Perhaps, Frank thought, this man was indeed a serial killer, and the reason that Frank had not been able to find any cases matching was simply, that the prior murders had been committed elsewhere. Had the reporter not mentioned a heavy accent?

Half naked, his hair still dripping with water, he abandoned the task of trying to match the very few clean clothing items he had, grabbed his phone and called Elouise.

As he told her about this new idea, asking her to start an international search on unsolved homicides matching theirs, he could feel her getting as excited about this new direction as he was. Getting the information might take a long time, and that was on the off chance that someone out there would recognize the modus operandi, be able to match it up with an actual case and turn up new leads or perhaps a suspect from all of it. He was now hoping that somewhere out there, one of those homicide detectives who took their work too personally, had an unsolved murdercase involving a woman dressed up as a ghost. And that this someone would get on the horn to Seattle as soon as he heard of the case of Caroline Saunders.

After drying himself off and finally settling on a pale blue shirt, a darker blue tie with some kind of abstract pattern on it and an old but not terribly crumpled grey suit, he had not worn in a while, he poured himself a glass of red wine, trying to calm his nerves. It was not the date that made his hands shake and his bloodpressure go through the roof, however. Frank was already trying to think of the best way of handling it, if he got the call, he was hoping for.

It took him only a couple of minutes to empty the first glass of wine, and immediately, he poured himself another glass, which he sipped from while pacing up and down his living room floor. Part of him was annoyed that he reacted like this, when he was supposed be to getting ready to go out with someone, and whenever he did pause to think of her, he felt a tingle inside, he had not felt in a long time, but the sensation soon went away again, as his thoughts drifted back to the case. Another part of him was wanting to postpone the date and just start calling Interpol and various homicide departments overseas. Langley had said the accent sounded German, so that is where he would begin.

After the second glass of wine and another call to Elouise, to tell her to concentrate on Germany, he slowly began to calm down. He started to feel a little ashamed of his childish excitement over something as vague as this, and as he caught his own face in the mirror, he stopped and forced himself to breathe slowly and let it go. For a moment, he feared that he had indeed become one of those people, who lived only for the job. At least, he said to his reflection, he was still able to get dates.

The Buenos Aires Grill was a steakhouse with a latin flavor. Frank had never been there before, but he immediately liked the warm ambience of the place and the thick aroma of sizzling steaks. The place was fairly small, just one room with a bar on one side and tables on the other and in the back. A couple of waiters seemed to be extremely busy, but still managed to smile and linger at each table. The place was packed and the air was thick but not stuffy. Frank spotted her waving once and saying something, which drowned completely in the noise of the room.

Mary London sat in the frontmost corner facing out towards the street. She was sipping on a glass of wine, she sat by the window Frank had just walked by on his way in there and now he felt guilty for not having seen her then. It was a stupid thought, he decided, and replaced it with taking in the full figure of his date, as she rose to shake his hand.

"Good evening, detective Cash."

"Call me Frank."

He thought it was a bit awkward to shake hands with her like this, as if they were complete strangers. Hers was a grip that would put many men to shame.

The awkwardness was soon replaced by something else, as Frank began to take in the sight of Mary London without her lab coat. She had an hour-glass figure with just a hint more weight on her hips than the women you would see in magazines, but well displayed nonetheless in her black outfit. Her shoulders were bare under the a small jacket, which she had taken off and hung on the back of her chair. They seemed smaller without the coat and gave her a certain amount of fragility, which Frank had never seen before. His eyes drifted to her chest. The dress was cut just low enough to a little bit of cleavage, without giving too much away. He liked women to have a little cleavage. Right below the chest, the dress got tight and perfectly followed her body down to her waist, where it seemed to loosen up and fall in soft curves down over her thighs until it opened up at the knees. Part of her was still, he thought, a mystery.

"Have you ever been here before?"

"I'm afraid not," he said, "but I hear the food is to die for."

"The perfect place for a homicide detective and a medical examiner then!" She said and sat back down laughing.

He laughed with her.

"I am glad you accepted," he said.

"I couldn't help it," she answered. "It's not often I get invitations. I was wondering if it's the smell of death on me, that scares the men away."

"I'm from homicide," he said with a smile on his face. "I'm used to death."

Part of him cringed at that remark. Did he just say, he was used to death? The truth was, that he was anything but used to it. His mind started to wander back to Caroline Saunders. She would probably have gone to a place like this with one of her dates.

"I hope you're hungry," Mary smiled and raised her glass. "The steaks here are as huge as they are good."

As they ordered and waited, the conversation was light and casual. He wondered about an awkwaredness, present under the calm surface. Not quite like the classic first-date nerves, which always made him clumsy and had him fidgetting. This felt more like caution, and then he realized that it was a little too close to dating a colleague, and that it was this awkwardness of suddenly letting go of that professional politeness, that made their conversation feel a little forced now. He knew there would be talk, if news of their date got out to the other homicide detectives. They all knew who dr. London was, and he could already hear the jokes about dating the pathologist.

"I must warn you," Mary said after the first few bites had been taken. "I am a strange person."

"I've noticed," Frank answered. "It's part of your charm."

"In the past, others have blamed it on my job," she continued, "but the truth is, that I picked this job because I am strange. So, it's the other way around."

"Are you worried about it?"

"No. I am merely warning you. Getting it out there."

"Alright," he said and smiled. "It's noted."

Over the next hour the two discussed very little work. Instead, they talked about annoying in-laws, art and travel. It turned out, that Mary London had been a lot of places and seen a lot of things. Frank had no doubt, that she was both smarter and more well-travelled than him, but she never came off as arrogant because of it. As they talked about Europe and the cultural differences between here and there, Frank noticed that she laughed a lot. She had lived all over Europe for almost a year, starting out in Germany, then moving to France and finally spending a couple of months in northern Italy with a quick trip to Greece. As she talked about the cultural differences between here and there, making jokes about everything from French food to Italian men, Frank caught a passion in her eyes, which made him wish she would never stop.

After an empty bottle of what had once been a very delicious Merlot and the wooden planks, on which their bloody but wonderful steaks had come, had all been removed from the table, Frank was about to pay for everything, and she slapped him on the wrist and would have none of it. They would share it, she said.

"I no room for that kind of romance in my life, Frank."

"Are you accusing me of trying to buy you?"

"No. But before you get any ideas, just know I'm not for sale." She smiled.

"Well, can I at least drive you home?"

"You bet your sweet ass," she said again and giggled.

The drive was a short one, to an apartment complex with a view of the sound, just a few blocks away. They sat on the curb for a while in silence, listening only to the sound of the Mustang's engine humming.

"There's parking just around the corner," she finally said. "I think, you should use it."

"Are you inviting me in for a nightcap?" he asked, trying hard to supress a huge grin.

"No," she answered. "I'm inviting you to stay the night."

Without a further word, he put the car in gear and found the parking lot. They got out and walked back to the front, arm in arm, but still without saying a word to each other. It felt better than he had imagined to be that close to her, Frank thought, and he could only guess how it would feel to make love with this woman.

"You know," she said, picking up the conversation as if there had never been any pause at all. "For a detective, you pick things up rather slowly."

"I'm off duty," he said, and as he did so, he realized that he had not thought about the case at all, since he had sat down at the table.

Chapter eighteen

Branko takes a train from the central station right next to his hotel. It feels good not to feel anything, he thinks to himself, as he boards the red carriage that takes him to the suburb, where Jacob Hansen lives. The red trains run through Copenhagen like blood through veins. Inside, people sit lost in their own worlds, listening to music on headphones or writing text messages on their cellphones. A few people read books or type on laptops. Some just stare into nothing. The Danes stick to themselves and no one speaks to each other, even if they are seated right across from one another. It is easy for Branko to blend in here. He gets off at Brøndby Strand station, which when compared to the central station is little more than a slab of concrete and a set of stairs. It fits well with the surrounding apartment blocks. After the train leaves, the only sound is the wind howling. He has already been there two times before, walking around, trying to connect what he has been studying on the maps with what his eyes see. Spending the extra day is better than risking getting lost in the repetitive, concrete landscape that is Brøndby Strand.

Jacob Hansen lives a few minutes from the station, in a concrete building with around 13 stories and in various shades of grey depending on how the layers of grime and dirt have settled over the years. Still, it looks exactly like the building next to it, which in turn looks exactly like the one next to that. Everything is the same here, grey and dirty concrete. Even during the war, Pristina was a prettier than this, Branko thinks to himself.

To navigate the area, he has memorized a few landmarks. There are the larger ones, like the towers that seem to mark where a new block of buildings begins. Each tower has a different pastel color on its side, undoubtedly to make it possible for the people who live here, to find their way home. And then there are the smaller landmarks, like grafitti tagged on a wall. Signatures left by bored kids, testimonials to their lack of direction in life, perhaps, or a desperate cry for any kind of attention or respect. Maybe Branko is just reading too much into it.

Two keys are needed to gain access to Jacob Hansen's apartment. One to get into the entryway and another for the apartment itself. He has neither, so he waits for someone to enter or leave the building, slipping in with them. He did the same on his last visit to the area, just to see if it would work, and just as predicted, the person who let him in, did not even seem to notice. It is the same this time. A middle-eastern man comes out and Branko slips in, letting out a mumbled sound that could be mistaken for thanks, only to be completely ignored. That saved him the first key. The second lock is the real problem.

Brank is looking at the flimsy door, seperating him from his target. He could easily kick it down, but that would make too much noise and attract too much attention even in this neighborhood. Next option would be picking it, but he does not have the tools and even if he did, he would still have to practice somewhere else. Another option is to knock and wait, but there is a peephole in the door, and Branko has a feeling that Jacob Hansen might be the kind of person who check before opening the door to a stranger, and if that stranger just happened to be holding a hand over the peephole, the door would most likely remain shut. Lastly, he considers knocking and listening for noises on the other side. He could chance it and fire straight through the door, like in the movies, hoping to hit his target. But he knows this is a ridiculous idea. He would basically be shooting blindly with very little chance of actually hitting anything but the door itself. Besides, Branko wants more than simply to kill mr. Hansen.

So, he waits.

The hallway is all dark-brown tile and more dull grey concrete. But it is wide, and it is easy enough to find a dark corner to stand in. He decides to stay until someone either enters or leaves Jacob Hansen's apartment. No matter how long it might take. He recalls the nights he spent in freezing foxholes, where he as a soldier would wait and watch, knowing that falling asleep might mean death to himself and his comrades. In comparison waiting in the hallway is no challenge. Branko's mind goes into a state, where he is still but not bored, ready and awake but not restless, as he settles himself in the darkness of the concrete hallway, a hand inside his sweatshirt holding the grip of his Walther PPK, which has the silencer already attached, the safety off and a bullet in the chamber. It is just like the war, he says to himself, but inside his pocket, his other hand is shaking so bad, he fears his rattling bones will give him away.

Hours pass by and Branko's legs start to grow numb. He wants to sit down, but he knows he cannot. He needs to be able to move fast, when the time comes. Instead, he allows himself small exercises, that do not require much movement but still gets the blood flowing. He notices that he is sweating in spite of the unheated hallway being almost as cold as the February night outside. Darkness has fallen now, and a pale yellow light falls from metal lampposts on the concrete buildings outside. Very little spills into the hallway, but there are timed lights here, that people can turn on, when they enter. Branko decides to quickly unscrew the bulb in the lamp nearest to himself.

He is still holding the lightbulb in his hand, when he hears someone on the other side of Hansen's door. There is no time for him to step into the dark or even get the gun out of his pocket.

The man opening the door looks surprised for just a second, as he sees Branko just outside his door. He is in his late thirties, thin except for a potbelly, unshaven and unkempt. He is leaning on a crutch. Their eyes meet and it is as if the other man knows why Branko is there, as he throws himself backwards, slamming the door on his way. But he is not fast enough. Branko gets a foot in. It hurts, as the door slams into it, but he blocks out the pain and opens the door back up instead, just in time to catch a glimpse of the other man hobbling out of the hallway into an adjacent room.

This is Branko's only weakness. He does not know the layout of the apartment, or whether or not there is a weapon inside. Knowing which kind of work Jacob Hansen used to do, Branko assumes that the man has something to defend himself with. He closes the door behind him and pulls out the silenced Walther PPK. From the next room, it sounds like pieces of furniture are being moved and knocked over. Then a sudden silence.

"Jacob Hansen?" Branko shouts.

No one answers him. That, to Branko, is as good as a yes.

He could move the half-size mirror on the wall in hallway and use it to peek into the other room, but he would need both hands for that. Branko weighs the pros and cons befire, being as quiet as possible, peeling the mirror off the wall. He angles it to see around the the corner of the doorway and takes babysteps forward, inching the mirror forward. He catches a glimpse of a tipped over couch, pulls the mirror back and tries to decide on the best course of action. He knows that the longer he takes, the more time his opponent will have to come up with a plan of his own.

Hansen had probably gone for one of the windows, stumbling on his way to it, knocking the couch over in the process. He would be wedged between the wall and the couch now, most likely trying to figure out how to get up, open the window and escape through it, before Branko would have shot him. He had not moved already, Branko decided, because he was afraid. And he was afraid, because he was unarmed. This would not be as hard, as he had feared. Except for his sister's voice inside his head now. She was asking him to reconsider, telling him that it was still not too late to quit, go home and make a new life for himself. It sounds like she is begging him, trying to say that she is not worth it. And then there is that other voice too. The Ghost whispers.

"Yes," the Ghost repeats. "She is not worth it. She was not even worth the air, she was breathing. And that is why I took it from her."

"Forgive me, Jovana," he says out loud, as he steps through the doorway, holding the gun straight out towards the couch.

Chapter nineteen

Frank arrived early at the office, coming straight from Mary's apartment. He had not shaved or showered, and thankfully thought of the cheap deodorant, he kept in his bottom drawer for times, when a case would keep him at the office all night. As he put it on, it made him think that this was the first erased trace of last night's adventures. Still, his clothes were sticking to his body, almost as if he had slept in them, but now that he no longer felt self-conscious about the sweat from last night's adventure, he did not mind having his clothes remind him of it.

There had been few words spoken between them, after they had entered her apartment. The place was had so little furniture, that he at first had thought the apartment half-empty and maybe she was still in the process of moving in. Then he had realized, that this was how she liked it, to not own anything that did not serve a purpose, and she had kept everything black, white or bright red. Not a single stray magazine or day old coffee cup in sight. Had it not been for what was about to happen, he doubted now, that he would have been able to relax at all. In the background, some classical piano piece had been playing from unseen speakers, but it had done nothing for the place. Still, when they had gotten into her bedroom, where the music was still playing, and they had begun their silent and voracious lovemaking, the setting had somehow heightened the experience. Afterwards, he had wondered if she had done her interior decoration with this specific purpose. As they had laid there, both pretending to be asleep, he had started thinking that perhaps there were other reasons for her simplistic taste, but he was too tired to really care.

Frank found himself drifting between the fresh memory and the case. His body was still tired, he had never slept well in other people's beds, but his mind was too busy to let the body rest now. He wondered if Elouise had sent off the request to Interpol and wanted to call her. But he knew that she was probably already on her way to the office, so instead he got up and made a fresh pot of coffee.

One of the other teams had had a late night, apparently. They had left a mess of pizzaboxes and soda cans and there was a faint smell of stale cigarette smoke in the air. He passed some more time, cleaning up their mess. Maybe one of the others would bring doughnuts.

Joel was the first to arrive, looking like something the cat had dragged in, but not like he wanted to talk about it. Frank served him a cup of black coffee so strong that just the smell of it made his stomach tighten up. Joel sniffed it hard and long before sending Frank a thin smile. Next was the profiler Christina who was almost too fresh. He heard her chattering even before he saw her immense figure come through the door. The looks of her enormous body made him almost not want the doughnuts she was bringing. Joel shot her a look, like being that awake this early in day was crime for which he would most certainly arrrest her, as soon as he was awake enough to do so. In the middle of her good-mornings and what-a-wonder-days however, she did not appear to catch it, so eventually Joel gave in and reluctantly grabbed a jelly doughnut.

While Joel was focusing hard on drinking and eating and Christina was talking about traffic, Frank nodded and kept looking at the door, just waiting for Elouise to come in. Before she did, however, Christina Quick switched to talking about the case.

"I was thinking about the victim," she said.

"What about her?"

"I don't think her position is irrelevant. Her place in society, as a seemingly successful and independant woman. The fact that she's a shrink makes it even more obvious."

"What is obvious?" Frank found himself getting irritated with ms. Quick's way of talking like she expected everyone to follow every train of thought. Maybe it was just the tiredness. Maybe it was waiting for Elouise.

"That he is telling us something here. He is showing us that he is the strong one. That this successful and intelligent woman, who specialized in therapy for men, had no power over him."

"That would support the former patient theory," Frank noted. "And exclude anyone who really knew her."

"How do you figure?" Joel asked, looking like he had just woken up from a bad dream.

"Well, we know from Anna, that Caroline had issues of her own. She might have been successful on the surface, but beneath that, she had serious problems."

"Ah yes," said Christina, "I do not believe that the killer knew her that well. But well enough to have made up a fantasy about her. He might've been a patient at one time, but he could just have read about her somewhere. I think he probably stalked her for a while though."

Frank didn't say anything. Outside the office window it had started raining, and he could hear the sound of the raindrops on the glass. It was heavy rain, the kind that only comes in short, violent showers. For a split second everything turnned white, as lightning struck somewhere. Counting slowly, he got to three before the soft rolling sound of thunder mixed in with the rain. He wondered what was keeeping Elouise and then remembered, that he had completely forgotten to tell the others about the overseas theory.

"How good of you to suddenly remember that the guy was European," Joel said. He was on his fourth doughnut and second cup of coffee, and the sugar and caffeine seemed to be helping. "Way to omit important details, Fax."

"Sorry, Joel, I don't know how, I forgot," he said, but at the same time he felt a stab of guilt. He knew perfectly well, why he had forgotten to tell the others. His back ached, as he once again thought about the night he had spent on Dr. London's black sating sheets.

"Let's just hope that someone gets back to us on that."

As if on cue, Elouise walked in, shaking an umbrella and looking like she might use it to stab the first person to stand in her way. Bu at the sight of coffee and what was left of the doughnuts, she dropped her weapon, smiled and waved at her co-workers. Frank and Joel just watched her, as she gulped down a cup of now lukewarm coffee and winced at its bitterness, quickly adding a sprinkle covered doughtnut to the mix. In the meantime, Christina Quick had gone back to chit chatting, this time about the weather in Seattle and how she was originally from inland California, where it rained much less. Nobody listened.

"So?" Frank said, looking at Elouise.

"Oh," She answered. "Yeah. I faxed off a description of our crime last night. Would have hit Interpol in Europe early this morning for them."

"Any replies?"

She got up and walked to the far end of the office, where the fax machine was. Below it was a small basket, designed to catch incoming messages.

"Nope," she said. "Nothing."

"Give it some time," Joel said. "Probably takes a few days for it to filter through the bureaucracy over there. They've probably got more red tape than we do, when we deal with the feds. Them being different countries and all."

By saying that, Joel had pointed out what they all knew by now. There was a real risk that this case would drag on, the crime growing a little colder with each day, until they either had a major breakthrough or other, more recent cases eventually took over. Often it would take less than a week to find a killer, sometimes only hours, since most homicides are commited in the spur of the moment, with little to no planning and by someone close to the victim. Usually there would be obvious suspects, traces of blood, fingerprints and witnesses. This one was different, more sinister and everyone on the team knew that the killer would most likely strike again, before they would make any definitive progress. Unless they got saved by Interpol.

"You've been going through the former patients, right?" Christina Quick asked.

"Yeah," Elouise and Joel answered in unison. "Some of them," Elouise continued. "We've picked the most obvious ones, judging from your profile, but there really weren't any good matches. From what we know, she did not see any actually ill patients."

"Have you had access to her records?"

"Yes," Joel took over. "Although I don't know if we can actually use any of that stuff. I'd have to check that with the DA."

"What I am thinking is," Christina continued, "that the killer might have been to see her just once or twice, or even regularly. But he would not have appeared to have serious issues."

"So, you're saying we should check again?" Frank asked.

"I would like to take a look at the records," Christina said, "and see if anything sticks out to me."

"Sure," Frank said. "Will you look at it with her, Elouise?"

Elouise nodded and suddenly everyone was smiling. As long as the case was in motion, there was still hope.

Like every other detective who has worked homicide for a number of years, Frank had his number of cold case files locked away in a file cabinet. And like so many others like him, he would take one of them out every now and then, just to read through it again. It was rare that anything came of it, but if nothing else, it helped him to understand his own work, when he saw the summaries and analyzed the order in which things were done. Solving homicide was always a race against time, and the more of it that passed by, the smaller were the chances of finding the killer. And sometimes the badguys got away with it. Gangmembers covered for each other, neighbors were too afraid to talk, random robberies gone wrong left no witnesses. Sometimes the killer would fuck up later on, and they would be able to tie him to an older case. Frank did not want the case of Caroline Saunders to be one of this. This killer was meticulous and had obviously given some thought to both his victim and the method used. Just because they could not find evidence that he had killed before, did not change the fact that they all expected him to kill again. This was no sudden fit of rage. This was evil. No stone would be left unturned on this one, he swore quietly. Looking down, he realized he was clenching his fist so tightly, his fingernails were digging into the palm of his hand.

Chapter twenty

Branko was expecting his target to either pop up from behind the couch, holding some kind of heavy firearm, or that he would make a jump for the window, but Jacob Hansen has yet to show his face. There are no other doors than the one he just came through, no other exits of any kind. He keeps the Walther PPK aimed straight at the couch as he calls out in English.

"Come out, mr. Hansen. Hands first."

There is no reply and Branko starts sidestepping around the end of the couch. He feels adrenaline pumping through every part of his body, keeping him on edge. It feels like he could dodge bullets, if he had to. He recognizes the sensation and knows that he must keep his cool. He has seen comrades fall in the past, because they too thought themselves invincible. Inside his head, he keeps chanting Jovana's name to stay focused. Meanwhile he seems to be aware of every little gurgle from the heating system's waterpipes, every breath being taken, every heartbeat.

He catches a glimpse of metal behind the couch. For a moment he thinks it could be a rifle, but then he realizes it is the crutch laying on the floor. There is a man next to it, keeping completely still, staring straight up, eyes wide with fear and anticipation.

Branko is surprised at how light the man is, as he pulls him up against the nearby wall. He presses the muzzle of his gun up under the target's chin, and target stays completely still.

"Just do it," Hansen says. His voice is dry and raspy. "Get it over with."

"Sit down," Branko says. "I have a few questions for you."

The target spits in Branko's face, daring him to blow his brains out, and instinctively, he feels his finger tighten on the trigger. Hansen knows that a quick death may well be preferable to answering questions. Not yet, Branko thinks to himself. For Jovana. He must have his answers first.

"Sit down, mr. Hansen," he says again. His voice is so cold, he does not even recognize it as his own.

As Branko takes a couple of steps back, leveling the gun at Hansen's forehead, the man slowly flips the cheap couch back upright and sits down in it. He has his legs up and his arms crossed, trying to appear completely calm, but Branko smells the fear on him. He will not be hard to break.

"What do you want?" Hansen asks. "If you were here to kill me, you would have done it already."

"I am looking for someone," Branko says. "And you can help me find him."

"Fuck you."

"The man is a rapist and a murderer."

He reaches inside his jacket and pulls out the photos of Jovana. He tosses the envelope to the man on the couch.

"I am told, the man I am looking for was once a friend of yours. Someone you trained as a Spectre. Maybe his work looks familiar to you?"

Hansen's eyes have become slits, as he stares at Branko, as if trying to decide whether to take him seriously. Then the skin around his eyes slowly relaxes and he reaches for the envelope. Branko keeps his eyes on the target's face, as he looks through the photos, but there is no emotion to be read at all.

The man looks long and hard at every picture, before putting them back into the envelope.

"I have no idea," he says and tossses the package towards Branko.

"In my file about you," Branko says, "it says that you were wounded in combat. Almost killed you. Right leg, right?"

The target does not reply. He looks straight into Branko's eyes, his own once again narrowing, trying to read the situation. His are light blue, almost grey. Like the rest of him, emotionless. Branko lifts up the Walther PPK and points it between his target's legs.

"I bet you can still fuck," he says. "The blast didn't take your cock off, did it?"

The silence is so heavy, you can almost hear the dust particles floating in the air. Branko moves his hand a little to the side and pulls the trigger. There is a short whistling sound and a crack, as the bullet fractures the kneecap of the man on the couch. Jacob Hansen crumples up in pain and starts to scream.

This is not good. The screams might attract unwanted attention. Quickly, he moves up close to the couch. Once more, he presses his gun against Hansen's forehead, now covered in the kind of bittersmelling sweat that comes from raw fear.

"Shut the fuck up," he says through his teeth, trying not to yell. "Next time, I will aim a little higher. Now shut up and start talking."

The screams subside and turn into sobbing noises. Hansen has more self control, that Branko had expected. Not that it will save him in the end. He leaves the man and goes to the kitchen. In the freezer, he finds a bag of frozen peas, which he wraps in a stained dishtowel and tosses to his target on the couch. Jacob Hansen presses the towel against his shattered knee, his knuckles and face the same white color, and the action seems to calm him a little.

"Let's try again. What can you tell me about the pictures?"

"Emil," he says, stuttering and choking on the two syllable word. "Emil Ravn Jensen."

"Who is that?"

"That's his name. I used to know him. A friend. Got in trouble here in Denmark, so I took him in and brought him down to Bosnia."

"He did this?"

"Looks like his work," Jacob Hansen says and then seems to get a new shock of pain. He clenches his teeth and is breathing hard through his nose.

"Where can I find him?"

"I- I don't know."

Again Branko raises his gun, pointing it straight at Jacob Hansen's face. He holds his other hand up to his ear, as if to indicate that he did not hear what his target just said.

"Honestly," the man gasps, "when I got wounded, he stayed behind. He couldn't return to Denmark. The police was looking for him."

"Go on," Branko says, his voice once again cold and the gun still pointed between the eyes of his target.

"He had raped some girls. They wanted him for it."

"When was the last time you heard from him?"

"He sent me a postcard a few years ago."

"Where is it?"

"In there," Hansen says and nods. Branko notices that he has difficulty raising his head after nodding in the direction of a set of drawers. He knows there is a chance the man will pass out from bloodloss and the pain in his knee. Lowering his gun, he walks to the bureau and opens the top drawer, which seems to hold a collection of things, from a bag of marijuana to a Browning 9mm automatic with extra clips and ammo. But no postcard.

"Which drawer?"

"Top," his voice is thick. "In the back somewhere."

Branko pulls out the drawer a little further, until it almost falls out of the bureau, and then he sees it. A postcard with a picture of a sunny beach on the front. As he picks it up, he is at first disappointed that it is written in a language he does not understand, but seeing that it is signed 'Emil' is good enough. The postcard was written by his sister's killer. A rush flows through his body now, as he sees the man's handwriting. One step closer, finally. A direct link to the Ghost.

"Read it," he says, holding it out in front of the bleeding man on the couch.

"I can't focus," he replies, "but I remember what it says. Some bullshit about him having found his calling. That he is travelling a lot and is happy. I think it says, that he is going to France."

Branko looks at the card again. The stamp is Spanish but he cannot make out the date.

"When did you get this?"

"Years ago," he says. "'96, I think."

"And this is the last you heard from him?"

"For Christ's sake!" The target screams, holding out his unused hand palm up. "What the fuck do I have to lose? Emil was a friend of mine, but that was years ago, okay? Can I call an ambulance now? I'm fucking dying here!"

"I know," Branko says, points his Walther PPK at the target's forehead one last time and pulls the trigger. The soft sound of the silenced pistol is followed by a wet crack, as Jacob Hansen's skull tears open, spraying the couch with its contents.

Chapter twentyone

The day dragged on slowly, in spite of Frank's determination. Impatience, he thought, was brought on by the scent of a killer, and now it seemed that time had slowed down as if to test his ability to avoid juming to any conclusions, while he waited for the case to progress naturally. He joined in with Christina and Elouise in going through Carolyn's list of patients, trying to figure out how they could use the list to their advantage, without actually breaking any laws in the process. It was a frustrating task, even if there was no immediate suspects on the list. In the meantime, he had sent Joel out to talk to Darryl the clerk and the neighbor again, this time leaning a little harder on the latter of the two.

The hope was that Darryl would be able to remember something that might fit into the newest additions to the profile of the killer. And as for the neighbor, they simply hoped he had been too scared to say anything at first, and that a little pressure from a man with Joel's skills of persuasion might help jog his memory. Christina's latest theory was, that the killer might be another psychiatrist or somehow connected to that profession. He might have met her at a convention or lecture, she suggested, or even gone to school with her. Though things were moving slow now, they were still in motion. All focus was on any foreigner showing up in Caroline Saunders's life, especially within the last six to twelve months.

Frank called up Caroline's friend Anna, asking her to put together a list of any foreigners, she ever heard Caroline talk about, whether it be a patient, a lover or something different. He remembered her behavior during the interview and decided she was as qualified to help as any of them, as he filled her in on their theory. Frank hoped that she would remember someone who fit the picture right off the bat, but even when that was not the case, he was still happy to have talk to her. Just the fact that he was letting her know, they were making progress and getting closer to identifying the killer, helped him realize it too. Closure was out there, and they would find it. She thanked him with a voice that sounded as tired as he felt. She probably had not slept well since her friend had been murdered. Who could blame her.

After a couple of hours or pouring through records and journals, they had come up with nothing new to go on. Joel called in and said, that Darryl had no recollection of anyone ever visiting the clinic, who spoke with an accent. With the exception of the hispanic cleaning lady. For good measure, Joel had gotten a hold of her too and cleared her.

At around three in the afternoon, the lack of any real progress was catching up to Frank. His sticky clothes no longer reminded him of the night's adventures, but simply clung to his skin, making him sweat even more than before. He was irritable and snapped at his team-mates, catching himself doing it and in turn getting even more angry. Even the coffee he had been drinking was starting to upset his otherwise hardened stomach. He was sitting at his desk alone, pinching the bridge of his nose with his eyes closed, when the phone on his desk started ringing. After three rings, he picked it up with his free hand.

"Cash, homicide," he said into the reciever, his eyes still closed.

"It's Anna," a familiar voice said, "I have been thinking about that list, you asked me to put together."

"And?" he asked.

"I've got a couple of people. Some are pretty far fetched, but I figured..."

"Nothing is too far fetched, Anna," he said, cutting her off in the process. He caught himself doing it and hoped she did not take it the wrong way, as he opened his eyes and straightened himself in his chair. This was not the time to lose focus. "Look, I didn't mean to cut you off there. We're very interested in anything, you can come up with. It's been a long day here."

"All I have is three people," she said. "One is her mechanic. I'm not sure where he is from, but I heard Carol talk about him from time to time. I think the place is called 'Wally's Wheels' or something."

"Thanks, I can find that," he said.

"The second guy has a restaurant not far from her office. A greek place. Can't remember his name, but we used to eat there now and again, and he would always come over to greet us."

"Greek, you say? If it's near her office, it shouldn't be too hard to find either."

"Okay," she said. "This last one goes back a few years. Some guy she met at a convention here in Seattle. He was a representative from some pharmaceutical company. I remember him, because she told me how he had been trying to pick her up all during the convention, and how she was playing along, only to let him down on the last night."

"Do you remember what happened?"

"Yeah," she said. "He got pretty upset. Almost turned into a fistfight between him and the guy Carol ended up going home with."

"Got a name?"

"I've been trying to remember, but the only thing, I can come up with is the name of the company he worked for. I think that was 'Mind Ease Inc' or something corny like that."

"Do you remember when this was and the name of the convention?"

"It was here in Seattle, back in 2000. But I don't know the name of the convention."

"Okay," Frank said, still catching up on the note taking. "Thank you very much, Anna. You've been a great help so far."

"Anything for Caroline."

"I'll be sure to let you know, if any of these pan out. In the meantime, I have another favor to ask. I'd like you not to pass any of this on to any one. We don't want to advertise to the public, that we're doing. Okay?"

"You didn't have to ask that of me, detective."

"I'm sorry," Frank said, tapping a pen on his desk. "I know."

They wrapped up the conversation, and Frank sat there for a bit, thinking about what Anna had just told him, not even noticing that he started tapping the beat of "I Will Survive" with his pen, humming low along with it. It took a while before he noticed lieutenant Redding looking at him from across the room, one eyebrow raised.

"I'll take that as a good sign," Big Red said and sent him a smile.

Late in the afternoon, the final follow-up report came over from forensics. Elouise and Frank both poured over it, looking at both the autopsy report and the findings from the search at the office. But as expected, there was nothing new and exciting in there.

Another hour was spent going through the a good handful of messages taken over the phone during the day. They had come from callers, who had heard about the case on the news. Most of them were ridiculous and some even had the two detectives laughing. Two were from patients of Caroline's, who both thought Darryl was a good candidate for the role as the killer. In a matter of minutes, Elouise had done some background checks and called them back, only to end up discarding both as either reliable witnesses or possible suspects.

Before calling it a day, the three detectives met up in the office to gather what they had to update the summary report. Joel had gone to lean on the neighbor and had come away with absolutely nothing to show for it. He was cursing and talking about wasting his time, until Frank reminded him about covering all the bases and filling in the blanks. Even if it meant another dead end. Joel knew as well as any, that murder investigations often ended up being a process of elimination, and after chewing on Frank's words for a while, he seemed to shrug off whatever irritation he had brought into the office with him and lit a cigarette, knowing full well that smoking was not allowed inside the building. The other two seemed to think it was best not to remind him of that.

Finally, Frank brought up the new information he had gotten from Anna. He figured it would be the best find of the day, and he had purposely saved it for last, to end the meeting on a positive note. And his suspicions had been right. Both Elouise and Joel clapped their hands and nodded to one another, and Frank saw the same reaction in their faces, he had felt when hanging up the call. A new hope, a new lead. What a job this was, this constant fight for even the slightest hope of a new direction to go in. He loved it.

Frank jumped straight into the shower, when he got home. The water finally cleaned last night off of him along with a long day of phonecalls and paperwork. He was slightly disappointed that they had not heard anything from Europe, even if he knew it was asking a lot. Still, the more he thought about it, the more certain he was that something would eventually show up. He could hope, that whatever they got, would get them closer to getting their guy.

Dried off and clean shaven but still naked, Frank poured himself a glass of wine from the same bottle, he had been drinking from before he had left for his date with Mary. The skin on his body was still pink and slightly tender from the steaming hot water, the way he liked it sometimes. The almost burning water was like meditation to him, washing away all unwanted thoughts and renewing both body and soul, and afterwards he was full of renewed energy. He took a long sip and tried to push the case out of his mind for just a moment. It felt good to be home at a decent hour for once, being able to relax and just enjoy the memory of Mary's smile and the softness of the skin on her back. He wondered if it would come to more with her and whether he should give a call. The unwritten rules of the whole dating game had always been a mystery to Frank, and just trying to decide on something as simple as making a phonecall made him uneasy. Eventually, he decided against it. It wasn't that he was putting it off to play some kind of game. It was more that he just did not want to talk to anyone. Instead, he enjoyed the mindless entertainment unfolding on the television screen in front of him and secretly praised the inventors of sit coms.

The soft knocking on his door, could not have come at a worse time. He knew who it was, and he was in no mood to be neighborly. Still, he also did not feel like offending anyone. Especially not Rosa Perez, who was probably the best neighbor he could ever wish for. So, he put on his robe and opened the door. Get it over with and go back to the re-runs of The King of Queens.

When she saw him, she immediately blushed.

"So sorry," she said. "I did not mean to disturb you."

"That's okay," he lied. "What's up?"

"I tried to bring you dinner last night, but you were not in."

"That's right," he said, not really wanting to share the details of his personal life with her, simply because she made a mean burrito.

"So, I thought, I would do it today instead," she sent him a cunning smile, but then suddenly held a finger to her lips, looking past Frank into his hallway. "You don't have company, do you?"

"No no," Frank smiled. "it's just me."

"Okay," she said and handed him the plate of food.

"This really is too much," he said, trying to appear half-hearted in accepting the plate. "I am capable of cooking my own food, you know."

"You can cook?" she asked him with a raised eyebrow.

"Sure."

"You can invite us for dinner some night then." She smiled as she said it and with that mrs. Perez turned her back on Frank and disappeared into her own unit across the hall.

He went back to his tv and ate his food, while he considered whether or not Rosa Perez was making a move on him, and how he could avoid it turning into a problem if that was the case. The last thing he needed was the next door neighbor stalking him. Or maybe he was just getting paranoid with age, he thought, unable to suppress a small grin. Who was he to think so highly of himself anyway? That both Dr. London and Mrs. Perez would have the hots for him suddenly seemed laughable. Still, it was better to be safe than to be sorry. He decided not to accept any more free dinners for a while.

Chapter twentytwo

BARCELONA, MARCH 2004 – There is a fly bouncing against the window in Branko's motel room, but he does not get up to open it. The air feels thick and sweat seems to seep from his skin, even though he does nothing but sit. The only movement comes from the ceiling fan's slow rotation and grainy images flickering across the bolted down tv-set. The news are in Spanish of course, but the images speak for themselves. Once again, conflict has broken out in his home region, after three Albanian boys were found dead in the river. The people are blaming the Serbs. There are riots in the streets and Serbs are being driven from their homes. Just like they had driven the Albanians out ten years earlier. There will be no returning to Pristina for Branko now.

He never really felt involved in the conflict. As a child, he had had friends that later were supposed to be his enemies, just because they were not Serbs. It had all seemed pointless to him. His parents were the same way. Even as the Albanians were being driven out of Kosovo in the early ninetees, their coffee shop was still open for all, no matter who or what you were. In the beginning, they had been convinced that it would pass soon, always believing in the best in people. The truth was, that evil had been allowed to grow in a lot of people then, until there had been nothing good left in them. And those who felt like Branko and his family, ended up having to pretend otherwise. Many of his old friends turned their backs on Branko, and finally his family had to only allow Serbs in as customers at the café, out of fear for what would happen otherwise. He remembers his father talking about it at night, after he had closed up shop. Had humanity not learned anything from the second world war, he asked no one, shaking his head.

Branko remembers being confused and hurt by what was happening. People he thought cared about him, were no longer talking to him at all. And he questioned his own father's judgement. Surely there were reasons, why the hate had been allowed to grow. His father had been a kind man, but also, Branko had thought, naive. He had joined the army, to learn for himself. Looking back now, it seemed like such a stupid thing to do. He had learned alright. About the atrocities which every human being are capable of performing. It was easy now, in hindsight, to see that he had been wrong, and that he should have listened to the old man. But it was too late now. His family was all but wiped out, himself a mere shadow of himself. He no longer remembers what he had wanted to to with his life, before he had joined the army. Had it just been to walk in his father's footsteps and take over the café, or had there been more.

Everything was clouded by the memories of war. The endless nights of not knowing whether you would be alive to see the morning light. The sound of mortar fire, always seeming to get closer. Grown men crying, others losing their mind completely, becoming nothing but monsters and ghosts.

For years, Branko has been able to live with these experiences, but lately the faces of the many victims are starting to come back to him in his dreams. First among them is still the bank manager, and now Jacob Hansen. Perhaps, he thinks, these two have brought the others back with them. He prays to God every night, hoping that He will find it in his heart to bring peace to Branko's mind. Without warning the tears start rolling down his cheeks, while the tv in his room is still displaying pictures of riots in his hometown.

There is a church in Barcelona, where Branko goes every day now. He knows, he must find peace of mind, before he can continue on his mission. He likes to sit there and and just take in the peace of being on the Lord's house and finds comfort in knowing, that though he has lost everything, he has not lost his faith. Though he knows some of the things he has done were wrong, being here, praying and listening to the choir as it sings in His honor, Branko cannot help but feel, that God has not left him either. He has donated a third of what he was given for his business in Denmark to the church here, and he takes comfort in knowing, that some of that money earned by blood, can still be channeled into something good.

If he could, he would get the priest to assist him in confessing his sins, but the priest does not speak enough English or German, and could not offer guidance. So, Branko is relying on prayer and the guidance of God himself until he has learned enough Spanish to try again. He does not believe that God speaks directly to him, but he feels His will nonetheless. It is time to spend some time doing penance for his sins. It is time for prayer and devotion. Branko wipes the tears off his face, turns off the television and picks up the Gideon's Bible, he found in his nightstand drawer. That too, is in Spanish, but he still flicks through the pages, trying to read the words. The labor itself is in His name and it calms him.

In the meantime, the photos of his murdered sister and the postcard from her killer are hidden away in the same drawer, where he found the bible. He has not forgotten about her or his quest, but he feels that he must wait now. When the time is right, he will take it out again and start looking for clues. For now, he is happy to be in Spain and to see the spring come. Branko puts down his Bible and goes to open his window, watching the fly finally finding its freedom, he wonders if it is capable of feeling relief. And standing there, looking out over the sunny rooftops, he realizes that it a moment of relief is exactly what he needs too.

Chapter twentythree

When Frank picked up the fax, he could hardly believe his eyes. The fax had come from the Spanish police, who had not one, but two matches to the case in Seattle.

In both cases, the women had been bound on hands and feet. Both had also been raped and left with a sheet over them, holes for the eyes and everything. It was a perfect match, but in Spain, the killer had not been as careful and both seamon and fingerprints had been obtained from the scene in the first of the cases. Neither DNA or fingerprint matches had been made to anyone known by the Spanish police and no one had ever been arrested. Both murders were from 1995 and were commited within Spain but in different parts of the country. The first killing had been in Tarragona and the second in Madrid, the papers said, but Frank had no idea where those cities where. It took him nearly twenty minutes to locate an atlas with a decent map of Spain, and by the time he was running his finger over the map, his heart was beating so hard, he thought it might break down on him. Tarragona was a coastal town, bordering the Mediterranean Sea wheres Madrid was further into the country, nearly three hundred miles away.

The rest of the team were called in. Frank said nothing, as he waited for all of them to get in and get seated. It felt like they were taking forever. Elouise's eyes drifted to the pen in Frank's hand, tapping non-stop on the desk, but she did not say anything. Lieutenant Redding was the last to arrive, looking slightly disappointed when he realized there were no chairs left. Only when everyone had settled down, did Frank start. He held the papers in front of him, as if they were a map to the holy grail, as he briefed everyone on their contents.

"This is a major breakthrough," Frank finished. "We may not know the exact identity of the killer yet, but we know about his past now, and with a little luck, we may be able to get copies of the fingerprints or the DNA, obtained in Spain."

"I'll get on the horn to Spain," Redding said. "See what I can do."

"The bad news," Frank continued after nodding his acknowledgement to the lieutenant, "is that we also know for sure that this is a serial killer, and that he will probably strike again. I hope we can get something out of this, that will help us catch this guy before that happens."

"Isn't this atypical behavior for a serial killer?" Elouise said. "Most of them operate within a fairly small area. Spain is hardly in the neighborhood."

"Also," Frank said, tapping the pen again, "these two murders happened ten years ago. From what we know, serial killers don't go that long between killing."

"Not true," Christina Quick said. " It all depends on a number of stimuli in the killer's personal life. If this is the same guy, he could have moved here and started a new life. For a while, that might have provided him with all the excitement he needed to control his impulses."

"Do we have any Spaniards on our list?" Joel asked Elouise.

"I have Antonio Banderas on my personal list, but I take it that's not what you're asking?"

"Very funny," Joel replied.

"No, to my knowledge we have no Spaniards on any of our lists," she said, putting humor aside. "Also, wasn't he supposed to have had a German accent? I'm no expert on European languages, but from what I know, the two don't sound anything alike."

"So where does that leave us?" Joel asked, now looking at Frank.

"We continue doing what we've been doing. And we go back and doublecheck everything in the light of this new information."

Based on what Anna had provided them with, the team set out to find the three foreigners she had described. 'Wally's Wheels' was easy enough to locate, and they would be going through Caroline's stuff, hoping to find anything with the name of the mechanic that had been working on her car, before actually approaching the shop itself.

Next on the list was the Greek Restaurant. Looking at a local guide, they found that the only one in the area was the 'House of Athens' only two blocks from her office. The place was owned and operated by a married couple, who said they would be happy to meet with the police, when Frank had called to enquire.

Finally, there was the mystery pharmaceutical representative. They were unable to find anything on a company called 'Mind Ease Inc.' And therefore could not find their guy either. Again, they would rely on going through any notes left behind by Caroline, as their first step towards finding the man.

Elouise had already left for Caroline's office, to look for anything they had left behind the first time. Joel and Frank drove with her and walked to the 'House of Athens'. The owners were already there. Both were in their mid to late thirties. The husband introced them as Rick and Helena, they both smiled and the husband had a hand on his wife's shoulder. At a glance, they appeared to be a perfectly happy couple. But Frank knew that looks could be decieving and tried to focus on the husband without the wife. Like on cue, Joel asked the wife if she would join him in the next room.

Rick gave Frank a firm handshake and introduced himself with a broad smile. He was built well, like someone who used to work out a lot, when he was younger, but who had probably been too busy with both his business and his family, to keep up with it, and now parts of him had started to sag. He had big hands, Frank noticed, like someone who was not afraid of hard physical work, his dark brown and curly hair and unshaved chin fit well with the stereotypical Greek image. Only a pair of shiny, green eyes set him apart from the stereotype.

Small talking about Greece and food, Frank first listened for an accent. There was a hint of one, but it was too vague for him to place. Rick told Frank, that he was half Greek and half American, and that was his excuse for the faint accent and the green eyes. Frank wondered if perhaps the German accent had been a deliberate red herring.

"It works wonders at the tables," he said and overdid it on purpose.

"Did you know Caroline Saunders?" Frank asked, changing the subject. It often worked well to use surprise changes to the conversation like this.

"Not well," he said. "She came in here maybe once a month. Sometimes with company, sometimes with a girlfriend."

"When you say company-"

"I mean men," Rick said and smiled. "We take pride in our romantic atmosphere, detective."

Frank looked hard and long at the potbellied restaurantowner, but saw nothing but genuine pride in his eyes. The place did have a romantic atmosphere, he thought, looking around at the whitewashed walls, decorated with dusty old port bottles, rope, fishnets and other Mediterranean nicknacks. This was the second time today, he had come across the Mediterranean. Could this be more than a coincidence?

"Is there anything else, you can tell us about her or any of her dates? Anything out of the ordinary?"

Rick seemed to think about this for a minute, before scratching his head and replying.

"It was my impression that she intimidated men," he said. "I notice such things, you see. Who controls the conversations and stuff. It helps, of course, that she almost never brought the same guy in twice."

"That's a good observation," Frank agreed.

"She always seemed happy though," Rick added. "and very intelligent. I could tell from her face, that she had decided which way her dates were going to go in the time it would take me to take take an order for some wine, pour two glasses and return to the table."

"Did you always serve her personally?"

"Heavens no," Rick laughed. He had a loud, almost theatrical laugh, probably honed through years of casual smalltalk. "We are too busy for that kind of service. But I do try to be the good host and welcome most of our regulars."

"Do you have anything else to add?"

"I'm going to miss her, detective Cash. She was a good customer and a friend of the house."

Frank nodded an turned to walk through the door, to the front room where Joel and Helena were waiting. Halfway out, he had an idea and turned back towards Rick.

"We have a suspicion that Caroline's killer could have been a regular here," he tried to be as matter of factly as possible, never taking his eyes off Rick's face. What he had thought of was a quick and dirty test, to see what kind of man Rick was. Or whether he was to be considered a suspect or not. "If we're right," he continued, "there is a good chance he might come back to this place."

"Like I said," Rick said, scratching his curly hair. "I haven't noticed anything, but if there is anything I can do to help..."

"That's very nice of you," Frank said. "If we decide to follow up on this, we might want to put someone here to do surveillance. It would be an officer posing as a customer. Would that be alright?"

This was the test. Rick thought about his answer for a while, tilting his head slightly as if waiting for some sudden inspiration.

"Sure, I guess," he finally said, shrugging. "If you think it might help."

"You never know."

On their way back to Caroline's office, Frank and Joel discussed what they had learned, agreeing that her bringing the men to the same restaurants made her a creature of habit. And thus an easy target for anyone wishing to stalk her. As for the restaurant owner himself, Joel had studied the man's bodylanguage through the doorway, from the other room , where he had interviewed the wife, but he had not picked up anything unusual. Helena had said more or less the same things as her husband. Caroline was a regular, visiting about once a month, often in the company of gentlemen. She was always polite and friendly to the staff. Helena doubled as hostess and would sometimes welcome and smalltalk with her, just like Rick. Frank told Joel about the test, he had given the restaurant owner. If Rick had something to hide, he would probably react nervously to the idea of having a cop sitting right there in his restaurant, but there had been no nervousness or hints of a guilty conscience.

Elouise was waiting for the two others, as they came back to Caroline's office. She had already gone through everything there was and found nothing. Next stop would be Caroline's apartment, where they would all go together.

The place had a haunted feel to it, as if part of Caroline Saunders was still around. Somewhere in the background, Frank could still smell death in the air, even if it had been dilluted with time and disinfectant. The place had already been turned over to Caroline's parents, but apparently they had not yet set foot in the apartment.

"Has she been put in the ground yet?" Frank asked.

"Tomorrow," Joel answered. "I was planning on attending."

"We will all go," Frank said, "but not together. I want the ceremony covered. Our guy might show up for a peek."

"Good idea," Elouise said. "I'll gladly hang back in a car somewhere. Funerals are not my thing."

"A homicide detective who's afraid of funerals?" Joel looked at her.

"None of your fucking business," she said to him and left for a bookcase, where she started taking books down and leafing through them one at a time.

"Let it go, man," Frank put his hand on Joel's shoulder. "Just get to work."

About an hour later, they had found what they came for: A reciept from Wally's Wheels and a folder with notes from the convention. The receit did not have a name on it, but an employee number. That was just as good. The notes from the convention would take some closer study before they knew, whether they would produce anything, but it was still a good catch. As they returned to the office, the two locations were split. Elouise would go with Frank and see if they could find the man from the convention. Joel would handle the mechanic.

Chapter twentyfour

BARCELONA, MAY 2005 – A little over a year in Spain has taught Branko enough Spanish to get by. He has been helping out at the church, getting to know some of the locals and even moved out of the motel room and into a room with one of the local families. Their family is much like his own used to be. Two children, a boy and a girl, and the boy is just around the same age Branko was, when he took off to join the army. He almost never thinks about that these days. They treat him more as one of their own, than as a tenant, he pays no rent but helps out at the family bakery instead. For the first time in ten years, Branko is happy. The nightmares have subsided and only the envelope containing his sister's police report, the postcard from her killer and the pictures from where she died reminds him of his quest. He always carries them with him, to keep her close by, and to make sure he never forgets his most important purpose in life.

Branko the baker, he smiles at the thought of this newly acquired title. Working with the dough, learning the family recipes, breathing the smells of the baking bread and seeing the happy faces of those who buy it has made him happy. Life has been hard, he thinks to himself, but without self pity. The horrors of the war, the fate of his family members and his own fall after that, Branko is convinced there is a purpose for all of it. Amsterdam would have killed him, had it not been for the German. A man he had been willing to kill earlier. Instead, he ended up killing someone else for the German, which in turn brought him to this wonderful country, where people are so welcoming and there is peace. God truly does work in mysterious ways.

It is Jovana's birthday today. She would have turned thirty and the whole family and all their friends would come for a party she would never forget. She might have been married now too. Maybe even have had a couple of children of her own. Branko looks out over the calm, clear blue water, and realizes that he has found was he needed to find in Barcelona. Today, he knows, the time has come to move on. He must dive into the past once more, and find one Ghost to give rest to another.

He tells his new family about his sister, that she was murdered and that today would have been her birthday. They are good people, and together they pray for her soul. And then he excuses himself, saying that he needs time alone, to honor her memory. "Go with God," they say, and he knows that God is never far away.

The public library is where he chooses to go. He has gone there before, to pick up books on Spanish and children's books to help him learn to read. He likes it there, almost as much as the bakery and the church. Every place serves its purpose. In the bakery he works hard using his hands. With all the evil he has seen and done, it is good to use the hands for good work, for feeding people. The church was the first place he found peace here, and he still goes every week. As soon as his Spanish was good enough, he confided in the the priest there. Being able to confess his sins helped to serve as a strong motivation for learning the language, and when he was finally able to ask the Lord's forgiveness, tears of joy streamed down his face.

Since that day, father Alvarez and Branko have had many long conversations about God, war and honor. Though the priest has never been in combat himself, Branko has great respect for his more theological approach to the subject. Alvarez says that God never starts wars, but that he will help the willing to steer through them, to survive. And he says that the will to stay on

God's path is the most important part of worship. Everyone sins, he says, but those who learn from their sins will still find forgiveness. Branko has wanted to tell father Alzarez about his quest many times, but for some reason he cannot. Still, the more they talk, the more Branko feels that God has put him here for a purpose, and that He condones finding Jovana's killer. Perhaps the father already suspects, that Branko is on a quest, but Branko knows that he would never ask about it.

At the library, Branko is just himself. It is here, that he can escape into a closed world of words and knowledge. He never talks to people there, except to ask where to find certain books. The more he goes there, the more he realizes his love for studying life and world he lives in. For nearly three months, he studied the Spanish civil war, trying to learn about the nature of war. Alvarez got him curious about what drives men to kill each other in the name of an idea, but the more he reads, the less he seems to understand. And what was the idea he was fighting for? Certainly not freedom for his people. Or hate for the enemy. Eventually, he found that studying war brought back the nightmares and the Ghost, and he started reading about baking instead.

Today, he asks the librarian to help him find newspaper articles. He does not wish to divulge the exact story he is looking for, so he says, he wants to study the more recent local history, starting from 1996. And the librarian smiles and asks him to wait, while she disappears into the archives, only to return fifteen minutes later, pushing a small table on wheels. On it is twelve leatherbound volumes, one for every month of the year in 1996, each volume holds all the issues of the major Spanish newspaper, El Pais, published that month. Branko begins from January first, thumbing through the pages as he looks for anything familiar.

It does not take long, before he finds what he is looking for. A follow-up article on two murders that happened the year before, catches Branko's interest. A woman was killed in Tarragona and a month later, another one in Madrid. The article contains very little information about the actual murders, except the police believe the two are related, and the journalist who wrote the article calls them the Ghost Murders.

Politely, Branko explains that he would like to go back another year, and the librarian rolls the newspapers away, only to return once more, with a new stack of leather tomes. She makes a comment about the weight of the books and Branko apologizes for putting the fragile woman to work like this. Again, she smiles. Branko suspects that she likes him, and though he is flattered by the thought, there is no room in his heart for another woman. Jovana still takes up all the space there is. Flashes of the black whore, he nearly killed in Amsterdam play themselves out and he feels a chill run down his spine.

Using dates given in the first article, it only takes Branko a few minutes to find the articles he is looking for. Soon, he understands why the murders are called the Ghost Murders. It is as he suspected, that each of the women were covered by a white sheet, where holes had been cut for the eyes. As he reads on, he sees that the women were also raped and suddenly the connection becomes so clear, it is almost unbearable. To think that was that easy to find traces of the Ghost here makes the guilt well up in him. Guilt that he waited this long to check.

Branko's hands are shaking uncontrollably and his eyes are watering. It seems almost impossible, that he should confirm the identity of his sister's killer here, in a library in Spain and after having travelled all over Europe. He is so far from home, more than ten years have passed since Jovana's murder, and on the very day she would have turned thirty years old, there is a break in the chase. He gets up and staggers outside. He does not hear the librarian call to him, asking if he is okay. If he did, he would not have known what to answer.

His only thought is to go to the church and talk to father Alvarez. If ever he needed guidance, it is now. On his way, he stops to look out over the Mediterranean Ocean reflecting the afternoon sun that will soon go down over the rooftops on the other side of town. Barcelona is a great metropolitan city, but still its beauty is not spoiled by modern lifestyle and today, it feels like every inch of it is screaming to Branko. He feels God everywhere, and He is telling him to let go of the fear, that he has done well. Jovana must be watching over him today, he thinks, by God's side.

From father Alvarez's surprised look, it is clear that he can see that Branko is upset. He comes over right away and puts a hand on his shoulder. Branko has not felt a more soothing touch in years. Let go of the fear.

"I must talk with you," he says. "It is about my sister."

"I understand," the priest says and smiles. "I know today would have been her birthday. If you need to talk, I will gladly lend an ear."

"No father," Branko says. "I know who killed her. I know." And as he says it, he hands the envelope to the priest.

They are sitting in father Alvarez's office. The priest is whitefaced and massaging his soft hands vigorously. On the desk in front of him, the pictures speak their own language. Branko takes them away and puts them back in their envelope. He watches as the priest is searching for words.

"This is complicated," the priest finally says. "From my point of view, you understand that I cannot condone revenge. God will punish the man who did this." He points at the photographs without looking or actually touching them.

"Take another look at those pictures, father. If this was your sister, would you be able to let it be up to God? Or would you take matters into your own hands?"

"I trust God, my son," Alvarez says, still not looking at the prints before him. "But I am also human, and I see why something this horrible would make anyone seek the man responsible."

There is an awkward silence in the room. For all the conversations the two men have had over the past months, this is the first time there has been any awkwardness between them. Branko sees the priest's dilemma, and he appreciates it. As he interprets his words, the priest is really saying, that he sympathizes with Branko's quest, although he is not allowed to say it outright.

"I need guidance, father," he says.

"For this matter," Alvarez replies, looking suddenly stern, "I do not think spiritual guidance is what you need. And I do not believe, that I am the best man for the the job either. But I do know who might be."

"Who?"

"His name is Alejandro Herrera, and he is a regular in the church. I am sure the two of you have met, even if you have never talked. I will be happy to make the introductions."

"And how can he help me?"

"He is a lieutenant with the police," the priest says. "A good man."

Branko thinks about this before answering. After all, he is a fugitive, a killer, a robber and travelling with false papers. But eventually after a couple of minutes of silence, he decides to trust the priest, and gratefully accepts the kind offer.

That same evening, he visits with the Herrera family. Alejandro is a big, barrel-shaped man in his early fifties. They have passed each other many times in the church, like the father said, but never spoken. Branko has come after dinner, bringing a bottle of wine. The two men sit, each nuturing a glass on the porch behind Herrera's house, while his wife is putting the children to bed. Like most other people Branko has met, the Herrera family has immediately let him in and treated him like a most welcome guest. The introduction by Alvarez was all that was needed. They talk about the priest and life at the church, and Alejandro talks about his children. Finally, he asks about Branko's family. Father Alvarez has already briefed the policeman about what Branko is doing, and Branko knows the question is an invitation to move on to his reason for being there.

It takes the better part of an hour to tell the big policeman about the last ten years of Branko's life. He leaves out the bankrobberies and the work he did in Denmark, but is otherwise so honest, that it even surprises himself. It feels good to tell the story, almost as if by telling it, it becomes a memory from the past intead of a burden on the present. As he gets near the end of his story, he produces the manilla envelope again and shows the contents to the lieutenant, who looks at them without even the slightest trace of shock or surprise. The wrinkles in his face are deep and makes his olive skin look almost like the bark of an old oak. His deep voice seems to rumble from the bottom of his round belly.

"This is certainly a similar case. I would guess that the same killer is behind this one and the murders here and from what you've explained to me, it sounds like we are dealing with a serial killer. You've brought a lot of information to me, señor Petrovic."

"I am not sure what to do now," Branko says. "I like it here. This is the first place I have felt at home since leaving Pristina. A place I can never go back to now. There is nothing for me there. But I can not let go of this task of finding my sister's killer."

"I understand," says Alejandro and as if he was able to read Branko's thoughts, he adds, "and I would not try to stop you."

"Is there any way, you can help me then?"

"I will make a few calls for you and see, if I can find anything. With my contacts, I may be able to find information, you would not find as easily."

"Thank you," Branko says and feels a burning behind his eyes. It is such a strange thing, to be among such helpful people, who do not want anything in return. He thinks of the German and the other characters, he has met during his years of travelling. "You are a kind man, lieutenant Herrera."

"Have another glass of wine, my friend. You will see. Good things happen to good people." The big man smiles and refills Branko's glass.

Chapter twentyfive

There was nothing in Caroline's notes from the convention mentioning a company by the name of "Mind's Ease Inc", but Frank and Elouise found another name on the listing of represented companies, and decided to go with that. Mind's Eye Inc had an address in Tacoma, not long from Seattle but still, too long to drive without a little research first.

It took a while to go through the company's website, but eventually, he found what he needed. The company had indeed been represented at the convention in 2000 by a man named George Patterson who now held the title of vice president. Sounding as official as he could, he called the company and asked to be forwarded to mr. Patterson. There was a click, two rings and then a voice.

"Patterson's office," the perky tone told Frank this was most likely a secretary.

"Hi, my name is Frank Cash, I'm with the Seattle police department. May I speak with George Patterson, please."

There was a silence on the other end.

"Hello?" Frank asked.

"I'm sorry," said the now not so perky sounding woman. "Did you say police?"

"I did."

"Anyone can call and say that," the secretary said. It was a song he had heard many times before. He knew this would not be as easy, as he had hoped.

"Is there anywhere, I can get a hold of him?"

"I can take a message," the woman said.

Frank decided not to leave any messages. Instead, he asked, if he could schedule an appointment the following afternoon. It always both annoyed him and raised his suspicion, whenever a company would act protective and secretive. Most often, he had found, the reason seemed to be merely to appear more important than they really were, but it was still his job to wonder. With a sigh, the nameless secretary set up an appointment the next day, warning Frank that it was only if nothing last-minute came up.

And so it was. Frank hung up and ran a hand down his face. Everything seemed to be moving at its own pace, almost regardless of his own efforts. He was happy that the investigation was still moving, but he still had no idea if they were actually getting anywhere. And meanwhile, a killer was still on the loose in Seattle.

In an effort to try and think about more positive things, he turned his attention to Mary London. She had made him nervous. No woman had done that to him in a long time, and he knew she had already taken place among the special few, that would leave a permanent mark. They had crossed a line, when he had stayed the night, and even if nothing more ever happened, the fantasy that had been Dr. M. London, medical examiner turned lover, had become real. That did not happen often in life, but instead of getting his ego boosted like a man's man, Frank sat there hoping it would evolve into something else. Something more. Though maybe it was just him. He had been the one with the fantasy after all, and the more he thought about it, the less certain he became of what she might have felt or not felt. When his thoughts about her started going in circles, he quickly decided that the waiting was over and gave her a call.

The conversation lasted only a few minutes. Her answers were short and Frank could not help but feel, that he was somehow disturbing her, but he did not ask why. Instead, he had invited himself over to her place that same evening. She had welcomed him in a way that was just as hard to interpret as the rest of her, but just the thought seeing her again caused a slight tingle in his groin.

"All is well that ends well," he said to no one.

"Let's just hope it has an ending," Elouise answered from across the room, where she had been busy working on the case file. Her reply had caught him off guard, and he wondered if she had been listening in on his conversation with Mary, but he still smiled and nodded and Elouise made no further comments.

On his was to Mary's apartment, Frank stopped to pick up flowers. Knowing her simplistic taste, he went for something that would match. It had to be red, but he did not want to get roses. For some reason, he did not see her a roses kind of girl. Instead, he asked the florist to mix it up with other red flowers.

She greeted him with a smile and quick but warm embrace. The flowers made her smlie even brighter, and she laughed and joked about how Frank was a hopeless romantic.

The rest of the evening, however, did not go as he had hoped. She sat him down for a talk, almost as soon as he entered. It was one of those painful ones. If only she had regretted being with him, it would have been easier to accept, but Mary told Frank about an ex that still haunted her somewhere in the back of her head. She said, that she was attracted to Frank, and that she did not want to stop seeing him, but that she would have to take it slow, until she had worked that other guy out of the system. She did not give him a name, and Frank did not ask. They talked for hours, both of them playing the role of the understanding and mature adult, and meanwhile Frank was picturing her naked, wondering if he would ever get to experience that again. Probably not, he concluded.

Frank ended up going home just before midnight. He drove home in silence, preferring the hum of the engine and the rumble of the tires against the road to music. His apartment seemed empty and cold. He poured himself a glass of wine, cranked up the heat and sat in the couch, looking at a turned off tv, when his phone rang.

For a second, he hoped it would be her.

"Hello?" he said.

"Detective Cash?" said a deep voice with a heavy accent.

"Speaking," he said. "Who is this?"

"My name is Alejandro Herrera, I am a leiutenant with the police in Barcelona, Spain."

And just like that, Dr. M. London was out of his thoughts, if only for a while. Frank thought desperately to remember the name from any of the information, he had recieved by fax, but the name did not ring any bells.

"I am sorry to disturb you at this hour," the voice rumbled.

"That's quite alright," Frank said, realizing that it was almost one in the morning for him. In Spain it would be just a couple of hours before lunch. "How can I help you, leiutenant?"

"I think it may be me, who can help you."

"Oh?"

"A colleague of mine from Interpol sent me a copy of your fax regarding a murder. Your dead matches something here."

"Yeah," Frank said, "I got a reply from you guys this morning."

"I know, but I may have a name for you," the rmbling voice continued.

"A name?"

"Emil Ravn Jensen. He is a Danish national. You may be able to get more on him from the Danish police."

"How did you get this? Interpol did not have this information."

"You are not the only person looking for this man," the Spaniard said. "I met a man named Branko Petrovic, whose sister apparently got killed by the same man."

"In Spain?"

"No, in Pristina, Kosovo. During the conflict there. He has been tracking the killer for several years. I don't know much more about him. But I do know this: The killer moved north from Spain and killed another girl in Paris. Or so we believe."

"When was this?"

"Not too long after he killed here. 1996, I think. You will have to call France to get the complete file on that."

Frank asked leiutenant Herrera as many questions as he could think of. The Spanish police and co-operated with the French for a while and had even gotten in touch with the Danes, but it had not led them anywhere. The killings, in the meantime, stopped, and eventually, so did the investigation. The vigilante from Kosovo had come to see Herrera a while back, and they had discussed the case. It was just after two in the morning, when Frank finally hung up the phone and looked at the several pages worth of notes he had written down during the conversation. There was a lot of information there, possibly more than he could see at this point, he thought and poured himself another glass of wine. It would be a while before he would be able to sleep.

Chapter twentysix

PARIS, JUNE 2005 – From the hotel window, Branko can see the Eiffel tower, like a gigantic homage to the male reproductive organ towering over the city. He finds it mildly amusing, and just that fact, that he is able to find anything amusing at all, is a testament to the time he has spent in Barcelona. He owes a lot to the people there, and can hardly wait to return to them and to the place, he now considers his second home. But first there is a killer, he has to kill. He is close now, so close he can almost smell him. Lieutenant Herrera had called him as promised, and he had told Branko about yet another killing done by the Ghost Killer. This time it had been in Paris, so that was where Branko had gone.

At the public library, he has talked to a young girl working there. Her English is better than his, so every now and then, he has to ask her to slow down or explain the meaning of certain words, but she is very patient with him. The girl is helping him find articles and any other public documents on the murder in Paris. He has told her, that he is making a study of unsolved murders all over Europe and is using this case as an example, and she has not asked him anything else about why he is so interested. For some reason, he is reluctant to share the truth now. He feels torn between his quest to restore his family's honor and the fact that he plans to kill a man. This feeling came after he and father Alvarez started having their long discussions, and he knows that he is really torn between the love of his sister and a fear that God might not really want this. But he is too close now. He must finish what he has started.

"For Jovana."

"What?" the young librarian asks.

"Nothing," he quickly replies, snapping out of it. "What have you got?"

"Well," she says and takes a deep breath. "The murder happened here in Paris. The lady was the owner of a bed and breakfast and the police assumed it was a tenant, who had killed her. For two months, the newspapers followed the story. Police interviewed as many current and former tenants, as they could find, but eventually came up emptyhanded. The case is still open."

"That's all?"

"For now," she says. "I am still digging."

Days pass by and turn into weeks, and Branko is suspecting that the librarian's newly found boyfriend is taking away some of her focus. He does not blame her though, but only wishes, he too would be able to feel like she does. But she is young and has never had a hard day in her life, and so she is easily distracted. Branko knows that he has lost his aura of mystery for her, and over time, he gets the feeling that she is trying to avoid him. At night the ghost whispers. She is ripe. Just like Jovana was, when he took her. And how he had taken her, ravaged her body even as she was being choked underneath him. The whispers become so loud some times.

Using the same story, he told the librarian, he contacts the French police, hoping they will let him in on what they have on the killing. At first they brush him off, but as he keeps coming back, they begin to take an interest in him. Finally, he gets a meeting with one of the detectives who worked the case. But the meeting is a disappointment for Branko, as he quickly learns that the French police only granted it to him, to see if he was a possible suspect. They ask their questions about who he is and where he is from and he explains it to them. Going to the police was a mistake, he realizes. Some of the men who investigated the murder in Paris still hope to find whoever did it, and he fears they will take his passport and find out that it is fake. It could be the end of his quest, and so he shares his story with them, trying to steer the interest away from him as a suspect. He shows them the photos, the police report and even the postcard, and does his best to make it sound like he just wants to help. Maybe give them some new clues. Until finally, they end up letting him go, encouraging him to do the same with the case.

He goes to pray. God must help him now, he thinks, as he remembers what happened to him in Amsterdam, when he ran into another dead end. How he degraded day by day scares him, and he swears that he will never again let self-pity get a hold of him like that. Never again, will he give in to the temptations of drugs and gambling or seek the company of prostitutes. He knows now, that he has passed that test, and that God is still on his side. The whispers subside.

Chapter twentyseven

It was another cold and rainy November morning in Seattle. The grey clouds lay as a thick blanket over the sky as far as the eye could see, and a steady stream of drops fell on the silent crowd gathered in front of the black casket. Frank kept his distance, so he could get a good view of the scene, but not doing anything to try and hide. He had Joel doing that from across the street.

In the group of mourners, Frank only recognized her parents, Anna, the neighbor and Darryl the receptionist. There was a handful of people, he had never seen before. Perhaps they were colleagues, people she had studied with or even patients. He had shaken the hand of the parents before the ceremony and eavesdropped on as many conversations, as he could, withdrawing when the eulogy was about to begin. Before it was all over, Joel or himself would get the names and addresses of all the attendants. It was part of the job that made any detective feel out of place, but it had to be done.

As Anna was finishing the eulogy, Frank recognized the expressions of the people around him. This was a funeral without closure, as he had seen it before in other murder cases. Everywhere he looked, he saw anger behind the eyes, as much as he saw mourning. That anger would only subside, he thought to himself, when the news of Caroline's killer being caught finally reached these people. Only time could take away the sorrow.

As ceremony ended and the crowd began to disperse, he felt a buzzing in his pocket, telling him that Joel was calling his cell. He was supposed to do so, only if he spotted someting out of the ordinary. Frank had the phone in his hand in seconds, not bothering with hellos, he just listened as his eyes started scanning the surroundings.

"Lone guy came in a little after the rest of you. Just left ahead of the group. He is in the parking lot right now. Looks like he is talking to himself or something."

"Keep an eye on him," Frank said, as he started walking. "Which car?"

"Black Ford Explorer. Older model. I can't read the plate from here."

"How is he dressed?"

"Black jeans, grey sweatshirt and open black jacket. Leather. He is wearing a purple baseball cap. Big guy."

"Got him," Frank said and hung up, as he entered the parking lot. As he put the phone away, his hands automatically travelled from his pocket to his gun on his hip. The man had his back halfway turned, yet Frank got the impression that he was well aware of Frank's presence. It was indeed a big man. His shoulders were wide and his body looked like it had been put together from large crates. Blocks of pure muscle, but on a tall, long frame. Two lines of cars away, Frank held out his badge.

"Police," he yelled.

The man looked up slowly from under the cap, turning to face Frank. Bright blue eyes shone even in the shadow it cast on his face. The two men studied each other. The man was around Frank's age, yet deep lines and thick, leathery looking skin made him look lot older, as if the man in front of him had lived many lives. Facing Frank, the man stood completely still.

"Are you Frank Cash?" the man asked as Frank was still inching forward.

"That's right," Frank said, hoping Joel was close enough to hear this. "who are you?"

"My name," the man answered with a heavy accent, "is Branislav Petrovic. Or Branko."

"Okay, mr. Petrovic," Frank said, realizing in that moment, that this had to be the man that Adam Langley had been contacted by. "What are you doing here?"

"Looking for you," the man answered.

The air in the interview room was charged with electricity as they all sat down. Joel was there with them and both Elouise, Big Red and Christina Quick were on the other side of the one-way mirror. Everyone knew that this man could be the key to solving the case, that was, if he was not the killer himself.

"Would you like a cigarette?" Joel asked.

"I don't smoke," Branko answered.

"Let's get started," Frank said. "What do you know about Caroline Saunders?"

"I know nothing about her, except that she was killed by the same man that killed my sister."

"Your sister?"

"In 1994, in my home town, Pristina."

"Can you tell us a little more?"

"It was during the time when Milosevic was in power in Kosovo, and there was a lot of Albanians being driven out of Pristina. Not war yet, but everyone knew it was coming. People were preparing themselves."

"Kosovo, you said?" Frank asked, having noticed that the man had a German passport.

"Yes. But this man also killed in Spain and France. Maybe more places."

"And you are looking for him?"

"We share that," Branko said, smiling for the first time. His teeth were short and tightly set in a wide grin that reminded Frank of a turtle's beak.

"But you arrived in the US before anyone was killed here," Frank said, trying to make it sound more like a statement than a question.

"That is correct. I knew he would be here and that he would kill again. In fact, I am surprised that he waited so long."

"Who is this guy?" Joel asked Branko.

"Emil Ravn Jensen, Danish."

They had a name. If this man was telling the truth, he had more or less just handed them the identity of a serial killer. The Ghost Killer, as he would no doubt be called. But the name was new to everyone in the room but Branko. They needed to know more.

"What were you planning to do, once you found him?" Frank asked.

"Kill him," Branko said flatly.

"Just like that?"

"Yes. I have been tracking him for years to do this."

"You realize, that if you killed him, we would have you arrested for murder. Regardless of the fact that the guy is a serial killer."

"I know," Branko said and shrugged. "It does not matter to me."

"In fact," Frank said, sensing that Branko was starting to shut them out, "we could detain you here, just for saying that you intend to kill this guy."

The interview went on for another half hour, before the first break. Branko was being matter of factly, apparently willing to share his knowledge and intentions, but without giving them anything solid to go on. In the meantime, Elouise had contacted Denmark and asked for a check on the name given by Branko. The search had given some interesting results, which she ran by Frank during the break.

Emil Ravn Jensen was a suspected serial rapist currently wanted by the Danish police. When he took it one step further and killed a Swedish woman in 1992, he also became wanted for murder, but before they could catch him, he disappeared. Danish police never found him, in spite of keeping his family under surveillance for some time and putting him on Interpol's most wanted list. They had noted that another man, whom the police knew as an associate of mr. Jensen disappeared around the same time. That man, whose name was Jacob Hansen, re-appeared in Denmark a couple of years later, now disabled from an injury that did not appear in any of his medical records, but that police reported was consistent with rumors, that he had worked as an independant mercenary in the war in former Yugoslavia. Danish police questioned mr. Hansen on the fate of Emil Ravn Jensen, but learned nothing.

A few months ago, Jacob Hansen was found shot dead in his apartment outside Copenhagen, Denmark. Ballistics confirmed that the gun had been silenced, which combined with other circumstances surrounding the murder led police to believe that the murder had been an ordered hit. Further investigation had led to evidence hidden by Hansen himself, prior to his death, which unraveled a network of criminal activities spanning the entire European continent. This investigation was still ongoing, but among the things believed about this network, was that they ran organized trading of women, weapons and drugs. Danish police had set up a task force, collaborating with police departments in the other countries involved and Elouise had been granted access to the protected site, where they shared notes and leads. So far, the ongoing investigation suggested ties to already known gangs of organized crime all over eastern Europe, Italy, Germany, England and throughout the Scandinavian countries as well.

Following the murder of Jacob Hansen, the international case had grown from evidence left in a bank drop box in Copenhagen. This was where Jacob Hansen had kept his life insurance in the shape of collected names, addresses and a few pictures, though in the end it had failed to save him. In the material the investigators had found numerous references to a German national named Jürgen Schweitzer, who apparently had provided women and others with false passports as well as other documents and services.

Schweitzer had been arrested in Hamburg, Germany, and on his way to a hearing in the German courts, was attempted assasinated. This attempt eventually made Schweitzer strike a deal, offering information in exchange for protection.

There was more to this story, but Elouise was not finished collecting it all yet. Frank wanted to get back to the interview with Branko, but stopped by Christina Quick on the way into the interview room. One question was all he had for her, and he had asked Joel the same thing: Was Branko's story about his sister to be believed, or should they assume that he himself was the killer? The answer would affect the strategy used in the rest of their interview with him, and both had agreed that he came across as believable.

"Do you know a man named Jürgen Schweitzer?" Frank asked, as he sat back down and handed a cup of coffee to the man sitting across from him. Frank had gotten a picture of Schweitzer from Elouise, taken by German press shortly before the assasination attempt. He slid it across the table, towards Branko.

"The German," Branko said. "That was how I knew him."

"So, you do know him?"

"He is the reason, I am here."

"How so?"

Branko told the story of how the German had been the one, who had provided him with his German passport.

"He is an influential man," He finished his story. "He led me to a few people, who were able to help me track down the Ghost."

Frank noted the reference to the killer as a ghost, but decided not to comment on it. "Did you know, that he is part of an organized crime network in Europe?" he asked instead, keeping the focus on the German man.

"No," Branko said. "But I always suspected it. During the conflict, he was an important man in Pristina. He helped a lot of people for a price. I guessed he was probably working for the Russians."

"Did you know he was arrested a few months ago?"

"Yes."

"He has been connected to the death of another Danish national, named Jacob Hansen." Frank said. "You wouldn't happen to know anything about that, would you?"

"No." Branko said, his face completely motionless. Frank had hoped for more, but knew that nothing was coming. It was likely that Branko had been the hitman, he thought, since the connection to both Schweitzer and Hansen had already been established. But he was not interested in finding Jacob Hansen's killer. All he cared about was Caroline Saunders.

"Let's take another break," Frank said to Joel, and they both left the room.

Frank's head was spinning. This case was suddenly growing faster than he had ever imagined. When asked, Joel agreed that Branko had to have been connection to Jacob Hansen's death somehow.

"Maybe he did it, thinking this guy was his sister's killer," he said.

"Maybe," Frank said, "but then why is he here?"

"No matter what, we've got to decide what to do with him. So far, he is here on a voluntary basis. He could leave at any time. I think we need to charge him with something, but I'm not sure, I want to charge him with the murder in Denmark. That would only complicate matters here."

As the detectives settled into their chairs once again, Branko looked at each one of them, as if sizing them up for a fight. Then he smiled and nodded.

"You are thinking about arresting me?"

"We haven't decided yet," Frank said, holding out his hands palms up, surprised by his own honesty. Perhaps the question had taken him by surprise. "Tell us how you ended up in Seattle."

"What do you mean?"

"How did you know this man, you are looking for, would be in Seattle?"

"Schweitzer told me."

"When did you speak with him?"

"Just before he was arrested. Two days or so before."

"How did he know?"

"I did not ask. If he says it's so, I believe him. He has no reason to lie."

"But what was his reason to tell you?"

"Men do strange things, when they know their end is near," Branko shrugged.

"Do you know a man named Alejandro Herrera?" Frank asked, hoping to catch Branko off guard. The only reaction was a slight pause.

"No."

"He knows you. Yesterday, before we saw you at the funeral, Herrera gave us many of the same pieces of information, you are giving us now. Only, he said, he had helped you learn about Paris."

"Okay," Branko said. "So, I know him. What of it?"

Frank had already gotten what he wanted with that answer, namely confirmation that this was the same person, Alejandro Herrera had told him about on the phone the night before. Instead of answering Branko's question, he decided to once again change the tactics of his interrogation.

"You said, you were looking for me, when we met in the parking lot. Why did you say that?"

"I was," he said, "because I thought you might lead me to the Ghost."

"The Ghost?"

"The one who killed my sister. The one who whispers."

Chapter twentyeight

It had taken a few phone calls, but with the backing of Big Red, Frank had mananged to set up a suveillance team in only half an hour. As they let Branko Petrovic leave, after handing him a businesscard and politely instructing him not to leave town and to call, should he find out any more, the surveillance of him begun. Frank had a firm belief that this man knew more, than he was telling, but no matter what angle he had come from, he had not been able to make Branko crack. Joel was now silently protesting, that Branko had been let go, but both Elouise and Quick agreed that it had been the right thing to do.

"If this doesn't prove, that three man teams are too small, then I don't know what will," Frank said to Big Red. "Do you want to release any of this to the press?"

"I was thinking," the plump lieutenant said. "I don't want to reveal anything new about our investigation here, but we might still be able to use the press to our advantage."

"How so?"

"We could make sure that the story of the European crime syndicate hits the newspapers here and see how our suspects react to that."

"You forget two things," Frank answered.

"What's that?"

"First of all, all my guys are now tied up in another surveillance. I need Joel and Elouise to be ready now, and the other thing is, that we don't have a suspect to follow."

"Nothing on the name he gave you?"

"Not yet. I've contacted Homeland Security. If anyone by that name entered the country, we'll know soon enough. But I doubt it though."

Joel had left to talk to the mechanic from Wally's Wheels and Elouise had finally been able to get an appointment with George Patterson from Mind's Eye Inc. Frank had wanted to tag along on that one, but since they were now shadowing Branko, he would have to stay on that. Even though he was not actively following the Serb around, he would have to be ready to drop whatever he had been doing and go if something happened with Branko. If he was in Tacoma, he would be too far away, so in the meantime he was stuck in Seattle, standing by. How he hated standing by. He passed time reading through and updating the paperwork.

Soon after he had put himself in front of the now thick binder containing all the notes on the case, his thoughts began drifting towards Mary London. There was another situation, where he had ended up in stand by position. Deep down, he already knew that nothing would ever come of their one night together. He had been a victim of bad timing, she had told him, but he was beginning to think that there was something else too. Something left unsaid. Maybe she had some rule about not dating cops, maybe he had scared her off or bored her. Maybe the sex had not been good enough. He could already see them meeting over an autopsy, himself awkwardly trying to stay professional. She would know what he was thinking, of course, but be ice cold. She would distance herself as much as possible from now on, and it did not feel fair that he had actually started hoping something would come out their meeting. Something more than a one night stand.

"What a load of crap," he said to himself, once more trying to focus his attention on the paperwork, but was again distracted. This time by dull drumming sound from his window. The winter rain was still beating down outside. Branko would probably stay indoors, but suddenly Frank wanted nothing more than to be out in it. The rain might clear his mind and wash away all those things that kept bouncing around in his brain, cluttering up everything. They were building a new skyscraper downtown. Maybe he would go down and take a look at that, he was thinking as he stepped out into the wet world outside.

Walking through the financial district of downtown was like walking through a modern ghost town. There were very few pedestrians here on a normal day, and on a cold and rainy day such as this, it was all but deserted. A few cars drifted by slowly. One homeless man emerged half-way from an alley, but seemed to sense that Frank was a cop and sank back into the shadows. Frank thought about buying an umbrella, but there were no shops around here, just corporate workhouses and half-empty Starbuck's coffeehouses. He stepped into one of them, had an americano with no cream or sugar, just to warm him back up, before stepping back out on the streets.

There were messages waiting for him, when he came back to the office, which immediately made him check his cellphone. Both the surveillance team, Joel and Elouise had been instructed to call him up, if anything new came up, but he had missed no calls. That meant, he could take his coat off and get himself a fresh cup of hot coffee, before checking who had been trying to reach him.

As expected it was nothing interesting. An in-house collection for the retirement present of one of the former detectives from the homicide department. One of the guys who had not made the cut, and was now supposed to be getting transferred to another deparment. But because of his age, someone had suggested he retire instead. Frank suspected, that since he had already been taken away from what he loved doing, he would have been an easy push. That was another way of cutting budgets, Frank thought to himself. Frank called back and said he would put a hundred in the box, which was more than usual. As he hung up, he could not decide if he had done it, because he felt sorry for the old guy, or because he felt sorry for himself.

Joel was the first one back. His account was that of a man, who had just wasted two hours of his life, on the same day his boss had chosen to let a man go, he felt should have been locked up. He always called Frank boss, whenever he disagreed with a decision he had made. With as few words to Frank as possible, he made it clear that the garage had been another dead end, and then sat down to write the report about it.

Elouise returned a little later, while Joel was still typing. She sighed heavily, as she planted herself heavily in a chair across from Frank. George Patterson had been flirting with her during the entire interview, knowing full well, that he was being interviewed as a possible suspect in the Caroline Saunders case. He showed no remorse for what happened to her, Elouise had noted. He had actually smiled, when Elouise had first brought up the murder case she was investigating. When asked about her, he had called her a bitch and a cock tease. He accused her of leading him on, only to dump him at the sight of something better. But he also insisted that he did not kill her, although he had no alibi for the time of her murder.

"Let's do some checking," Frank said. "and see if the two of them ever crossed paths again, had similar hang-outs or friends. And see if he fits into the European angle in any way."

He immediately ran Patterson'a name through various databases. The man had no criminal records, apart from one unpaid parking ticket, which was currently being contested. Once again Frank got on the phone with special agent Jeffrey Bernstein.

"Frank!" said Jeffrey. "This is becoming a bad habit, my friend."

"Put it on my tab, Jeff," Frank said, knowing full well what Jeffrey was really saying.

"What can I do for you this time?"

"A bunch of things. I need info on three things. First up is George Patterson, vice president at Mind's Eye Inc, based in Tacoma."

"Uh huh," Jeffrey said, and Frank could hear pen on paper at the other end of the line, as notes were being taken. "What else?"

"I need information on a Branislav 'Branko' Petrovic," he said. "A foreign national. Says he is from Kosovo but his passport says German. I've got him running around here in Seattle with a couple of guys following him around."

"Alright," Jeffrey said. "Sounds like I should call the wife, and tell her not to expect me home for dinner. Do you have anything else for me?"

"One last thing," Frank said. "A large European crime syndicate is being torn apart these days. Based on witness testimony of a German by the name of Jürgen Schweitzer. I need to know everything you can get me about that case and Schweitzer himself."

"Is that all?" Jeffrey said. "Listen Frank, this is huge and frankly a little outside of my usual playground. What's going on?"

"I don't have time to explain," he said, cutting Jeffrey off. "Except to say that these things all appear to be connected to my case and that I will be sending you a card for Christmas."

"I shall see what I can find, but don't expect any miracles here" he said.

"One more favor," Frank said, just a Jeffrey was about to hang up.

"Yes?" The voice was flat and Frank imagined Jeffrey was talking through a clenched jaw.

"I would like you to run the name Emil Ravn Jensen for any possible matches in your database. I don't care how vague the match might seem. Anything is good at this point."

As they hung up, Frank knew that he had pushed Jeffrey's will to help to the limit here. He just hoped, he had not exceeded it. He made a mental note to send him something nice as a thank you. Maybe a nice bottle of single malt scotch, which if Frank remembered correctly was Jeffrey Bernstein's favorite vice. Not that this would be enough in the long run, he knew that, but it might serve to smoothen things out here and now. Frank put it on a post-it note, so he would not forget.

The three detectives went through the paperwork one more time, adding their latest reports along the way. It was much easier to concentrate now, when working with the others. Little things were bounced back and forth, jokes were cracked and for a while it almost seemed as if they knew what they were doing. But as they were finishing up, it was clear that this case had become one of the most far reaching and complicated murder cases in Frank's careeer.

"First we didn't have shit to go on," Joel said. "Now we have too much."

"Is this even our juristiction now?" Elouise asked.

"As far as I see," Frank said. "We still only have on crime one US soil, and that is Caroline Saunder's murder right here in downtown Seattle. And last I checked, we were the homicide division."

"Glad we got that settled," Joel said grinning. "Now, how does a few detectives in Seattle tie the murder of a troubled shrink into organized crime networks in Europe?"

"A little at a time, Joel," Frank said. "A little at a time."

Joel was to take first watch by the phone, in case the surveillance team came up with anything. He would physically be joining the team in the field as soon as he had had his dinner. Next in line was Frank, who had volunteered to take the nightshift and at seven in the morning, the morning crew would be headed by Elouise.

"This might be the last we see of each other for a few days," Frank said. "You know that means, the paperwork has to be right on the money. I don't want to call you up in the middle of the night, if something looks strange in the reports. But I will, if I feel I have to. Keep in touch, guys."

"We've heard this song before, remember?" Joel said.

"I know," Frank said. "but we're only half the people we're used to being, which in my book means twice the risk of someone fucking up."

Joel nodded and excused himself. It was time for him to find some food and then go find the surveillance team. Elouise got up and declared she was going home to get a few hours of sleep, before it was her turn to take over.

Only Frank stayed at the office a little longer, finishing up the summary for Big Red and the boys upstairs. He tried the best he could, to underline the difficulty they had being only three detectives on the team, emphasizing the fact that they had to call in extra surveillance teams, effectively drawing manpower from other departments. This type of thing would lead to trouble in the long run, when departments began to feel that they were 'on loan' more often than they were working their own cases. Frank wanted to plant that seed as soon as possible, hoping what anyone in his situation would hope: That the powers that be would reverse the cutback on the manpower, or at least try to find some other way to restructure the department than simply cutting it in half.

Even after he was done and had put the report on the lieutenant's desk, he still stayed behind. For some reason, he did not feel like going home. Perhaps it was his too friendly neighbor, he wanted to avoid. Maybe he wanted to avoid thinking about Mary. No matter what the real reason was, Frank told himself, that he wanted to be around in case the phone rang.

From what he knew about the case so far, the man who called himself Branko had been chasing the killer for years. He had followed the man from country to country, from murder to murder. The remarkable thing was, that he had reached Seattle before anyone had gotten killed there, and from what Frank had learned, this had been on the word of some German by the name Jürgen Schweitzer. Clearly, this Schweitzer was an important character. Not only had he been able to provide Branko with information on the whereabouts of a serial killer, but he had also been tied to a network of organized crime. And he was so deeply involved with them, that whoever he could point a finger at wanted him dead. What troubled Frank was, that organized crime and serial killers usually did not go together. In an effort to learn more, Frank googled the German's name, trying to find more information in the newsarticles published after the assasination attempt.

Most of the results he got, came from various European newssites, and the articles were in German, French and other languages he could not identify. But the articles he did find, had little new. Jürgen Schweitzer had been all over Europe, apparently involved in all kinds of shady business. News agencies tied him to document forgers and suspected arms dealers, which led to speculation of his involvement in private military companies or PMCs. Sources placed Schweitzer in the Balkans during most of the 90's.

All this fit perfectly with Branko's story. Frank was guessing that the man Branko was chasing had been in Kosovo as a mercenary, and that the German would have known about him that way. He might not have known the killer personally, but he might have known someone who did. And that person could well have been the now dead Jacob Hansen.

Frank was quite aware that Branko most likely had pulled the trigger on Jacob Hansen, even if he did not have even the slightest evidence. It seemed logical, that he would have seeked out Hansen to get information on the killer, who was also from Denmark. He could have killed Hansen out of spite, because he suspected he might be the killer or any number of reasons. Clearly, Hansen had expected that someone was going to try and kill him, and had taken the precaution of storing as much information about the criminal network, as he possibly could. Information that pointed back to Schweitzer.

Maybe, Frank thought, Branko had been nothing but a tool for the network to clean up a mess. Maybe they just wanted Hansen dead and had manipulated Branko to take care of business in exchange for information.

In the information he found on Schweitzer, he also read about he murder of Jacob Hansen, and Frank paid special attention to the fact, that

Hansen had been shot in February 2004. More than a year before the murder in Seattle. Schweitzer himself had not been arrested until June, most likely because it had taken a while for police to connect the dots left behind by Hansen and gather evidence. The fact that they were investigating a whole network but only arrested one man, indicated to Frank, that they had had a hard time finding anything solid. That would also explain why whoever was behind the network, had tried to take Schweitzer out of the game. Without proof they were safe, but with Schweitzer caught, they suddenly had something to lose.

It was a lot of information. There were too many ifs and maybes. Too many theories and ways to connect the dots for anything to be solid. Frank told himself to cut away all the organized crime angles and look at what he had in front of him. A dead woman in Seattle, one in the former Yugoslavia, two in Spain and one in France. A serial killer on the lose, most likely a Danish citizen. A Kosovo Serb chasing the Dane for a murder he had commited in 1994. Those were the facts. The rest was, he told himself, nothing but backstory and fluff. He even had a possible name on the killer. But that had not helped any.

Chapter twentynine

Branko knows they are following him. If they are trying to hide it, they are not doing a very good job. He was expecting them to, and does not mind it at all. All part of the plan, actually, and he smiles at the thought of how predictable it all was. When they had tied him to the murder of Hansen, he had thought the game was over, but as soon as he realized that they were not going to hold him for it, he knew his plan would work. But now that he thinks about it, it becomes clear why they had had to let him go. Suspicions were all they had. No evidence. And besides, Jacob Hansen is not their priority. Police was police after all, no doubt overworked and underpaid and with little time for old cases on other continents. With the cops following him now, Branko is ready to move on to the next step.

The plan is a simple one, but Branko is still nervous. He is gambling everything on this in the hope that Emil Jensen is still in Seattle. If the Ghost slips through his fingers this time, he knows there will never be a new chance. In the end it was unexpected help, that had brought him to where he was now. God's work, no doubt. He had convinced the German to lend a hand, as penance for his sins perhaps. Branko thinks back to that day in June, when the German had called him in Paris.

"I have decided to help you one last time," The German's voice had been strained and almost a whisper.

"How so?"

"I know that the man you are looking for now lives in Seattle." There had been a pause, while Branko let it sink in. "I have known for some time."

"Then why are you telling me now?" Branko had asked, not sure what to believe. Was this genuine help or part of some bigger scheme?

"Something is about to happen, and I won't be around much longer. Consider this a dying man's last attempt at saving his soul."

That sentence had stuck with Branko, and in the end it was those words that had convinced him, it had all been an act of God. But he is not about to assume now, that God will make him succeed no matter what. It is all a test. He must remain humble and do his best, or the Ghost would win. The Devil's man.

The day after the phonecall, the German had been arrested by German police, though Branko only found this out later on, when the story about the attempt on his life had been on the news.

During their conversation, Branko had asked how he knew about the location.

"I knew even before I sent you to kill Hansen," The German said. "Frankly, I was surprised you did not go straight to Seattle from Copenhagen. There were certain people, who were concerned about mr. Hansen, and they asked me to take care of it."

"So, you sent me to kill him." Branko had at that point still been wondering how this was supposed to have led him to Seattle, but decided to hear the German out before asking any more questions.

"Not right away. I needed to find out a few things before any action was taken, and I sent someone else to do look around. This man discovered quite a few interesting things. One of these was, that mr. Hansen and the man you are looking for still kept in touch, and that this man now lived in Seattle. And it had been easy to find out. Apparently mr. Hansen had liked to brag about knowing the man responsible for the murders in Spain and France. It is possible, he thought it would protect him."

When the German had learned this, he had gotten the idea to send Branko to do the hit on Jacob Hansen. Unfortunately, the hit on the Danes had had some unfortunate after effects, which the German assured Branko had nothing to do with the job heh ad done, but things that had occurred after the police had gone through the Dane's items.

"Mr. Hansen had some life insurance stashed away, that I did not know about. When he passed, information came out that put me in bad spot. My business associates will not let me forget this." There had been no self-pity or even anger in the German's voice, though Branko had gotten the sense that there was a lot more to this story, than the German was telling, but he knew better than to ask. "You are one of the only people I have met in recent years, who actually believes in something. You have a calling, Branko, that goes beyond mere greed and lust for power. That is why I have chosen to call you now, to offer my help one final time."

And so, Branko had taken the German's word for it and gone to Seattle. But he found, that once he got there, that it had been another dead end. He had tried to get a local journalist to help him search for murders matching his beloved sister's, but that had revealed nothing at all. He had searched all phonebooks and registries he could find, for anyone named Emil Jensen, Ravn Jensen or any other combination of the Ghost's names, but that had not helped him any either.

When the woman had been murdered, Branko had actually felt lucky. He had followed the press carefully, but very little information had been revealed. This made him center his attention on Frank Cash, who according to the papers was the detective in charge of the investigation, and he had followed Cash around for a few days. And Frank had seemed like a good, honest cop, dedicated to his case just like Branko was dedicated to his. Perhaps he had even begun identifying with the detective a little, and maybe that was how he had come up with the plan, he was now carrying out.

He looks out at the car outside his rented room. The two cops look bored, he thinks. One is looking towards the entrance of the motel with a blank expression on his face. The other is looking out the side window. Through his binoculars, he has noticed that the two never seem to talk. He guesses they are not happy to be there. Not everyone has the same dedication as himself and detective Cash.

Branko makes the phonecall short and sweet. After introducing himself, he is put through to mr. Langley's desk right away. As expected, the journalist is there, probably writing on the day's story. Branko tells him to trash that story and turn his attention elsewhere. He begins with the story about the murders in Spain and France, but Langley does not seem as interested as he had hoped. But there is more to come. When he adds information that no one else has ever printed: That the killer is a former mercenary, who fought in the war in the former Yugoslavia, Langley sounds excited and asks if there is any way to confirm any of this.

"You are a smart man, mr. Langley. I am sure you can find information about the murders in Europe on the internet. Detective Frank Cash also knows about the identity of the killer. Even if he won't admit it, I am sure you can tell the truth when you ask him. You can quote me, if you think that might help."

"I can come to the motel you're at and interview you right now," the journalist says, which throws Branko off for just a second, but of course any reporter will have caller identification.

"No," Branko says. "Go ahead and use my name if you like. It does not matter to me, but I have nothing more to add."

That is enough. Branko hangs up knowing that the seed is planted. There is no way, the paper is not going to print this story. And just maybe, it will be enough to draw the Ghost out of hiding.

Now it is time to make the policemen work for a living, Branko says to himself as he puts on his clothes and leaves the Days Inn. He is happy to have found, that he has a place to pray in Seattle. He walks for a while, while there is a break in the otherwise continuous rain, before flagging down a cab to take him to the orthodox church. Once there, he folds his hands in prayer. He prays that his plan will work, that detective Cash and his men will arrive just a little too late to save the killer's life. And he prays for Jovana's soul. He knows there is a chance, the Ghost will simply be scared off by the newsstory and disappear once again. But he is not counting on it. So many conversations they have had, the Ghost and him. Many night, they have fought a never ending battle of wills. The Ghost lives inside Branko now, and he knows the Ghost will be unable to resist him now. The Ghost will come, and when he comes, Branko will be ready for him. Even now, sitting in the church, he feels the gun in the lining of his pants.

Getting a gun was easier than he had imagined. It took him one night of hanging out in a bar, to be told that he should go to Rainier Valley, if he wanted one with no questions asked. Once there, he found a new bar to frequent. He shot pool for a couple of nights, lost some money, bought some rounds and befriended some people. Finally, after a couple of weeks, he asked one of the patrons where to go.

The place was like something out of a Hollywood movie, he thought.. A seedy little pawn shop owned and operated by a hugely fat man wearing a dark red, crumpled and sour smelling flannel shirt and a nicotine stained mustache. The place had everything from electric guitars and diamond rings to sniper rifles, some of it secured behind bars or glass display cases. Branko wondered how many of the items had been stolen, as he looked through the windows. He would not go inside. Only someone known by the shop's owner, would be able to buy an unregistered gun. That was why, he had brought Victor.

Victor was a stocky built Mexican construction worker with a too mouth that was too broad for his face and strong arms. He was also a very good pool player, married to a woman Branko had heard a lot about but never seen. Victor liked to drink Seven and Sevens, and the more he drank, the better friends the two became. That was all Branko knew about him, even after having spent night after night with the man. But Victor was a local, known by the pawnshop owner. It took him less than fifteen minutes to reappear with a loaded 9mm pistol.

The two of them had tested it that same night, firing at garbage dumpsters in an alley. They had been drunk and stupid. Branko thanked God, that no one had called the police that night, or it almost certainly would have been the end of his hunt for the Ghost, but now instead, it seemed like another sign, that the He wanted Branko to succeed. But he not touched alcohol since that night, nor returned to the bar or seen Victor. Branko includes the Mexican and his family in his prayers now, not to thank him for what he did, but in the hope that God will bless his family with a life free from sin.

Chapter thirty

No matter how badly he wanted to, Frank knew there was no way to stop the article about which Adam Langley was calling. They were so close now, that one wrong step could bring it all down, and Frank had hoped they could have kept it out of the press until it was all over. But apparently Langley had done some digging of his own, and the possible connection between the murders in Europe and Caroline Saunders was too good of a story to let go, and given that all the pieces of the puzzle were already out there, it was too much to even ask the reporter to hold on to it. Who knew when the competition would piece it all together.

Adam Langley listed some facts from the European cases to Frank over the phone and wanted a comment on them. And he was asking about the latest developments in the case of Caroline Saunders. And as he had probably expected when calling, Frank would neither deny or confirm anything, except to say that the investigation into the murder of ms. Saunders was still being actively pursued.

"Come on, detective. Give me a little more than that."

"I can't do that, Langley."

"I know you guys are close to -"

"And how would you know this?"

"I have my contacts..." It was a weak reply from the journalist, but it seemed that Adam Langley was vested in the story, and when reporters got vested, they were damn hard to get rid of. It was understandable though, Frank supposed. After all, he had been contacted by Branko long before the first murder.

"Off the record?"

"Sure. We still have an agreement about an exclusive later though, right?"

"There will be a press release, possibly a press conference, but I'll try to slip you a little extra, if you do good."

"What've you got?" Langley was no longer able to conceal the excitement in his voice, which made him sound slightly out of breath.

"No," Frank said. "First you give me something. That's how it works, so get used to that."

"Alright," Langley gave an impatient sigh. "The guy I mentioned before called me again. He's the one who dropped the new info on me and got me back on the story. I don't know if you can use that for anything?"

"When?"

"Today."

"Okay," Frank said, nodding to himself as he tried to make it all fit. "We are close, as you have guessed. We believe that there is a connection to Europe, but we are not quite there yet."

"Is my source a suspect?"

"We're not sure, but personally, I don't think he's the guy."

"Can I qoute you on that?"

"Not yet."

Langley understood what Frank was saying. He would not stop the story from going to the press, but he would angle it more towards the European link than the current investigation. Frank was not exactly happy, when he hung up, but he knew that it was the best, he could expect to get. He also knew that as soon as the public knew about the link to Europe, all eyes would be on Frank and his team. But that did not worry him too much. He had handled high profile cases before, including the press which would turn up in hordes soon, not all of them as respectful as Adam Langley. Perhaps there was still hope that he might turn into a decent reporter after all. As decent as they came, at least. When it came to the more ruthless journalists, what worried Frank was the hint of the killer's identity, in case Branislav Petrovic's identity became publicly known. There would be speculations about him, of course, as Frank was sure there already was. Could he be the Ghost Killer? Frank did not think he was. The statement from Herrera, the crime scene photos, it all indicated that Branko was telling the truth. Besides, Frank found himself liking the idea, that if someone killed his own sister, that he would do what Branko had done, and not stop hunting her killer down, until he found him.

Frank was afraid that all this new attention would cause the real killer to skip town, before they found him. Now, the cat was out of the bag and the media would keep digging. It would be on tv as soon as the local networks saw the article, and from that point on, there would be no more controlling the flow of events.

Frank got on the phone with Christina Quick and asked her to go out for dinner with him. He would have invited her to the Hurricane, but the fact that that was just across the street from where Branko was staying, made it a bad choice. Instead he would meet with the profiler at '13 Coins', another of Frank's favored restaurants. The privacy of the booths there, with their high, leatherpadded walls, made them feel more like little rooms than booths. It was a perfect place for the kind of talk, they would be having.

The classically black and white dressed waiters were polite and observant. After drinks had been served, they did not disturb the table unnecessarily. And the clams were to die for. As Frank dug one after another out of its shell and dipped it in the melted butter, he explained the nature of his dilemma to the gigantic woman across the table, currently busy stuffing her face with a large burger, dwarfed in the hands of Christina Quick. Now was a very good time, he said as he studied how big those hands really were, for her to come up with a prioritized list of possible actions, the killer would take.

"Since he has been going for so long without killing," she said, "I think we can assume that he has found something else, that has kept him busy. Something that until recently provided him with enough contentment, that he was able to surpress his urge to kill."

"But how does that affect him now that he *has* killed again?"

"It means that he is very likely vested in this place," she said, talking with her mouth full. Frank could not help but think, that Christina Quick as a competent although not very appealing person. "He may have friends here that he cares about. Or maybe even a family of his own. In spite of everything, he might not be willing to give those up."

"So, you don't think he will run?"

"No."

"What then?"

"As I see it, he has three roads to take," she began, pausing only to take another bite of food. "He could lie low for a while and hope that this all blows off and that his identity will remain a mystery. However, I doubt that will happen."

"We are too close, and he knows it," Frank said.

"Exactly. The reference to Yugoslavia is too close to home for him. His second option is turn into a Zodiac type killer."

"How do you mean?"

"The Zodiac killer sent letters to the press, bragging about his work and taunting people with things to come. A well worded article in the paper could push our guy over the edge, making him do something like that."

"How likely would you say that is?" Frank asked, already having visions of a spreading panic throughout the greater Seattle area.

"It depends on a number of things. He might be too afraid to get caught, to make such a bold move. But then again, they never did catch Zodiac."

"How comforting. What about the third possibility?"

"This is most likely the one mr. Petrovic is counting on," she said. "It centers around the killer wanting right the wrong. Serial killers are typicallly proud of what they do, and they don't like people messing with their pride. He will want to clean it up and take charge of the situation. And that would involve killing off anyone, he considers behind making the mess."

"Like Branko Petrovic."

"Exactly," Quick answered. "And if Petrovic figures, he is being watched by the police, he is really just using himself as bait to lure out the killer."

"The man's got ball," Frank said, as he emptied his emptied his glass of Mac 'n' Jack's. Christina was done with her burger and was eyeing Frank's clams hungrily.

"What about the investigation here? How will he handle that?" Frank asked, trying to block out the image of her stuffing clams into her mouth.

"I don't know. He might try to kill you as well."

"That won't stop the investigation," Frank said.

"You and I know, that an investigation is like a big train that keeps running until it either arrives at its destination or runs out of of steam, but our guy may not see it that way. The killer will tend to personify the whole deal, focusing on those who are providing the public with facts. Those who are reaping the fame for his work."

"What about Adam Langley then?"

"He might be on that list as well."

"Great," Frank said, thinking of what would happen if a journalist got killed by a serial killer. His eyes wandered to the coins embedded in the table in front of him. Matching the name of the restaurant, each table had thirteen coins from all over the world in them. Frank noticed that he was looking at a Danish coin and wondered for a second if there was some kind of hidden message in that.

Going out for dinner was the perfect excuse for not going home, which still for some reason did not appeal to Frank. After saying goodbye to Christina, he took a cruise north from downtown to Ballard and then round, back down through Queen Anne and back to downtown, just to drive and let his thoughts wander. Some of his best ideas had come to him whilst driving, and looking out at the city as it rolled by reminded him of why he was doing what he was doing. He did it for them; the people out there from the homeless veterans begging for quarters to the Caroline Saunders of this world. No one was safe from murder, but Frank had long ago sworn to try and make their world just a little safer. It sounded like a cliché, but it was the truth nevertheless. Whether it was by foot or by car, a trip around the city always reminded him, that what he did was important. But there was something else, too. Another reason he had needed a drive. Though Quick had not said it directly, Frank felt that he had been given a death threat, and knowing that his life might be in danger, made him want to be reminded once again, of why he was doing this. When risking your neck, he thought, it was good to know that you did it for a reason. Frank had done a lot of driving around, in the months after he had gotten shot. Now, he thought back to looks in eyes of the people at Caroline's funeral. The lack of closure he had seen there. If he did his job well, those people would be able to go on with their lives. Again, he thought about his own closure. The whole reason, he had joined the force in the first place. His entire career might be a hunt for closure, for all he knew. He wondered what someone like Christina Quick could out of that.

At ten thirty, he joined the surveillance team and relieved Joel. Frank realized that he would be completely drained by the end of his shift and very likely would be one of the last people to see the article in tomorrow morning's Times, which meant he would probably also be sound asleep when the rest of the vultures started calling and hanging around the station. He would have to trust that Elouise was going to call him, if things got out of hand.

"Anything?" He asked as Joel was getting ready go home.

"Nope," Joel said. "He went to church for a while. Very exciting."

"I bet it was. Did you send anyone with him inside?"

"Sure did. The guy spent an hour praying. Then went for a little walk around the area. Didn't stop to talk to anyone, didn't make any phonecalls or anything like that. Got in a cab and drove back home."

"Put it in writing, Joel," Frank said. "Before you go home."

Frank could have sworn he heard a few profanities, as Joel walked over to his own car. Filing a report after having been sitting in a car for hours might not be what Joel wanted most right then, but with what was about to happen to the case, Frank would not have it any other way. And though Joel probably cursed him all the way back to the office, Frank knew that the work would get done. In the end, that was all that really mattered.

The surveillance of the Days Inn was split between two cars. One was placed inside the parking area of the hotel itself. The building was raised one story over streetlevel, and cars could park under it. The result was a shadowy parkinglot, where an officer sitting behind the wheel of a parked car could easily go unnoticed, even by someone walking right by it. The second car was parked across the street, in the parkinglot of 'The Hurricane Café'. This was an even darker parking lot, largely empty most of the time, away from the streetlights and without any other buildings right next to it, other than the one story building housing the diner. From a surveillance point of view, Branko could not have picked a better place to stay.

Since this was the late night shift, there was only one man in each vehicle. To make sure the other one stayed awake, Frank would click his radio every ten minutes and his unseen partner would click back.

Chapter thirtyone

In his dream, Jovana comes to him, as she sometimes does. She never speaks, but she takes his hand and leads him through the streets of Pristina. As they walk, she points details in the city out to him. Houses he has walked by a thousand times suddenly appear new. And in the windows, he sees friends and family long gone. He waves at them and they wave back.

From the streets of the city, they go down to the river, where they used to play as kids. Some of his childhood friends are already there, and they are all little boys again. They are a tight gang, sharing secrets and adventures and always fighting the other gangs of boys. But it is never serious fighting. Most of the time, they yell at each other and call each other names. Once in a while a fight breaks out and someone gets bloody nose or a black eye, but mostly they taunt each other like boys do.

A few years later, some of them would be shooting at each other.

Jovana takes his hand and leads him away from his friends, heading back home towards the coffee shop. They are met by their father who smiles his big smile and hands them each a cup of hot chocolate. The smell is thick and rich and sweet, and he hears his father's warm laugh, as he closes his eyes to savor the aroma, before taking the first sip. Mom is in her room upstairs, embroidering like she always did. Branko watches her hand guide the needle in intricate zig-zag patterns, hearing the sound of the it moving steadily in a dull rythm until the world around him starts to fade and there is nothing but that shining thin needle moving back and forth, up and down, in and out in slow motion. And then the sound begins to change.

It becomes sharper, like firecrackers at first and then, as Branko realizes his sister is gone and the darkness twirls around him, the sound becomes louder still. Machinegun fire. The sound of bullets tearing through the air, whistling through leaves and ripping men apart. With it comes the screams of his comrades falling around him, and suddenly the needle is back, sewing someone's wound together. The medic looks from the wounded man at Branko and shakes his head slowly. The inferno grows louder, as he hears the wailing sound of incoming mortar rounds and he starts to run. She can not be far away, he thinks to himself. He screams out her name, but his yelling is drowned out by the sound of the incoming grenades exploding all around him. He stumbles on a treeroot and for just a second everything goes black. When he gets up, he is back in Barcelona.

Jovana is with him again, smiling as if to say that everything will be alright. The horror is over. She gives him a soft kiss on the cheek, and as she pulls away, she whispers a single word.

"Soon."

It is the day he has been waiting for, when his story will finally be told. He woke up later than he thought, he would. It is almost noon. As he gets out of bed to take a shower, he looks out at the police car still parked in the lot across the street. Perhaps he will go to the restaurant there and have breakfast. The black girl in the reception, said it was a cool place. Branko thinks there is no better time to visit a cool American place for breakfast.

Chapter thirtytwo

The sound of the phone ringing jolted Frank out of bed. Before he even knew his own name, he had picked it up. Being the practical man, that Agent Bernstein was, he went straight to the most important news.

"We believe Emil Ravn Jensen is indeed living in Seattle under an assumed identity."

"How the-"

"Turns out the Danish police were still actively looking for him, and contacted us about it several months ago. Apparently, some a man named Jacob Hansen had let it slip, that he knew the whereabouts of the man, and the Danes had gotten a tip about it."

"Lucky break," Frank said, sitting up now.

"Not only that, but it seems he might have had something to do with the recent killing of the same Jacob Hansen, who spilled the beans."

"How so?"

"Jacob Hansen was shot in Denmark some time ago. We believe Emil Jensen ordered the hit from right here in Seattle."

This did not make any sense to Frank, who was fast becoming more and more awake. He rubbed his eyes and tried to make sense of it.

"I thought Schweitzer's gangster-friends had Jacob Hansen killed?"

"No, no mob hit was ever put on Hansen. I have it on good authority, that Emil Jensen actually ordered the hit through the German, who in turn went out and got someone else to pull the trigger."

"That makes sense, I guess. But how and why?"

"None of this is public," Jeffrey said, as if he was talking to a journalist. "But I've been told Schweitzer confessed it during interrogation. Probably as part of a witness protection deal."

"Has he said who got to be the triggerman?"

"No."

"Anything else come up?"

"I doubt, I have much, you don't already know. I'm sending over a copy of everything now."

"Thank you," Frank said and hung up. He was wide awake now, trying to make sense of this latest turn of events. After a couple of minutes, he concluded that coffee and perhaps a shower would make these new pieces of the puzzle easier to fit into the bigger picture.

The story took up the front page of the Times, above the fold, as Frank had expected. He skimmed the article while driving to the office. Traffic was unusually slow on the bridge due to the rain which today seemed meaner and more aggressive than usual, but Frank hardly noticed the inching cars on the road with him, his thoughts completely focused on the case. It was all about to come down, he felt it in his gut, and he did not like to see new twists at the point. He imagined that the office would be pure chaos by now.

Even before he set foot in it, he knew that he was right. He had just left his car in the parking lot, when he was ambushed by a couple of reporters demanding updates and news. Frank said it like it was, that he was just coming in to work and that he had nothing new to add. When asked about the contents of the article, he gave them the classic 'no comment' and 'following several promising leads' line. It would work for now, although he knew that in the long run, something would either leak or the press would dig up the details by itself. Hopefully, the killer would be caught before then. Until then, it was a race against time. Another complication.

Elouise was still with the surveillance team, so Frank brought Joel, Christina and Big Red up to date without her. In as few words as possible, he retold what Jeffrey had said that morning and when he was done, looked to Christina for more.

"Well," she said, "last night we discussed the possibility, that this guy would be the type to clean up any potential mess by killing off the witnesses. If Jacob Hansen knew the identity of the Ghost killer, Emil Jensen would have motive to have him taken out of the picture."

"It's a possibility," Frank said. "But that would mean that the information that lead to the bust of Schweitzer and those guys got out by coincidence."

Joel shrugged and Big Red was scratching his neck, looking at Frank as if he had just fallen from the sky.

"What matters," Christina said, "is that no matter who ordered the hit on Hansen, we should now assume that Emil could be coming after either Branko, Langley, Frank or all of the above."

"The hunter becomes the hunted," Joel said and hummed a little, dramatic melody.

"Very funny, Joel." Frank said.

"So, what do we do now?" Joel asked, this time looking at Big Red.

"Well, we still don't know where this Emil Jensen is, or even what name he is using. We keep someone on Branko and bring Langley character in for a word."

"What about Frank?" Christina asked, looking from the lieutenant to Frank and back again.

"We should consider this guy armed and exctremely dangerous," Big Red answered and turned to Frank. "If the prick comes at you, feel free to take him down."

With those words, the meeting was over.

Frank sat at his desk, nurturing a cup of cold coffee, asking himself the one big question he had left. Where was Emil Jensen now? The fact that they had a name got them no closer.

Suddenly, Frank felt very stupid, smacking himself on the forehead and drawing looks from everyone else because of it. But he did not have time to explain himself to any of them. After a couple of minutes of searching for the right contact information, Frank picked up the phone and called Denmark. Emil Jensen was wanted in by the Danish police, but it was more than likely that he had been arrested in the past, and that his picture was on file with the Danish police. Surely, they would have mugshot for him, and within minutes, Frank would know what the Ghost Killer looked like. It took the better part of an hour, several transfers and explaining himself slowly to distrustful Danish cops, before he finally got a hold of someone with the authority and ability to help him. Not that it was any help, really. Emil Jensen had no criminal record at all, Frank then asked about the items found in Jacob Hansens possession and was transferred around some more. In Seattle it was ten in the morning, but in Copenhagen it was seven at night. Half the people he was supposed to talk to, were at home with their families eating dinner. In the end, he ended up leaving a message, asking that whoever had access to the seized evidence would go through it, looking for anything that might have Emil Jensens picture on it. As he hung up, he felt as if the fate of the case was now resting on that one phone message.

Even though he knew that it was not as bad as that, Frank recognized this vaccuum in his gut that made him feel slightly nauseous. It was that time when all the pieces of the puzzle were there, and it was just a matter of time now, before they would start forming a complete picture. The excitement was already flowing through his system, and he needed a way to channel it out and clear his head. As he raised his head, he noticed that everyone was still staring at him in the office.

"How come no one thought of this before?" asked Joel.

Frank just got up and shrugged in Joel's general direction. He felt unable to speak. Whenever a case reached this point and the excitement became almost too much to bear, he liked to go down to the gym. He trained boxing there. The high tempo exercises and hard physical punishment burned off all the excess adrenaline and got any harbored aggressions and frustrations out of his system. As he went through the various exercises, he thought of all the things, that bothered him. From the recent cuts in manpower to the bad timing with Mary London. Oddly enough, the further into the exercises he got, the less the actual case took up in his thoughts.

Afterwards, following a steaming hot shower that left his skin pink, he found his mind sharper and more focused. He was ready now, to step back and look at all those puzzle pieces again, and start putting them together from the frame and inwards, until the last piece was in place and the Ghost Killer was caught.

As he stepped back into the office, he saw Joel waiting for him there, a curious expression on his face, fidgetting with a pen.

"What's up?" Frank asked.

"We can't find Langley," Joel said. "He left for lunch fifteen minutes ago, but no one at the paper knows where he went. And he is not answering his cellphone."

"A journalist not answering his cellphone?" Frank said, suddenly understanding Joel's concern. "One could easily jump to the conclusion that something wasn't quite right with that."

"Indeed," Joel said.

The two men sat quietly for a few seconds, until Joel picked up his phone and hit re-dial. The two detectives held eyecontact, while Joel waited for someone to pick up.

"This is Joel Burns from Seattle's homicide division again. Please call me back as soon as you get this message," Joel said and hung up.

"Fuck," Frank said, already calling up Elouise from his own phone.

The conversation with her was short. She was about to leave for home, after having run a double shift at surveillance. Branko had crossed the street, had breakfast and gone back to hotel in that time, and that was all she had to report. She was tired and grumpy, and Frank let her go with that.

There was nothing they could do but wait. Langley's cellphone might be on silent or out of battery, they told each other. They would be patient and keep trying, the first rule of any investigation, but with every passing minute he and Joel both knew that this did not bode well. On the day of his big front page serial-killer story, no reporter would disappear off the surface of the earth like that, knowing that people would be calling him all day with compliments or for comments on the story.

While they waited, Frank took time to look at the file Jeffrey Bernstein had sent over. He had been right. There was nothing new in it about Schweitzer or any of the other people involved. At least nothing that seemed to tie into the case. Schweitzer had been under observation on and off throughout the last fifteen years by various police departments and agencies in different countries, including both the Feds and the CIA. He had been suspected of ties to the Russian mob and several other, minor groups of organized crime, but nothing had ever been proven.

At two in the afternoon, Joel had already sent out a message to patrol cars in the city to keep an eye out for Adam Langley. He was still not answering his cellphone and no one at the paper had heard from him, since he had gone to lunch. The restlessness that Frank had worked out of his body earlier, was already creeping back under his skin.

Chapter thirtythree

The breakfast left him feeling bloated and tired. Everything had been fried and almost dripping on grease, and though it had been tasty, Branko still felt irritated that he had let himself eat that much. Back in his room, he is spread out on the bed, trying to pass the time in front of the television, but as usual it feels like he is watching commercials broken up by a few minutes of entertainment here and there. So, this is America, he thinks to himself. Greasy food and braindead commercialism. Some day, someone will have to explain the concept of the American Dream to him, he thinks to himself, but his thoughts are interrupted by his motel room telephone ringing.

"Hello?" He says, getting up slowly, picking up his binoculars with the other hand and looking out towards the parkinglot.

"Mr. Petrovic," Says the other voice, whost accent is faint but still noticeable even to Branko. "I am most anxious to meet you."

"Ghost," Branko almost whispers, feeling the chill run down his spine. His plan has worked and God has brought the man he has been looking for straight to him. "Just say when and where."

"Are they watching you?"

"Yes."

"Can you slip away?"

"I believe there is a back door."

"Excellent," his voice is cold and completely calm. Branko listens as hard as he can, but cannot find any trace of excitement or nervousness. "You will find a message for you at the reception. Lose the cops and go to the address specified there. I will be waiting."

A sudden click ends the conversation. Inside Branko is on fire. The simplicity of the plan had made him almost not belive that it could work. To reverse the roles and become the hunted had been the perfect idea. The Ghost could not pass up the opportunity to face off with his nemesis. He is too cocky and that will be his downfall.

The clock in Branko's room says half past six in the evening.

To get to the reception, he has to exit the main building and enter a small adjacent office, but Branko knows the detectives will see him do that, so instead he calls down and asks if he has any messages. The girl answers that an envelope was dropped off not too long ago. He asks her to open it, and though she protests at first, saying that she is not allowed to do that, he manages to persuade her with a bit of humor and flattery. Inside is an address. He jots it down on a small courtesy notepad next to the phone and hangs up. That was the easy part. Now he has to leave the building without getting noticed.

Out in the hallway, he follows the emergency exit signs to a stairwell at the far end of the building, opposite of the exit going towards the reception. Branko figures that he will emerge in plain view of the cops across the street, but it is still better than coming out the front door.

The emergency exit faces out towards 7th Avenue right across from the parking lot next to The Hurricane, so Branko waits as he looks out a tiny and very dirty window in the door. Of all the streets in downtown Seattle, this one appears to be one of the most quiet, even during the day, and it seems to take forever for decent cover to pass by, but finally a delivery truck passes outside, and Branko slips out and around the stairwell. Without looking over his shoulder, he turns the corner and crosses through the motel parking lot going the opposite way of the diner.

He walks four blocks without looking back. His heart is pounding so loudly, that he can hear it over the sounds of the streets. What is he going to say, if he is stopped by the police? How is he going to explain his concealed weapon? He cannot let them stop him now, that he is finally on his way to be face to face with the man, he has been looking for for so long.

When he finally stops, he sinks into a narrow alley, from where he can cast glances down the street he was coming from. But he does not see any police. The streets are almost empty, with only the occasional car cruising by. He spots a Starbuck's on the corner across from where he is hiding. Without hesitating, he walks in and orders a capuccino.

The American's must be a very busy people, he thinks to himself, noticing that everyone gets their orders served in paper cups. It reminds him of his father working in the coffee shop in Pristina. They never even had paper cups there. People took their time to sit down and enjoy their coffee. Maybe some day, he thinks, he will be open a European style café here and show the people how coffee is supposed to be enjoyed. As reddish blond, girl with spots all over her face serves him his order, he asks if he could get them to call him a cab. Using his accent, he does he best to look like another lost tourist. The girl behind the counter eagerly smiles and nods, and a few minutes later Branko is on his way.

The cab drops him off in front of an old brick apartmentbuilding that was recently given a makeover. He walks up to find the outer door held open by a folded piece of cardboard, doublechecks that the apartment number is on the fifth floor, walks past the elevator and takes the stairs. The thought of standing still inside that box right, does not sit right with him. He feels a buzz in every muscle in his body that he has never felt before. This could very well be the moment he was been waiting for for so long. His chance to finally restore Jovana's honor. To get even. He remembers his dream from the night before, and her last word to him. Soon. Sooner than expected, in fact, but he is ready. Branko never thought, he would be looking forward to killing anyone, but now he sees, that he does not even look at it as murder. He is doing the world a favor. It was left to him to do this. It is God's will and his sister's last dying wish. Even if she never got a chance to say so in life, she has told him so many times since then.

Once he reaches the fifth floor and sees the apartment door slightly ajar, the excitement is replaced with suspicion. He already knows that The Ghost will want to kill him as much, as he wants to kill The Ghost. Could this be nothing but a trap? An ambush perhaps? He gets out his gun and steps aside, listening hard for any sounds coming from inside the apartment. Somewhere in the building, someone is having sex, and he hears the faint moaning sound of a woman probably faking an orgasm. But those sounds are not coming from this apartment. This place is quiet as a tomb. He looks for a name on the door, but finds only the number. Without waiting any longer, he turns from the wall and into the dimly lit hallway, gun first, ready to pull the trigger at the first sign of movement.

Chapter thirtyfour

The call came in at a quarter to six. Petrovic had left the hotel, obviously trying to ditch the surveillance team, but not realising that there was a second car parked in the hotel parking lot. Joel was in the other car, so he had to stay behind, but as he called it in to Frank, who was in the middle of a not very good, overpriced delivery pizza, he assured him that car number two was in place. The second call came from detective Mendez in the pursuing car. Branko had stopped at a Starbuck's. Frank sighed in relief, only to hear that a cab was arriving and that Branko was getting into it.

Frank put on his hands free set and stayed on the line with Mendez, who normally worked vice and was more experienced in tailing people than anyone on the homicide squad. He jumped into the Mustang and set a course towards Pioneer Square, the old part of Seattle just south of downtown, which seemed to be where Branko was heading as well. Frank was instructing the others to stay in place when they got there, and wait for him to arrive, asking Mendez to keep Joel informed as well in case they needed him. Joel would never blow the shadow, even if the car he was driving had already been made. He knew how to keep his distance.

When Frank pulled his Mustang over, Mendez was already holding a heavy glass door open into an apartmentbuilding. Just as Frank stepped out into the street, it was as if the sky decided to come down. Drops that were too cold to be water but too soft to be hail, it seemed to be a special kind of rain designed purely to mock him and drench him, in the few seconds it took to get from the car to the doorway.

"The door was jammed open when he got here," Mendez said, almost yelling over the sound of the heavy downpour. "Like he prepared it or had someone do it for him."

"We'll know in a few minutes," Frank replied. "Call the other team in."

Mendez got on his radio and told Joel to go ahead and pull up. The two others waited for them to arrive, while keeping an eye out for anyone coming down the stairs. A few minutes later, they were ready to move up. Joel and Frank took the stairs while Mendez would take the elevator, leaving his partner on the street below. They all moved slowly and methodically, looking for anything out of the ordinary on their way.

When Frank saw the open door on the fifth floor, he clicked his radio five times, indicating to Mendez which floor to go to. At that moment, there was a loud thump from inside, and Joel and Frank did not wait for Mendez to arrive. Guns first, the two homicide detectives went in.

The hallway was empty and dark and holding four doors. First one was the bathroom, which was quickly cleared. Second would be the livingroom, followed by a kitchen and finally a bedroom. Both men turned into the livingroom at the same time.

Inside they found an unexpected mess. On the floor, between the investigators and a low dark wood coffeetable, was the lifeless body of a man, lying face down in a large pool of blood. The first thing Frank noticed, was the expensive designer suit, the body was wearing, and without seeing the face, he knew they had finally located Adam Langley. But both detectives knew that this was not the time to stop and examine the coprse. He was not going anywhere anyway. Instead they quickly went back into the hall and turned into the kitchen. It was tiny, clean and very modern. It looked like it had never been used, except for a single plate and glass in the sink.

Finally Mendez arrived.

This left only the bedroom, but the door at the end of the hall was closed. Frank put his gun back in his hip holster, and signalled to the others to be ready. In one fluid movement, he turned the handle, pushed the door open and withdrew to let the others go in guns first.

The room was dark and cold and Frank hit the light behind the two others. There was no one there, only an open window leading out to a fire escape. The three of them looked at each other for a second, before Mendez and Joel ran out of the apartment and back down on the street. They were still on the surveillance task, but it seemed they had just lost their target. Frank stayed behind, heading back into the livingroom, as he called back to headquarters.

While he waited for the forensic team, he looked around the apartment. There was no doubt that this was Adam Langley's home. Stuck in the side of a mirror in the hall, there were several pictures of him and a young woman, he recognized a Langley's nurse girlfriend. Last time he had seen her, he had been anything but friendly to her. Now, he might have to seek her out again, to bring her the worst kind of news you can get. He doubted, he would be man of the year in her life.

Adam, it appeared, had been a man who read a lot of books. Two walls in the livingroom and one in the bedroom were bookshelves. He found the expected books on journalism, a few books on photojournalism, a few on

English grammar and communicative writing. And there were books on history, a few biographies and even a forensics handbook. Not very much fiction, Frank noticed.

The crime scene investigators arrived and began their documentation of the scene, while Frank called up Elouise at her home. She was asleep and grunted something that could easily have been interpreted as an insult, when Frank described the situation to her and asked that she come back in and take charge in this part of the investigation. His next call was to Big Red. Frank would be needing more manpower now, if he were to investigate two murders and run a surveillance, which at this point was turning into a manhunt and a case of media hell. The lieutenant did not sound pleased, but promised to get a hold of the one of the other homicide teams and see what he could do.

A short beep told Frank, he had a call waiting, and he cut the call to the lieutenant short. It was Joel with more bad news. Branko had given them the slip and disappeared into the night. Mendez and Joel had gone back to his hotelroom and gotten access to his room there, but apart from some clothing items and a suitcase, they had found only one item of interest. A gun cleaning kit. Frank was happy, he had already made the call to Redding. Filling him in on this latest development could wait.

Chapter thirtyfive

The rain is very cold, yet Branko is sweating and breathing hard. He has been running for a long time now, and he has no idea where he is. His first thought is to go to the church, but he knows that he will not be safe there. The police will be looking for him now, thinking he killed that reporter. It had been a trap. Branko is trying to figure out, how the Ghost set him up in this way, when he had been the one with the plan.

His clothes are cold and clammy against his bakc, as he leans up against a wet concrete wall and his knees start to shake and he feels suddenly nauseated and dizzy. It is as if the whole world has been pulled out from under his feet, and he is falling through space. Suddenly, America seems like a very dark and strange place, so far from everything he knows and loves.

Moving again, staggering and almost stumbling now and then but staying upright nonetheless. He passes a few people on the street, who do their best not to look at him. As he passes an alley, he stops to throw up, his mouth filling up with the sour taste of defeat as tears stream uncontrollably down his cheeks and he cries out to God, demanding to know why this had to happen now that he was so close.

Branko pulls out the gun from his pocket and holds it to his temple. If he pulled the trigger, no one would ever miss him now. He has no family, no friends and no purpose in life. His hand is shaking so violently, that he is in fact hitting himself repeatedly with the steel barrel of the weapon, but his fingers refuse to pull the trigger. Letting his arms fall heavily, he feels all energy drain from within him and he slides down the wall. He sits in the wet alley, where the heavy rain almost washes away the stink of urine, garbage and Branko's own vomit. The last ten years of his life flash before his eyes, as he tries to make sense of it all. Why had he run away? He knew it was a trap of course, and that the police most likely would show up at any time. Running had been his only choice. Even if the police had believed his story, they would not let him go. But if it was all over anyway, why had he even cared about that. Branko tells himself that he ran, because a part of him knows that this is not over. This is all just another setback, he says to himself, even if he has no idea where to go or what to do now.

Time passes and Branko starts to feel more alive and clear headed as his body cools down. Struggling to get back up, his legs are still shaky and his muscles are stiff from the cold. He needs to re-focus, and make a new plan. Outside the alley is a 'Jack in the Box' and Branko goes inside. He is the only customer inside the brightly lit fast food restaurant, although there is a lot of activity in the kitchen, as they complete orders for the drive through customers. The plump guy with the bad skin behind the counter says something Branko does not understand, but he smiles and points to the big menu.

The burger is too greasy and Branko only takes a couple of bites before putting it down, but the fries are good and with the warmth of being inside and the caffeinated cola it gives him the boost, he needs. There has to be some sense to all of this. He had fully expected to outsmart The Ghost or at least get the chance to fight him man to man.

The Ghost had tried to get Branko arrested and either framed for Langley's murder or at least buy some time, while the police interrogated and investigated. Or perhaps the Ghost was counting on Branko to draw his gun on the cops and get killed by them. But then he starts to think about the dead reporter, and slowly Branko realizes how it fits together. The Ghost probably used the journalist to find out where Branko was and how to get in touch with him. He then killed Langley, as he would have anyway, and decided to frame it on Branko. It was a clever plan, he had to admit, though the police would no doubt see through it eventually. Maybe a slight delay was all the Ghost needed to get away again, Branko thinks to himself, staring out the window of the brightly lit restaurant. He had gotten away from the police and that part of the Ghost's plan had failed. It is not over yet.

Chapter thirtysix

"Petrovic didn't do this," Frank says to Elouise when she arrives at the scene. Her eyes are red and there are large, puffy bags under them. She rubs her temples, eyes and cheeks, as she looks down at the dead Adam Langley. "Langley was stabbed," Frank says, "with one of his own kitchenknives, looks like. We believe that Branko carries a gun."

"A gun?"

"That's right," Frank said, "and if he came here to kill Langley, he most likely would have shot him. Besides what would be his motive?"

"Maybe he got pissed off, that he was mentioned by name in Langley's article?"

"No," Frank said. "I think Branko wanted his name in that article, to help lure Emil Jensen out. I know that he contacted Langley and not the other way around."

"So, you think the Ghost Killer did this?"

"I wish you wouldn't call him that," Frank said. "You're just giving him what he wants. But yes, I think Emil Jensen did this."

"There is some sign of a struggle," Elouise noted. "The coffeetable has been pushed back about a foot. That chair was knocked over."

"My guess is," Frank said, having spent enough time in the apartment now, to have come up with a likely series of events. "That the killer waited in the kitchen and suprised Langley in the hallway, as he came home. He backed into the livingroom, where he tried to make a break for it, only to get stabbed to death."

"Sounds likely," Elouise said. "But what was he doing here on his lunch break? And how did the killer get in ahead of him?"

"That is why I put you in the lead of this one," Frank said. "Because you know how to ask the right questions. Now all you need to do is find the answers."

"Gee, thanks man," she said. "I think, I'll start with a cup of coffee."

Frank drove back to the office to update the boss. He had gotten a call back, with the message that the other teams were all tied up in their own investigations, and the chief was less than happy with the request for even more manpower, now that there was already people on loan for the surveillance. Big Red had ended up calling in a few favors from other departments and gathered a total of four more guys, who officially were working overtime on cases in their own departments, but who in reality would be working part-time for homicide. It seemed backwards and stupid to Frank, but he was too preoccupied with the case to really care. As long, as he had the people he needed, he could care less where they came from or how they had gotten there.

It was nearly eight in the evening, when he started briefing the newcomers on what was going on. He went through the case files so far, handed out photocopies of the case summary and gave them a quick update on the latest developments, that had yet to be added to the murder book. Then he sent two of them to join Elouise at Adam Langley's apartment and the other two were to join the surveillance team, currently circling around the area surrounding Langley's apartment, Days Inn and the orthodox catholic church, looking for their subject who was believed to be on foot. Frank stressed that Petrovic was most likely armed, but that he was to be brought in in one piece if possible.

Frank collapsed in his chair, as soon as the last of the detectives had left the office. The case was exploding around him now, and for every new twist and turn, he felt that he came equally closer to either finding the killer or losing control. The paperwork would as always help him stay on track, so he fired up his computer to get started on it.

Elouise would file a report on the related Adam Langley case later, so he simply filed a description of the events leading up to his discovery of the body, to fill the gap between Joel and Mendez's surveillance reports and the homicide.

It only took about fifteen minutes to do, so he spent another few minutes on the intranet of the SPD network, trying to stay up do date on what else was going on in the city. That was when he noticed the little icon at the bottom of his screen, indicating that he had new mail waiting. In itself, this was nothing special, since he got e-mails from various departments and mailinglists every day, but it had been a while, since he had checked his mail, and what he saw made him smile. There was an e-mail from his colleagues in Denmark.

The mail was short and to the point. In reply to his request for a photo of Emil Jensen, they had found a few images in Jacob Hansens private collection, from which Emil Jensen had been positively identified by his mother. Two pictures were attached to the mail.

The entire office was empty, when Frank opened the first of the two picture files. But even if the place had been bustling with activity, it would have all shrunk away from him at that moment. He was looking into the face of a man, he had been talking to only a couple of days ago. The picture, Frank guessed, was taken during their time as mercenaries. Both Emil and Jacob were in camouflage uniforms, assault rifles slung over their shoulders. There were rolling hills with scattered trees in the background, not unlike those you could find in all around Seattle. The image was a scan of an old print, but there was no mistaking the man next to Jacob Hansen. His face had been circled in red by whoever had sent the e-mail, but even that had not been necessary.

Emil Ravn Jensen was a strong man, by the looks of it. His buttoned down shirt showed a well toned body and tanned skin that the man obviously liked to show off. His dark brown hair and short, trimmed beard was in contrast to a set of shining, green eyes.

Chapter thirtyseven

He hates acting on assumption, but Branko has no real choice. Under the pale lights at the 'Jack in the Box', he has come to two conclusions. The first one is that only the police can find the Ghost now, and that they probably will before too long. The second conclusion is that he will not let that stop him. He has come a long way to get his revenge, and he will not give up now. He must play the cards, he has been dealt, and that is why he is now making guesses.

Branko guesses that if anyone is going to be present when the cops take down the Ghost, it will be Frank Cash. He is, as far as Branko can tell, in charge of the investigation, and if he cares about his job at all, he will certainly want to be there, when they close the case.

He knows that the police are looking for him now. Even if they know, he did not kill the journalist, they will be wanting to talk to him about his presence in the apartment. But that will also mean, that they will take away his gun and his only chance of getting close enough to the Ghost to use it. That cannot happen. Last night's dream comes back to him, and his sister's last word suddenly takes on a new meaning. Soon. Could it mean that he is going to join her soon? He sees himself waiting in the shadows as the police move in to arrest the Ghost, and he sees himself pull out the gun and shoot rapidly as he walks closer to the man who killed his sister, finally standing over the body as he fires off the final round at point blank range. The cops would certainly shoot him, if that is how it ended up going down.

Still, Branko is quite calm, as he stands across the street from the police headquarters, waiting for something to happen. Either Frank Cash will come out, and Branko will follow him, or maybe they will bring the Ghost in and past where he is waiting. Both are long shots, but they seem to be his only ones. He will take them, and he will react to whatever possibilities God sends his way.

Much to Branko's surprise, detective Cash comes out of the building within just a few minutes. As Cash heads for the parking lot, it occurs to Branko, that it will be impossible for him to follow the detective by foot or cab. For a second, he considers stealing a vehicle, but he has no idea how to do such a thing. Instead, he does the only thing, he can think of.

"Where are you going, detective?" He says, as he approaches Frank Cash.

"Petrovic!" Cash exclaims, looking genuinely surprised. "What are you doing here?"

The cop is moving his hand towards his hip, but he must see that Branko knows what he is trying to do, because he lets his hands drop, before getting his gun out.

"Don't worry, detective. I am not here to harm you."

"What were you doing in Langley's apartment?"

"Ghost told me to go there."

"How did he reach you?"

"He left a message at the motel. It should still be there."

"We've already searched your room. There was nothing there."

"The message is at the desk. I called down to get it, so I would not have to walk right by your men to get it."

"So, what are you doing here now?" Frank asks, his eyes narrowing as he sees the bulge in Branko's jacket pocket.

"The same as you, detective. Looking for the Ghost."

"Well, you can leave the looking to me."

There is something in the detective's tone of voice and an uneasy look on his face. Branko catches it and smiles.

"You've found him, haven't you?"

"That's not your concern, Branko."

"Oh but it is very much my concern," he says. "I have not come this far, only to trust a stranger to finish the job. As much as I respect you, detective, The Ghost is mine."

"That's not how we do things here," Frank says.

"It is now," replies Branko, finally pulling out his gun. "Drop yours and slide it over."

"Don't do this, Branko. They will kill you."

"Time will tell, detective. Time will tell."

Frank Cash does as he is told. When Branko has both guns, he tells the detective to go to his car. It suprises him, that Cash has one of the nicest cars in the parking lot. Branko has the barrel not two inches from Frank's ribs, as they pull out of the parking lot.

"Now," Branko says. "Tell me who he is."

"He is a restaurant owner," Franks says, without taking his eyes off the road. "He is married to an Ellen Johnson. They have a daughter who is eight. Her name is Katrine."

"And?" Branko asks. He is annoyed with what he is hearing. The man's family does not interest him. The Ghost does not deserve to have a family.

"That's all."

"Take me to him."

Frank hesitates and sighs.

"You know," he says. "I know what's going on inside you, Branko."

"Shut up and drive."

"I know about wanting revenge," Frank continues, looking out the windshield as he is speaking with a distant look on his face, like he is talking to himself. "My father was killed right here in Seattle, when I was just a kid. Did you know that?"

Branko does not reply. But he does not tell Frank to shut up again either.

"My family is from California," Frank continues, "but my old man was almost never home. He worked on a freighter. As a sailor. He had one night of shoreleave here and ended up getting stabbed and damn near gutted. They never found the guy, either."

Frank pauses, as they stop at a red light. Branko wonders why Frank is telling him this. Maybe he just needs to talk. Having a gun pointed at you can sometimes have that effect on people.

"I was too young to understand then, but from that day, all I wanted to become was a homicide detective. I even moved to Seattle, when my training at the academy was finished, just in case, you know."

"In case?"

"In case something came up. Like a clue. I know it sounds stupid and sometimes I even regret it. Maybe I could have had a better life being a carpenter or something. The thing is, I haven't even looked at my father's case file."

"Why not?"

"I don't know. Maybe I am afraid of failing. If my entire life is built up around some foolish idea, that I will some day solve my father's murder, and if I try and fail, what does that say about me?"

Branko thinks about it for a while, but has no answer.

"I know," Frank says. "I'm pretty fucked up, huh?"

"I guess we both are," Branko finally says.

"Would you mind pointing that gun somewhere else? I'm not going to do anything stupid and you're really freaking me out."

Branko stops pointing it directly at the detective, who lets out a big sigh at the gesture. Frank is sweating profusely, Branko notices. Maybe he was just nervous after all. He would have thought that a policeman would be calmer than this.

"I don't like guns," Frank says, as if he was reading Branko's thoughts. "But that's a whole other story, and I'm afraid we're too close to our destination to have time for it now."

Chapter thirtyeight

Frank looked over at the man sitting next to him. From what he knew, he had practically lived and breathed for this moment ever since his sister got killed. He was singleminded, and Frank had a feeling he would not let anything or anyone get in the way of what he had in mind for his sister's killer. It would not matter, that he had just shared his own story, and part of him was unsure why he had even told him. Honestly, Frank did not mind introducing Branko to Emil and let the pieces fall where they would, but the thought of the gun scared him. All he could do, was to play along and hope for the best.

Another few minutes passed by, during which neither man said a word. Frank thought about putting on some music or turning on the radio, but somehow he did not think it would ease the tension. The man next to him was no longer pointing his gun at Frank, but seemed lost in some internal monologue. Only when they pulled up on the curb and the car was put in park, did he seem to snap out of it, straightening the barrel once more.

The Johnsons lived in a small two-story house in Ballard, which also happened to be the Scandinavian area. Not surprising that the Dane would have settled there, Frank thought. As they pulled up, he saw light in only two windows. One on each floor.

"Let us not make this any harder than it has to be," Frank said. "For all I know, it might be his little daughter opening the door."

"What do you suggest?"

"We go up there together, and if anyone but Rick opens the door, I will flash my badge and ask to see him for a private word."

Branko nodded and the two men got out of the car.

"You might want to put those away," Frank said, nodding at the guns in Branko's hands.

Their knock was answered by Rick's wife. Chances were that she had no idea who her husband really was, and Frank hoped Branko would not accidentally give anything away and complicate matters any further.

"Good evening ma'am," he said, flashing his badge. "I don't know if you remember me. I came by the restaurant the other day."

"Of course I do," she said, looking from Frank to Branko and back. "what can I do for you?"

"We were kind of hoping to have another word with your husband. Is he in?"

"No," she said, "he is closing up the restaurant tonight."

"Ah," Frank said. "we'll just catch him there then."

He took a backwards step and smiled, noticing that Branko did not seem to move. Before anything could happen, Frank turned around to face him.

"Let's go."

Back in the car, the air seemed even more tense than before. Frank wondered what had gone through the mind of Branko, as they had been standing face to face with his wife. It must be hard, he thought, to see that the man who destroyed your family has moved on to start a family of his own.

"I don't want a bloodbath," he said, finally breaking the silence.

"What do you mean?" Branko said, his face turned away looking out of the window at the world passing by.

"This is a restaurant, we're heading to. I know you plan to kill him, but try to remember that there will innocent people there. Families. If you walk in there and start shooting, you will be no better than him."

Branko answered without raising his voice. "You have no idea what I have done to get here. And what I am willing to do."

"I am simply asking you to listen to this one thing. Innocent people could get needlessly hurt."

"What do you suggest we do?"

Frank liked this. He was getting Branko to listen to him, in spite of him being no threat at all to him. If he chose to, Branko could simply ignore anything Frank had to say, but the 'we' indicated that the big man was in deed listening.

"Let me go in there and arrest him nice and easy."

"He won't go like that."

Branko was right and Frank knew it. If he sensed, that he was in real danger of getting caught, he would either panic or snap. Either of those could be very dangerous.

"Let's wait then," he said. "Until the place closes down and he comes out to his car. Then we will take him."

He could see Branko struggling with this suggestion.

"It won't be that long," Frank added. "We'll have to wait outside for about half an hour."

"Okay," Branko finally said, and with that brought back the silence to the car. The silence remained there, even after they had pulled over to wait outside the Greek restaurant. It was already empty of customers and a couple of shadowy figures were moving around in there, sweeping the floors, wiping down the tables. It was impossible to tell if one of them were Rick or Emil og the Ghost, but most likely he would be in the back, counting up the day's money.

As they sat there waiting, Frank tried to think of a way to handle the inevitable situation, that Emil would appear from the building and Branko would try to shoot him. Frank never carried a back-up gun and only carried the one Branko was now holding, because he had been told to. And even that always felt heavy and cumbersome. Even more so than it really was. He knew it was a scar from the time he had gotten shot and that a few sessions with a therapist would probably cure him. Maybe Caroline Saunders could have made his fear of guns go away.

The two men watched as the first employees left the restaurant, some of them looked no older than their teens. Probably busboys. Joel called Frank's cellphone twice. The second time, he sent the man next to him a sideways look and answered the phone.

"Talk to me Joel."

Branko pressed the barrel of his gun into Frank's side as his way of telling him, not to do anything stupid. Frank was not about to.

"The guy is gone," Joel said. "We have cars looking everywhere man, we've asked patrol cars to look out for him. But he's gone."

"Alright," Frank said, concentrating all he could, so he would not reveal the fact that the man they were looking for, sat right next to him. Branko still needed Frank to recognize Emil, unless he somehow already knew what the killer looked like. "Just call it off and leave someone at the motel in case he comes back."

"Okay," Joel said and then seemed to hesitate. "Where are you, by the way?"

"I'm out driving around too," Frank said. "Just looking and trying to clear my head, you know?"

"I know exactly what you mean. This is one fucked up case."

Frank ended the conversation and shot Branko a look as he put away his phone. Branko slowly nodded as if to say, that everything was cool. Minutes later, Elouise rang too, giving an update on the Langley homicide. Nothing new there, and once again, Frank managed not to give anything away about what he was doing. He had just hung up the phone, when Branko suddenly sat up straight, like a cat spotting a mouse. Across the street, the lights in the restaurant had just gone off.

The next few minutes seemed to last a lifetime. Branko had one of the guns out and opened his door a just enough, that he would be able to either get out fast or shut it, in case there would be a pursuit. Frank held the wheel with both hands, his knuckles white and sweat forming on his brow. The scar on his cheek was itching like crazy.

A small group of people appeared from the service entrance in the alley on the side of the building, heading towards the street, it would be impossible to see who was who or if Emil was even among them, until they were all the way out on the sidewalk. But Branko was already out of the car, a gun in each hand, as he started going around the Mustang.

Then time sped up.

As soon as the group of men saw Branko coming at them with a gun in each hand, they scattered in all directions. Now, Frank thought, he would find out if Branko knew what his Ghost looked like. And no more had he finished that thought, before he started firing.

Branko's body moved in semicircle left to right, firing both pistols as he went. Frank saw two men go down, then he himself dropped to the bottom of his car and inched his way out on the opposite side. He dropped out on the ground and peeked over the hood, his heart pounding so hard in his chest, that he feared it might pop out. Right in front of them, he recognized Emil. He had been in the middle of the group, surrounded by his employees who had been turned into a human shield. Branko's arch of spraying bullets had passed him twice already, but no shots had hit. Even in the dim streetlights, Frank saw the gleam from those green eyes, as Emil reached into his leatherjacket and brought out a longbarreled revolver. The silver finish shone bright white, attracting Branko's attention. He swung both arms towards his center position, but it was too late. Frank saw a bright flash from the revolver in Emil's hand and the dark red spray from Branko, who went down immediately.

Frank had no time to check if Petrovic was dead or alive. Instead he dived back behind his car, hoping the slugs from the gun Emil carried were unable to penetrate the Mustang. There was another shot and a loud clunk as the car took a bullet. Another shot followed immediately after, going straight through the cabin, sending a cascade of shattered glass raining down on Frank. He fumbled with his cellphone, hitting the first speeddial number he could without looking, hoping it was not his sister's number, the only one on there, who was not a cop. If the gunshots did not attract the cavalry soon, maybe his phonecall could.

In the meantime he had enough to do just staying alive, and if Emil Jensen's slugs did not get him, there was still a good chance that he would have a heart attack, judging by the pounding in his chest. Frank wanted to move away from the car, around towards the guns perhaps, and be a hero. Or maybe just away from there. But he was unable to move. This was too similar to how it had been that day. The scar on his cheek was on fire.

"Come on out, detective," Emil yelled from the other side of the car. "No need dragging this out."

Frank did not answer, but tried to listen for footsteps instead. If he had owned a normal sedan like most of his colleagues, he might have been able to crawl under it to Branko and the guns on the other side, but the five inches or so under the Mustang was too tight. "Don't panic," he was whispering to himself. "Just don't panic."

"Give up, Cash," Emil yelled again, much closer this time. "There's no escaping the inevitable."

"Why don't you run?" Frank finally tried, his voice sounding strange in his own ears, as if someone else was speaking through him. "In a minute there will be cops all over this place. And if you shoot me, there's no way they'll let you live."

"Ah," Emil said, his voice giving away his short, hard breathing. "Maybe so. Or maybe you will end up being my ticket out of here."

As Emil got closer and closer he lowered his voice, but Frank could still hear him coming around the rear end of the car. For a second, he wondered why Emil did not just jump around and finish Frank off. Maybe he thought Frank still had his gun.

"I know you're back there," Frank yelled. "Stick your head around that corner and I'll blow your brains out."

"Uh-oh," Emil said. Frank heard a short, dry laugh, as he edged backwards towards the front end of the Mustang.

He was alongside the front wheel, now keeping his eye on Emil's shadow visible a few feet away. It showed him inching closer, silently and almost snakelike now, but seemingly unaware that the light was giving his position away. The ground under Frank's shoes made crunching sounds, every time he moved, so he tried to move all the time, closer and closer to the front of his car, away from Emil Jensen and the silver revolver in his hand. If he could just make it around to the other side, perhaps he could get a hold of a gun of his own.

In an instant, he caught the shadow speeding up and moving faster, and Frank crabbed his way backwards, reaching the front of the bumper just in time to catch a glimpse at the wild-eyed man coming around the back. For a split second their eyes locked. Emil's were glazed and feverish, his face was split in a wide grin as he fired off another round. Frank saw the gun go off at the same time he threw himself sideways, around to the front of the Mustang. He felt a sharp sting as he landed on the hard road. Frank quickly pulled up his legs and saw that the bullet had torn a hole in his pants and grazed the skin beneath. The pain burned but Frank still had full use of his leg and there was very little blood. He had been lucky this time and if he had counted corectly, Emil only had two shots left. But Frank was still unarmed and still had another corner to turn, before he would have any chance of getting his gun back. Oddly enough, he felt some of his fear evaporating. He had been almost paralyzed with the fear that he would get shot. Now that he almost had been, the curse seemed broken and his brain was kicking into survival mode.

Suddenly, the car rocked in front him and he heard the dull, metallic thuds of shoes climbing the car. Emil was coming over the roof, the top of his head already visible, as he was about to step over the slick rear window. Frank was standing up now, but there was no time for him to make it all the way around to where Branko's body lay in the street, to grab the guns. He had to come up with a new plan. As Emil half-way jumped to the top of the Mustang, Frank made his move.

Setting his good foot up the bumper of his car, Frank lunged forward like a football player, trying to tackle an opponent by throwing himself at him. Emil took a quick step backwards and avoided the grapple, but had to fight to keep his balance on the slippery roof of the rocking car, giving Frank enough time to get up and make another grab, this time for the long barreled gun in Emil's hands. Before Emil could move away, Frank had a hold of his wrist and was going for his other hand, but by then Emil had recovered his balance was ready to start fighting back.

Frank felt his knees weaken and his vision blurred, as he took a hard fist to the chin. But he did not let go of Emil's wrist, but tried instead to twist it as hard as he could, causing Emil to squeal in pain and tighten his grip on the revolver, firing off another shot in the process. Across the street a window shattered.

Emil pulled with all his might to get his gun back, but Frank refused to let go. The two of them were pulling as hard as they could, until suddenly Frank stopped pullling completely and instead went with Emil's pull, making the balance shift too hard. Both men went flying sideways off the car, Frank still gripping Emil's wrist.

There was a loud thump and a crack as the two men hit the asphalt below. Their eyes still locked, Frank saw the surprised look on his opponent's face, the green eyes flickered and rolled backwards, as Emil got limp beneath him. He had hit the road with the back of his head and Frank on top of him.

Frank pried the revolver from Emil's hand. As he was about to get up, he felt a sudden, sharp pain in his side and found himself splayed out on the road next to Emil. Above him stood the bloody mess that was Branko, apparently still very much alive, having just kicked Frank off of Emil, Frank saw him lift his left arm as the right one hung limp down his side, blood steadily pouring from a gaping hole in the shoulder. He growled something Frank did not understand and directed the gun in his hand at Emil.

Frank lifted Emil's gun up towards Branko, yelling at him to drop it and step away, but Branko did not appear to notice the detective. His finger tightened on the trigger, as Frank was screaming at him. There was a loud crack and a flash of light from Branko's hand, as his gun went off, and a second shot right afterwards, as Frank fired the last of Emil Jensen's bullets into the man into the man in front of him. Frank felt a warm spatter on his face. The recoil from firing the revolver had sent shockwaves through Frank's arm, but when he saw Branko's body jolt backwards and hit the car behind him, he knew he had hit him. Even before his body hit the ground, Frank could tell that Branko was dead.

Emil Ravn Jensen or Rick Johnson was not breathing either. When Frank finally looked over at him, he saw a face that was almost unrecognizable. One bullet had entered through his chin, in almost the same spot as when Frank had been shot. But the exit had not been as pretty. The top of Emil's skull had been shattered and its contents reduced to a pulp, now spread across the asphalt.

When Frank stood up, it was with the help of Joel. It had been him Frank had called on his speeddial, and with some quick thinking, he had had the phone tracked via the built in GPS unit. Joel had arrived just in time to see Branko keel over.

Chapter thirtynine

They took Frank to Harborview Medical Center, to take a look at his leg, and while a tiredlooking nurse cleaned the wound, lieutenant Redding got a statement. It surprised Frank, that he was so calm, now that it was all over. Maybe the real shock would set in later, or perhaps he was getting hardened. Time would tell.

"Let's see if we can put the right kind of spin on this, okay?" asked Redding.

"What do you have in mind?"

"If your team had not been cut in half, you would not have ended up in a situation that could have easily cost you your life. Wouldn't you say?"

Frank saw where this was going, and he like what he was hearing. This was their chance to get a story in the papers about how budget cuts had nearly gotten a detective killed, and with a little luck, the snowball would start rolling. Fingers would be pointed, blame tossed around and the public would be outraged.

The first reporters were already showing up, so they decided to smuggle Frank out the back way, while Redding went out and said his piece. Frank saw it on television, when he got home, and thought there was a good reason why Redding had made lieutenant. Some day soon, he would no doubt rise even higher in the ranks, which would be a loss to homicide but maybe a gain for the department as a whole. He just hoped, they would not want him to take over homicide, when the time came. Frank turned the tv off.

It was strangely quiet in his apartment, and it somehow felt lonelier than usual. Who had he saved today, he asked himself. Branko was dead, Emil was dead, Caroline was dead and so was Adam Langley. And for what? Was it really justice or was it something less. His thoughts drifted back to his own story, his dead father whose killer had walked, and in a way, he was not all that different from Branko. Only he had lost more than Frank, including his sense of perspective and reality. But then, maybe it was understandable. Would he not have sought revenge too, if he could?

There was a knock on his door. Softer than usual. In spite of his previous promise to cut down on socializing with the neighbors, he welcomed the thought now. Rosa had tears in her eyes, when he opened the door, and at first he thought they were for him.

"Do you have a minute, mr. Cash?"

"Call me Frank," he said and stepped aside. "And come on in."

"Muchas gracias," she answered, her voice barely more than a whimper.

They sat down across from each other, and she started to talk to him. She had heard the news of what had happened, but it was not Frank that she was afraid for, but her son Eric. This was the explanation for all the dinners, finally. Rosa Perez had never had any kind of romantic interest in Frank, and suddenly he was very glad, he never asked about it. Eric had been talking about becoming a police officer for a while now, and she had trying to talk him out of it, but the young man was past listening to his mother. So instead, she had tried to build up the courage to ask Frank to talk to Eric. Seeing the story on the news had reminded her, that being a cop was a dangerous job. Tears were running down her face along with an endless stream of apologies for intruding and putting all of this on him, on the same night as this terrible experience.

"Please don't apologize," Frank said, handing the sobbing woman a paper towel and a glass of wine. "I appreciate you asking me, but I'm not sure what to do about it. If Eric wants to become a cop, that's his own decision."

"But I'm afraid he will get hurt."

"All jobs have risks, Rosa. If he were a contruction worker, he would be around power tools all day. I don't know for sure, but I think more construction workers get hurt on a daily basis than cops."

This made her smile.

They spent another hour talking, about Eric and life on the force at first, Frank shared a few funny stories, and finally just talking. After all this time, they were getting to know each other as neighbors. Only when the long day and the red wine started to make Frank's eyelids heavy, did mrs. Perez excuse herself. Five minutes later, Frank was sound asleep on the couch.

They suspended him for a week, pending the mandatory investigation following the discharge of his firearm. In an exclusive interview with Seattle Times, he explained how Adam Langley had been a tremendous help. When asked about the budget cuts, Frank explained how his team had borrowed manpower from other departments, effectively breaking the rules to get the job done. The same day that article ran, lieutenant Redding called Frank back from suspension to give him an official warning him about making statements like that. But when he did, he did it with a smile, a nod and a handshake. The representative from Internal Affairs, who had been present in Big Red's office made no comment on the way, the message was delivered.

In the days following the Ghost Killer case, the media had a field day with the cutbacks on manpower in the police force. As a result, a compromise was eventually offered, and a fourth detective was added to every homicide team and a fourth team set up. The result was that homicide was now back up to a total of sixteen detectives, instead of the eightteen they had been. The mayor's office had issued statements, that no budget cuts were to become a hindrance in the excellent work done by the Seattle Police Department, though Frank had a feeling that the chief had been reprimanded behind the scenes, for cutting manpower in such a high profile department. No doubt the chief would have other, lesser important people than himself, to point to and blame. And Frank himself would most likely not be getting any promotions any time soon, which suited him just fine, though he would pretend otherwise, if that was what it took to make the brass happy.

The investigation ended as everyone had suspected. Frank was right to fire his gun when he did, and he was to return to duty right away.

Chapter forty

Frank was laying on his couch watching old reruns of Star Trek the Next Generation when there was a knock on his front door. He smiled to himself and got up.

"Are you ready?" asked mrs. Perez.

"Of course," he said. "Let's go."

As they drove, Rosa talked about her family of hard working men and women, about the prejudice she encountered every day, and how she imagined being a cop carried a lot of prejudice as well, as people judged you by the badge, instead of what was beneath. As a Mexican, she said, she was constantly met with suspicion, talked down to or even ignored. If Eric joined the force, she mused, it would only be more prejudice added to the pile. She worried that it would be too hard for him to deal with, being both Mexican and a police officer at the same time. Frank had taken Eric down to show him how homicide worked and arranged for him to go on a ride-along with officers on patrol. He had told him the story of how he had gotten shot and gone over the Ghost Killer case as well. Eric had sucked up all the information and impressions, but it had only strengthened his resolve. Eventually, Frank and Eric had sat down with Rosa together and laid it out to her. In the end, she had turned around on the subject and now seemed proud that her son was to attend the police academy.

The two of them grew silent, as Rosa parked her car in front of the cemetary. The aftermath of the investigation had delayed the release of

Branislav Petrovic's remains. Disposing of them would be paid for by the tax payers, his grave would be anonymous and soon he would be nothing more than a number. Grave number eleven thirtyeight. As expected, there were no one else at the cemetary. Frank's Mustang had been shot to pieces, when Emil Jensen's slugs had pounded into it, so he had asked Rosa to drive him. He was still not sure, why he had wanted to see Branko off. Maybe to let him know, that he would never forget the man, in whom he had somehow seen a mirror image of himself. How he could have been.

www.ingramcontent.com/pod-product-compliance
Lightning Source LLC
Chambersburg PA
CBHW031119030726
47496CB00002BA/595